FORBIDDEN BOSSES: THE COMPLETE COLLECTION

ROMANCE IN NYC

ANGEL DEVLIN

ALL RIGHTS RESERVED.
No part of this publication may be reproduced, distributed, or transmitted in any form or by any means, including photocopying, recording, or other electronic or mechanical methods, without the prior written permission of the publisher, with the exception of the use of small quotations in book reviews.
Copyright © 2018, 2022 By Angel Devlin.
Book cover design by The Pretty Little Design Company
Formatting by Andrea Long.

This is a work of fiction. Any resemblance of characters to actual persons, living or dead, is purely coincidental. Angel Devlin holds exclusive rights to this work. Unauthorized duplication is prohibited.

ABANDON

BOOK ONE

ABANDON
DEFINITION

to yield (oneself) without restraint or moderation; give (oneself) over to natural impulses, usually without self-control.

CHAPTER ONE

Ashley

Working for Aidan Hall kept me on the toes of my Jimmy Choos. You never quite knew what he was going to ask you to do next. As the owner of Abandon, a private members sex club, he'd inherited me as his main assistant the moment he bought the club from Henry Carter two years ago. I'd known Aidan a while before he took over and he was a great guy, though known to be impulsive at times. I loved my job, although it was busy and challenging. I was a shit hot assistant and Aidan knew it.

He'd been pre-occupied the last few days as he had finally begun a romance with a woman called Lori who he'd been giving puppy dog eyes to for ages. This morning he had called a meeting with me and said it was very important. I hoped he wasn't going to give me much more work to do as my schedule was brimming over.

I knocked on the door of his office, walking in when I heard his voice instruct me to do so. My dark-haired, dark eyed boss had stubble on his chin, a sign he'd been too busy with Lori to shave. It made me smile.

"Hey, Ashley. Take a seat."

Well, he looked in an amazingly great mood anyhow. Relaxed and with a smile that took up almost his whole face. Getting regular sex did that to you I suppose, though I found it hard to recall. The only relationship I had was with my job and that's how I liked it.

I sat in the chair opposite him, my iPad in my hand ready to take notes.

"You won't be needing that." Aidan smiled. "This isn't a PA thing."

I raised an eyebrow at him before sliding the iPad onto the edge of his sleek black desk, then I sat back crossing one leg over the other. Now I was intrigued.

He scrubbed a hand over his face. "Ashley, I want to start by apologizing."

I looked up at him with a query in my gaze. I could feel my eyebrows pulling tautly together. What did he need to apologize for? What had he done and how did it involve me?

He cleared his throat. "I think Abandon and its previous incarnation Club S, plus me and the previous owner, Henry, have largely taken you for granted. You do an amazing job around here, above and beyond what an assistant should do."

"I love my work," I said slowly and cautiously.

"It shows." He nodded his head.

I ran my tongue around my now dry mouth wishing he'd get to the point.

"Now, I'm planning on being out of the office more. It shouldn't come as any surprise to you that I'm looking to expand the business, given its success. So I plan to be out scoping locations for a new sister club to Abandon. I've also decided to extend this place..."

Fuck. I *was* getting more work. Did he think I could do without eating and breathing?

"To that end. I'm changing things around. Ashley, I want to invite you to take on the position of manager for Abandon, second only to myself. Abandon is extending to the floor above and I want you to oversee that development. There will be a VIP area for the elite there. Somewhere they can hold private parties rather than mix with everyone like they currently do on this floor. You'll negotiate with party planners and

PR in order to make Abandon XL *the* place for the rich and famous to party."

I tilted my head. "XL?"

Another smile came my way. "Abandon with gold dust. Extra-large, or extra-lust? Whichever. Just make sure it's dynamite. If you take the job that is." He scrawled some numbers on a piece of paper and turned it around to me.

"That would be your salary. Starting tomorrow." He searched my gaze.

My gaze that was wide-eyed. The number I was looking at was ten times my present salary.

Looking directly in my eyes, he ran a hand through his hair. "If you don't accept, I'll be doubling your present salary anyway. I'll also be backdating this to when I took over, so that's a two year backdate coming your way."

My jaw dropped. I was having trouble keeping up with this conversation. Aidan was so very enthusiastic about everything that he talked at one hundred miles an hour and went from one thought to another. After two years, I was largely used to him, but today his general happiness was making him even more tricky to keep up with.

I was getting a two year backdate. Twenty-four times my salary going into my account, and THEN double salary from now on, or even more if I accepted this new role.

I folded my arms across my chest. "I want to say yes, Aidan, I really do. But I don't see how I'm going to be able to take on all this extra work. I'm already here morning, noon, and night." Although I was his general assistant, our office building was on the floor above. The one he was talking about converting into Abandon XL. That made another question pop into my mind.

"Hey, what's happening to the other offices?" I asked. "If Abandon XL is going to be upstairs."

He shot me a grin. "Relocating. I've bought new premises near GoDown Productions. It's ready to move into. I want Abandon XL up and running in the next few months. Money's no object. I'm employing a project manager and they're waiting for my manager's call. In answer to your other question of how you would cope… If you accept the job, I'm getting you a deputy manager. You'll train them to manage Abandon and you can have Jessica to take over your PA duties. She'd be your assistant."

"Okay, yes, I'll do it." The words burst from my mouth before the sensible part of myself could take over. All I could think of was handling an exciting new project, being the boss, and having enough money to tell my present landlord to go suck a dick.

Aidan rolled out some plans across the table and

invited me to stand closer to look. I rose from my seat, smoothing down my skirt and stood at his side.

He gestured at the drawings. "If you can see, what I'm proposing is that these two thirds of the building to the right of the main lobby will be Abandon XL. At the left side, behind the elevators will be two separate staff apartments: one for the manager, one for the deputy. Obviously the manager's will have extra square footage." He laughed. "I will need one of you to be on site at all times. It would be up to you whether you used it full-time or just when you were on duty."

I gave a slow, disbelieving shake of my head. "There's an apartment too? That salary and an apartment?" I pressed a hand against my chest, fingers splayed out. "Aidan, could you slap me because I'm sure I'm dreaming."

He laughed again.

"Hey, you're not manic are you?" I frowned at him. "Do I need to call psych?"

A gleam in his eye, he winked at me. "What we are, Ashley, is on the up. Abandon is doing amazing. The elite are crying out for their own floor. You know how many times they make inquiries to get the place to themselves."

I nodded. There was always some VIP thinking they were important enough that we'd close the club for their sole use.

"Now we'll be able to offer them that as an option without it impacting on the other members."

"It's going to be incredible." I grinned.

Aidan looked up from his plans. "So, I'll need you to run any major ideas past me, but what I'd like you to do this week is meet with the guy who's going to be your deputy. I've shown him around Abandon, but he'll need showing the ropes of running the place. His name is Lucas and I've asked him to meet with us tomorrow morning."

"So you knew I'd take the job?" I smiled.

Aidan's eyes fixed on me. "No, Ashley, I got on my knees and prayed you'd take the job. I want you to work on ideas for what XL is going to look like and what we're going to offer. Come back to me with a mood board, presentation, or similar as soon as you can."

I tapped my top lip. "I could open a dialog with the VIPs who use the place already?"

"Love it. Do that, schmooze a few. Take them somewhere fancy on account. Find out what's hip and what's about to trend and get that in our club. Now Jess is going to be working for me, you, and Lucas so I've also increased her salary and she's ready to become a workaholic just like you." He reached over to grab his laptop bag. "I'm outta here. You have my schedule. I suggest today you take some time to process the morning and maybe take Jess to lunch? Chat about the future of Hall Enterprises and it's meteoric rise to the top."

He winked again, and with that he left the office. Picking up the piece of paper and the plans, I walked through to my own and sat back in my chair. I felt like I'd been whipped by a tornado. I stared at the piece of paper with my new salary written on it. Were those numbers real? I stuck my legs out, whipped them up and down, and let out an excited shriek. Oh my god, in the space of a few minutes my career had shot off into the stratosphere. The manager of Abandon! I loved this place. I'd been here from its inception right back when Henry Carter had bought it and first employed me as his assistant. I'd watched it morph into its current incarnation and now I was to be instrumental in its development to its next. I was excited to get started, but for now I called Jess, because us two girls needed to celebrate over lunch.

"I couldn't believe it when he asked me if I'd take on the position of PA to him, the new manager, and the deputy." Jess grinned at me then took a pull on her soda. "I asked him if you'd got one of the positions, and he told me if you said no, he was in the shit cos he'd just given your job away."

"Aidan Hall is one ballsy dude," I told her.

"Yeah, or he knows you so well, he knew you'd bite his right arm off to get a promotion."

My eyes widened. "I can't believe it, Jess. I'm going to be the manager of Abandon. Hey, it's not going to be weird between us is it?" My brows furrowed.

"Ash, you've been the senior assistant to me for years and to be honest this promotion for you has been a long time coming. I'm ecstatic for you. I'm getting a promotion myself, so, no, I don't think it's going to change our dynamic too much. Anyway if you get too cocky, can I have permission to tell you to check yourself before you wreck yourself?" She started to laugh.

"Please do. Seriously, Jess. I can't believe it. Do you know I get an apartment with my job?"

Her jaw dropped open. "An apartment? I want to be the manager."

"It's going to be on the same floor as Abandon XL. Aidan said I had the choice whether to use it when I was working because myself and this Lucas guy will have to take turns to be around for twenty-four-seven cover, or to live there. Well, seeing as I basically live there anyway and I swear my current rental has bed bugs, it's a no-brainer."

"Well, I'm happy for myself today. But I'm not only happy for you, I'm jealous to all hell."

"Hey. I haven't met this Lucas guy yet. This could be the worst business decision I've ever made."

"See this glass?" Jess shook her soda glass at me. "It's half full, not half empty. That's how you need to see things. Fresh starts and all that."

Jess knew that I came from a family of deadbeats that I had no contact with, and an ex that did the cheating-with-my-best-friend thing. The way I saw it, my work was social. I met hundreds of people a week. My life was busy, and I had a job I loved. What had happened today was some kind of miracle and I felt like I needed to keep pinching myself.

"We're going to be meeting all kinds of celebrities and getting to know all their kinks." Jess winked. "It's going to be like Abandon Enquirer in our office."

"Ah, we'll too busy to worry about that nonsense," I told her.

"What? You mean if we got Tom Hardy in there naked you wouldn't wanna look? Seriously, girl, you need to get back in the game and get laid. You have a whole sex club at your disposal. Go play."

I put my head forward a little and placed a hand over my forehead. "You just shouted that I had a whole sex club at my disposal. People are staring."

Jess snorted. "Sorry, got a bit overexcited there at the thought of naked rock stars."

"Look. We have to keep professional. There'll be no fraternizing with any members, or staff."

"Whaaat? That's not a rule, seeing as our own boss bedded the bartender! Plus, he used to take part in threesomes before he took over ownership. Aidan has a mighty fine ass you know?"

I shook my head. "Well, it's my rule anyhow. To keep work separate from my personal life."

"What personal life?" Jess quipped. "You oughta give all the new toys in Abandon XL a try and loosen up a little."

"Have you used the club?" Though I'd known Jess a long time, I didn't really know that much about her, other than she lived with a roommate called Sheridan who'd been her best friend since high school.

"Yes!" she said. "A couple of times on the masquerade nights. I don't think I could have gone in there with the possibility of anyone recognizing me, but with a mask on, it was different. Like no one knew it was Jess from Hall Enterprises."

"Really?" I was intrigued now. "Did it add to the excitement, people not knowing it was you?"

"Hell, yeah. Plus, well, some of the guys there just had the best bodies: really ripped, gym-honed, bounce-quarters-off-them bodies." Her face took on a dreamy look. "I think I might have to do it again this week." Her eyes widened. "Hey, why don't you join in on the next one? It's on Friday, isn't it?"

"No way." I put a hand up. "For me Abandon is strictly business. That's how it's always been and that's how it will stay."

Jess shrugged her shoulders. "You're missing out."

"I may well be, but I need my focus to be on my job, especially now that I have the promotion. I need to make sure this club is the best it can be."

"Which you'd know if you tested it." Jess winked.

CHAPTER TWO

Ashley

I'd found it hard to sleep that night. For one thing I'd kept looking around my squalid apartment thinking that I didn't need to stay here anymore. With all that money going into my account the following day, I could just forgo the rest of my lease in this shit hole and move to a hotel while I looked for somewhere else to rent before my new apartment was ready. We were looking at a few months before the club and apartments were done so I needed a short-term tenancy. In the meantime, I'd start packing up my stuff, and tomorrow evening, I'd book into The Global, a luxury hotel near to work. I'd treat myself to a suite for a week and live the high life. What the hell. I worked hard, had been saving, and hadn't been on vacation. It was time to celebrate my promotion and have a little splurge. My stomach fizzed with excitement and that was one of the reasons I couldn't sleep.

The other was the fact I had to meet this guy the next morning—Lucas. What if I didn't like him? Aidan hadn't told me anything about his past experience, so I didn't know if he had a background in clubs, knew about property, nothing. I didn't even know his last name! We would have to work very closely together, so I hoped he was a friendly guy who didn't mind the fact that he'd have a female boss. He was taking over management of the main floor but needed training up first, and so he'd need to be able to listen and follow orders. Once my own floor was up and running, I'd take more of a back seat with Abandon and concentrate on XL, but I'd still be in charge overall. New people brought new ideas and while I was more than willing to listen to them, Abandon was a tightly run ship and I didn't want that rocking.

I reached over to my nightstand and flicked on the light. Propping myself up against the headboard I reached into my drawer for a jotter and pen and began writing down ideas as they came to me. Thoughts about decor, little extras we could offer like a personal shopping service while the VIPs were in the club maybe? Perhaps a massage room etc. Top DJs playing sets in the main bar?

Finally, at around 3:30am my eyelids began to droop and I threw the jotter and pen to the floor, flicked off the light and slipped down under the comforter. My alarm was set for 6am and sure enough in what seemed to be the blink of an eye, it was beeping and I needed to get on with the day.

I wanted to make a good impression. The meeting was with Aidan, Lucas, Jess and myself, so we could talk about the future direction of the business. I flung open my closet door and stared at the boring black suits and white blouses inside. PA corporate wear had been appropriate before, but now I was the boss. Well, the manager of Abandon. I didn't need to remind myself that Aidan was the boss overall. He had a commanding and pleasant demeanor, but I knew he needed to start delegating to other people. Not only were all his businesses majorly successful and expanding, but his girlfriend Lori was training to be a photographer in New Jersey, and he wanted to spend time with her now he'd found the 'love of his life'. It was strange to see the change that had come over Aidan in the last couple years. From a playboy who'd enjoyed the fruits of the club, to the owner, and now to a businessman who wanted to cut loose a little and enjoy life. Yet another reason I didn't want to date. My own career was now taking off and I didn't need any distractions. I needed to make sure that Aidan wouldn't regret his decision to give me this responsibility, and that if possible, I could get him a return on his investment in the least possible time.

I decided on a red silky top with a high neckline and tie sleeves, and a pair of black pants. I added some simple jewelry, grabbed my black jacket, and with a purse, plus a pair of elegant flats on my feet, I made my way to the tall building that housed the two floors belonging to Hall Enterprises. I was near the elevator when the doors started to close. I let out a large sigh of despair as it could take a while to get another with how busy this place got during the day, but just as I was about to turn away, a hand waved through the door and they re-opened, much to the annoyance of the rest of the inhabitants of the car.

"Thanks." I squeezed in at the side of the guy who'd held his hand out.

"No worries," he replied, giving me a wide smile. I looked over and my floor number was already lit so I took a deep breath. My nerves were starting to kick in. I wondered what Lucas looked like. And then I had a thought. No. It couldn't be? I checked out the guy who'd opened the doors. He was around six feet two, really tall at the side of my five six. He was dressed in a gray suit, with a pale-blue shirt, and a silver tie. His hair was blond and a little wavy. He caught me checking him out and gave me a little smirk. *Fuck!* I wasn't checking him out in that way, but he didn't know that did he? Anyway, the chances of me being in an elevator with Lucas whatever-his-surname-was in a building that housed hundreds of staff was unlikely. So maybe I could just drop my head down and check out his package on my way down to looking if my own shoes were clean.

Hmmmm. Packing by the looks of things. Hey, just cos I didn't date didn't mean I was dead inside.

The doors opened to my floor and I stepped out. The hottie did too.

He turned to me and laughed.

I tilted my head toward him. "Hey, you're not by any chance named Lucas, are you?" I said, expecting him to tell me I was mistaken.

What I didn't expect was for his body to stiffen and for the smile to slide off his face.

"I am." He glared at me, his gray eyes appearing icy cold without the crinkles caused by a smile, at the side of them.

"Seems you have me at a disadvantage, seeing as I don't know who you are." His voice was gravelly and abrupt.

Well, talk about showing your true colors. I

decided that he could kiss my ass seeing as he was being a douche.

"You'll find out soon enough," I told him, and I stomped off ahead of him.

I grabbed what I needed for the meeting. Jess was already waiting for me in my office. "I ordered refreshments, they are in the room waiting," she informed me.

"It's so strange not doing that myself."

"Well, Boss Lady, you'd better get used to it because I intend to be the best assistant you ever had."

"You're the only assistant I ever had." I laughed.

"Holy fuck. Is that the new guy?" Jess had just caught a glimpse of Lucas through the window.

"It would appear so. I rode the elevator with him. He seemed really nice at first then changed into an ass."

"How so?"

"I don't have time to explain now. Let's go through to Aidan's office and we'll let you form your own opinion."

"You know what hassle I've been through and now I have this shit again." Lucas' voice rang out through the door.

I turned to Jess. "Like I said, ass."

"Yeah it's really nice."

"Not look at his ass. He is an ass," I pointed out, a little too loudly. The voices inside the office shut down.

Closing my eyes, I took a deep breath. Professional, Ashley, professional.

And then I pushed open the door and walked into the office.

Aidan gave us a warm smile as we entered the room. "Lucas. May I introduce you to your new assistant, Jess Wallis. As I said to you before she will be working for all three of us, so please use her for work and not picking up laundry or choosing Mother's Day gifts..." Jess nodded at him and leaned over to shake his hand. "And this is Ashley Jenson, my right-hand woman and the new manager of Abandon and Abandon XL. She'll be training you to take over Abandon while she works on developing the floor upstairs, so you're all going to be very busy over the next few months. Prepare to live in each other's pockets and have no lives. Not much different for you, hey, Ash?" He winked and looked at Lucas. "I hardly see this one go home. See if you can take some of the pressure off so she can have a life." He chortled. "I was going to say leave the building, but you're going to live here."

I smiled and reached out to shake Lucas' hand. "I look forward to working with you."

He shook my hand in return, though the reluctance to do so was written all over his face and in the fact he dropped my hand like I'd handed him a turd.

"Okay, take a seat everyone. We have a lot to get through this morning." Aidan indicated the chairs at the end of the large table in the room. I ended up sat opposite Lucas. Lucky for me—not. Jess got everyone a coffee and Aidan started.

"I'm going to be away for the rest of the week, so I need everyone up to speed with what we need to get underway. Ash, could you mainly focus on getting Lucas trained up on Abandon? Introduce him to the staff on the floor and show him how everything works. Jess, can you take him to meet everyone upstairs and fix appointments for him with human resources for his health and safety inductions, IT for passwords, etc?

"Yes, sir."

Aidan laughed.

"It's only Lucas, you don't have to call me sir in front of him."

Lucas pulled on the neckline of his shirt as if it were strangling him, and then looked at me. "I should only need a brief tour of Abandon as Aidan already showed me the place, Miss, er, Mrs. Jenson?" he queried.

"It's Ashley to everyone in this building. We don't do the formal thing here unless we're trying to impress investors." He could screw himself if he thought I was telling him my marital status.

"So if an investor calls in?" He quirked an eyebrow.

"Then you can call me Ms. Jenson." I tried to communicate 'go fuck yourself' through my glare, but all that happened was his mouth ticked up a little more at the corner.

"Oh, stupid me. I forgot to formally introduce you to Lucas." Aidan smacked his forehead. "I guess I'm so used to him, I forget no one else knows him. He slapped Lucas on the back.

"Meet Lucas Hall," he announced. "My cousin."

CHAPTER THREE

Lucas

I should have known my cousin would still be the same interfering little shit as when we were small. 'Come and work for me', he'd said, 'managing my club'. He'd told me I'd be trained up. He had not told me that I would have a female manager. After the shit I had go down this past year, this just wasn't fucking happening.

It was goddamn typical. Meet an attractive woman in the lobby, get her in close proximity, and then find out she was your boss. Well, I needed a job, but the quicker I learned the ropes and she was outta my hair the better. She needed to be kept at arm's length.

Then I find out that it's all informal there, first

name terms and shit. Great. Mind you, with the way she snarled when I asked her if she was a Miss or a Mrs., I think I'll call her Princess Jenson just to wind her the fuck up.

I turned to my new assistant, Jess. "Jess, I can see you're taking notes. Would you kindly come to see me after the meeting so we can go through making the arrangements for me to meet the other staff and get my passwords and security set up?"

"Of course, Mr. Hall." She looked from me to Aidan. "Oh, that's gonna be weird, two Mr. Hall's," she said, followed by a smile.

I liked her straightaway. You could see she was an open book. "You'll have to call me Lucas then," I told her.

I caught Ash doing an eye roll. I stared at her again, but she didn't flinch under my gaze.

"Get him to make an appointment with me, Jess," she instructed. "You have my availability. I'll meet Lucas whenever he's ready to find out what happens around here." The statement was loaded with the unspoken words, 'I'm in charge'. I had no problem with her authority, as long as she kept it professional.

You see I'd just gone through an ordeal at my last place of work, where I'd managed a bar and my female boss, the owner, had sexually harassed me. It had started with her standing a little too close, then accidental brushes of her arm against mine, before the final act where she'd called me into her office for a one-to-one. Unknown to me, she'd locked the door behind her before proceeding to try to grope my cock over the top of my slacks. Then when I'd shown no interest, she'd stripped off her top baring her breasts. Once she realized that even after her stripping, I wasn't going to do anything with her, she'd ruffled up her hair and declared I'd attacked her. A long and drawn out investigation had yielded no evidence either way and her allegations were dropped. However, Aidan knew all this and knew that a female boss was the last thing I wanted. So what was he playing at?

"Okay. Ash, after Lucas is as self-sufficient as possible, could you then set up meetings to chat with designers, focus groups, and the project manager. Can you also work with designers on the apartments and ensure they have everything you both need?" He turned to Lucas. "You'll need to give her a list of anything you can't live without, like a fridge large enough for lots of beer."

Way to make me sound like a drunk player rather than a professional businessman, cous.

"I'll dictate a list to Jess," I said.

"Actually, I'd rather show you around the space so you can get a feel for the place," Ash challenged. "Also, even though I'm running Abandon XL, I'd still like your input. We're a team here, and you may have useful past experience. Where did you work before?"

"I managed a bar in Queens."

"Oh," Ash replied. "Was it a large venue?"

"Does size matter? Surely it's what you do with it?" I said and watched as her eyes blinked fast. I'd got her that time. Then I checked myself. If I made her feel uncomfortable then I was no better than that bitch, Jo. "I apologize for that remark. It was inappropriate. Put it down to first day nerves."

She ignored me.

Good.

"Well, I think that's enough for you to be getting on with this week. I'll leave it for you two to organize what hours you're working between you. Just please make sure the club is covered. Henry is only ever at the end of the phone if you need him. He might have sold his club to me, but he still can't quite let go."

"Would you show me around upstairs, Jess?" I asked her.

"Sure."

"Thanks, Aidan. Nice to meet you, Ash. I'll get Jess to fix up some time for you to show me around."

She nodded, but didn't make any attempt to stand to shake my hand or anything.

I left the room, following Jess upstairs.

"You can tell me to mind my own business but what was with the frosty atmosphere between you two? You don't even know each other, do you?" Jess challenged.

I sighed. "It was obvious, was it?"

"I was shivering; it was Siberia in there."

"I think we're going to get along great, Jess. I like people being straight with me."

"We're a team here, like Ash said, so you're going to have to start thawing that situation out, whatever it is. What's happened between you?"

"Nothing." I chewed on my lip. "I'm bringing baggage from my previous employment here and letting it cast a cloud over my first day. I'll apologize to her later and start afresh."

"Good." Jess nodded. "I don't want to end up being the middle guy in a boss war."

Jess was fabulous. She introduced me to everyone I needed to know on the office floor and I spent the rest of the day getting set up with everything I'd need to start work tomorrow. What I hadn't done was visit the club during opening hours, so I figured I'd go get settled in my hotel room, grab something to eat and then return to the club later in the evening.

"Can you let Ash know that I'll be around the club this evening?" I asked Jess. "If she has any free time then she could take me on a tour. If not, I'll just look around myself."

"Sure thing, boss." She saluted and I laughed.

I was staying in a hotel that Aidan had recommended, just down the street from the club. I'd only had time to drop off my luggage and hadn't even gotten my room key card yet. I got this from reception and took the elevator up to my room on the eighteenth floor. The room was great. With a king size bed, a desk, tv, and WiFi, I had everything I needed for the foreseeable. I required an estimate of when my apartment would be ready though as I couldn't live in a hotel for weeks on end. However, this week, this would be my home and as I threw myself onto what proved to be a very comfy mattress, I felt satisfied that I'd made the move.

Aidan and I were close. He'd lost his brother in a motorcycle accident when he was fourteen and so our families had spent a lot of time together with our shared grief. As we'd gotten older and made our own way in life, we'd not seen each other as much, but texted and called from time to time.

It felt good that we were back in each other's lives. I didn't have siblings, and I admired Aidan as a person, not just a family member. He'd promised we'd go for a drink soon, but my arrival had coincided with him jetting off to look for a new club venue. That was one thing about my cousin; his business brain never switched off. I was looking forward to meeting his girlfriend, Lori, too. The one who'd finally tamed him.

My stomach growled and I realized I needed to get some dinner if I was heading back to the club. I debated on ordering room service, but after traveling earlier, I couldn't rule out falling to sleep afterward, so the restaurant looked to be a better option.

After visiting the bathroom to freshen up, I grabbed my wallet and rode the elevator to the second floor on which the restaurant, *Carlo's*, was located. The smell of tomato and garlic permeated the air and my stomach rumbled in anticipation. As I stood waiting for the Maître D' to allocate me a table, I startled when I saw Ash sitting by a table near the window. As if she detected eyes on her, she turned my way, and I received an eye roll as recognition hit her features.

Shit. I was going to have to sort this situation out.

"I'm gonna see if my colleague will allow me a seat at her table," I informed the Maître D' after giving him my room details and I made my way over to Ash.

"Well, I wasn't expecting to see you here," I said. "Do you mind if I join you? We seem to have gotten off on the wrong foot."

"Sure." She shrugged in an ambivalent fashion.

I took a seat opposite her and the waiter came up and took my order for a beer. "Do you want anything?" I asked Ash.

"No, I'm good thank you." She turned to the waiter. "Could you ask them to hold my food order until Mr. Hall's is also ready?"

I didn't want to delay her dinner and have her pissed at me for that too, so I quickly picked up the menu and ordered the first thing I saw, a lasagna.

The waiter left us, and I took a sharp inhale of breath before speaking.

"I want to clear the air. I've been an ass and it's not your fault. It's mine. I'm projecting shit from my past onto my future. I fucked up. I'm sorry."

She sat up straighter at the table. "Look, Lucas. I don't know anything about where you've come from. How you got the job. I'm clueless. Then you were fine in the lift but suddenly went artic on me. I'm committed to my job and you need to know that. I won't play games, I don't have the time. So if you have stuff to say, let's hear it so that we can get on with our work."

"You're the consummate professional, huh?"

"Completely, so don't mess me around." Her narrowed eyes showed me that she wasn't going to put up with any more douche behavior from me.

My drink arrived and I took a taste of my beer. It

was heaven in a glass. While I drank, I considered my position and I decided to be straight with her.

"I had issues at my last place of work." I looked directly at Ash even though I found it difficult to do so. "I was accused of sexual harassment by a boss who actually sexually harassed *me*—a female boss."

"Oh."

"Aidan didn't tell me that I was coming here and getting another female boss."

"Hey!" she barked out sharply.

I put up a hand to stop her. "You don't need to say anything. I'm not insinuating that you were going to molest me. It's just been a very difficult year and I'm still sore over it, wary." I decided I may as well be truthful. "Can I be candid, without you getting pissed at me?"

"You can try, but I'm making no assurances."

"Look, when I saw you in the lobby this morning, and held the elevator, well... let's just say I wouldn't have done it for everyone. When I then found out you were my boss... I reacted by going 'arctic' as you put it."

She took a sip of her wine and sat back in her seat. "Well, that makes sense so thank you for explaining that to me, but you can be assured that I don't shit where I eat. There's a relaxed rule about staff dating at Abandon, but I made my own rule a long time ago. No work relationships. What you see with me is what you get. I'm hardworking, obsessed with making Abandon the best there is, and I don't have time for relationships fucking with that. So can we draw a line under this now? I'm sorry you had that happen to you, it must have been very stressful, but no matter how hot a man is, if they work for Abandon, they're off the menu."

"Are you saying I'm hot?"

She flushed. "No. I meant *if* they were hot."

I started laughing and a smile finally broke across Ash's face too. I raised my glass and held it out across the table.

"Here's to a fantastic new *business* relationship." I stressed the word business and we clinked glasses.

We chatted while we ate dinner. "So how are you finding your room?" she asked me. "What kind did you book?"

"Just a standard, to keep costs down for now. Can we prioritize getting our apartments done though?" I wiped my mouth with a napkin. "Do you eat here a lot? I guess it's handy, being close to the club."

"Oh, I'm staying here. My treat for my promotion at work. I have the worst apartment, it makes you want to have a bath when you leave. So I decided I'd pay for a small suite for a week. I know I'm going to die when I get the final bill, but I have toweling robes, a jacuzzi bath, a huge flatscreen, a couch, desk, and the most comfortable bed ever. For once, I'm actually resenting having to go to work as I just want to starfish and eat chocolates—of which they left a complimentary box on my bed." Her eyes lit up.

"Hmmm, sounds a lot better than mine. So you're a chocolate woman, huh?"

"Yes." She patted her stomach. "Hence I'm not a gym bunny."

There was nothing wrong with Ash's body. She was tall and willowy, with long brown hair, but I refrained from commenting about her appearance. Just as we agreed, it was strictly professional.

She finished her meal and groaned. "Oh, I'm so full. I just want to go to my room and sleep for a week, but work awaits. Jess said you were coming over tonight to look around. I have time to show you a working night."

I indicated for the waiter to bring us separate bills. I would have paid for both, but could guess that Ash would demand we pay our own way. We signed the tab and then got to our feet.

I pointed in the direction of the exit.

"After you, boss. You lead and I'll follow."

For now. I thought. *Until I can run the floor my own way.*

CHAPTER FOUR

Ashley

So the reason for his sudden change in personality had been revealed. Now that was out in the open and the air cleared, I hoped we could begin a great working relationship. I was glad that Aidan had already showed him around the club when it was closed, so he knew what all the rooms were. It was a totally different experience to see the club full though and I saw his Mr. Cool persona drop a little as he walked into the main bar area where a guy was sitting at a table, his pants around his ankles while a woman blew him.

"I knew what the club was about and yet when you

see it directly in front of you, wow; I guess that takes some getting used to?" He looked at me, his head tilted.

"A week in and it'll seem second nature," I told him as we headed to the bar. I gestured to Damien, one of the head bartenders. "Can I have a coke please, and a beer for Lucas." I introduced him to the rest of the bartenders. We took our drinks and headed to a table away from the guy moaning in ecstasy as he prepared to shoot his load down the woman's throat.

"So, how long have you worked here?" he asked me.

"Sixteen years. I started off working for the original owner, Henry."

His eyes widened. "You must have been very young?"

"Yeah, eighteen."

"Did this not come as a shock to you then? All the sex and debauchery?"

I smiled. "At first. I'd taken on a job as Henry's assistant and I didn't know what all his businesses were. He was mainly a property developer; so yes, I admit I was a little shocked at first, but like I said, within a short space of time you just become used to it, seeing it day in, day out."

He leaned closer to me. "So, does the arousal wear off? Because seeing that guy over there being deep throated has me in the throws of what I think may be the start of blue balls."

I laughed at his honesty. He wasn't being lewd, just open, and I would be the same.

"At first you'll be constantly turned on, but after a while you'll become immune to most of it. All I find is that particular scenes might give me a frisson now."

"I guess something that you might be into would still turn you on, is that what you're saying?"

"I guess. Just occasionally I'll walk past something, and well, parts of me show they're still alive after all."

He took a drink of his beer.

"So, a week in and I won't have to walk around with my briefcase in front of my trousers?"

"Yes, you should be good by then."

There was a silence for a moment, then he broke it.

"So, my cousin bedded a bartender?"

"He did. Though she didn't work here very long. You know her other job, right?" I hoped he did, because it wasn't my place to tell him.

"That she was an adult movie actress? Yeah, he told me. I have to admit I took some convincing that he'd found the woman of his dreams."

"She certainly is and just as understanding seeing as her boyfriend owns a sex club and an adult movie company."

"He always was weird."

"You two were close I take it?" I realized I was

getting personal. "Sorry, you don't have to answer that. It wasn't a business question."

"It's fine. Yeah, we were. I kinda became a second brother to him after Rick died. But you know, time moves on and our lives went in different directions until recently, when he decided to bring me into his sordid enterprises." He smirked.

"It will be nice to have a team to work with. My job was getting ridiculously busy and given Abandon's future plans, I was due a breakdown anytime soon."

"See, now you won't have to have one. You can just call me on my cell and we'll go grab a coffee. Caffeine keeps me sane."

I couldn't help but study Lucas while I was directly in front of him. As long as the coffee we were grabbing wasn't back at his hotel room we were fine. *Stop your mind from going there right now,* I lectured myself. Seriously, I saw good looking men all the time, usually with their clothes off, so why was I getting flustered by this one? *Maybe because he has his clothes on and you're wondering what's underneath*, my traitorous mind replied.

"Right, shall I show you around the rest of the club? Then we could go up to check out the apartment space and you could let me know what sort of thing you're looking for? The sooner we can get plans submitted, the quicker we get our apartments."

"Are you living in yours full-time then? Not just when working?"

"I can't see the point of being anywhere else. I'm here most of the time anyhow. May as well live here, I practically do already."

He got off his seat.

"Come on then. Let's see Abandon in action."

The first place I took him to was through to the rooms with the large beds and big glass windows where you could watch the action.

Lucas groaned. "This place is going to kill me."

I laughed. I was so used to it all these years later, that it was amusing to see someone so affected by it. All the staff went through it, but it made Lucas seem more human.

"Seriously, is there a back office with photos of really ugly hairy bodies, and cold showers?"

As I looked at Lucas I was taken aback by the sheer hunger in his eyes. He looked at me through hooded lids. His voice was raspy. He was deeply turned on by his surroundings and I felt a stirring somewhere I shouldn't when I recognized his lust-fueled gaze. I quickly turned away.

"Look, let's have a break from this and go up to the upper floor."

It was strange going up to a floor usually busy with office workers. We exited the elevator into the lobby and were greeted by silence. It was eerie and I was pleased I hadn't come up here on my own. I could detect the close proximity of Lucas' body to my own, his heavy breath near my ear. I needed space.

I pressed a switch and light flooded down the offices as the main lights flickered on.

Lucas shielded his eyes from the bright glare after the dim golden ambience of the floor below.

"This way," I informed him.

He followed me down to the offices that would be converted to our apartments. We had to pass Aidan's office on this floor, and I headed inside to my desk and picked up a jotter and pen.

After I'd explained how the plans looked and what our apartments would contain, I turned to Lucas.

"So, any specific requests? Décor etc?"

"A hotel room look. Gray, black, white, chrome. All mod cons. I like to cook, so a kitchen is important. A speaker system where music can be heard in every room. A comfortable sofa and a massive flatscreen. I like to put my feet up when I relax. A large shower stall because I find in some hotel rooms or apartments I've rented that I'm squashed up against the glass when I'm trying to wash."

An image of Lucas' naked chest crushed up against the stall glass, water showering down on him came unbidden into my mind. I became aware of my breasts engorging, pushing against my bra, my nipples hardening. *I must stop this, I need to work with this man. I don't do relationships and Lucas has already taken me into his confidence about what happened with his last female boss.*

I took a few steps away from him.

That sounds good. I think I'll talk with the designer about both being like that. A hotel room look is a great idea. I'll make sure we get the workspace we'd get in a hotel room too. Once the designer has come up with some visuals, I'll get Jess to set up a meeting with us and Aidan so we can get everything approved."

"Good job I like you, given we're going to be working together and neighbors." He smiled.

"Well, a lot of the time you'll be working when I'm in my apartment and vice-versa so it's not like we're going to be in each other's space too much. I'll have my VIPs to entertain. Speaking of which, I need to get to my office and make some calls. I want to meet with some and get some idea of what my VIP club is going to look like. Are you going back to the club?" I asked him.

"I'll go and check out the rest of the rooms and then I'm going to call it a night and go back to the hotel. I'll catch up with you tomorrow sometime."

"I'll be in from 2pm. I'm working until 4am tomorrow."

"Yes, we need to get Jess to look at our schedules because I need to learn about Abandon as soon as possible so that you can be a little freer; get to relax now and then."

"That'll never happen," I told him. "This club is my life."

CHAPTER FIVE

Lucas

"This club is my life."

It was months now since I'd heard Ash state those words and yet they still held true. She was like a beautiful robot. As a businesswoman, I admired her greatly. She was professional—courteous but took no nonsense—and Aidan had been right to ask her to take on the role of manager. She excelled at it. I'd watched over the last few months as she'd held court over the many professionals we'd had to employ to see Abandon XL come to fruition. Tonight was the night of the first official booking. Ashley had already held a discreet opening night inviting only a select few guests and the place was already booked out for months ahead.

I had now taken over as manager of Abandon and we had staff in place so that both establishments ran efficiently and so we could actually see our brand new apartments from time to time. We'd both finally moved into them last week. Aidan had insisted on paying for Ash's hotel room when I'd told him where she was staying. She wasn't happy, but when he moved me to a suite on the same floor and I didn't protest, she stopped complaining.

We'd become friends and met for dinner when our work patterns allowed. Unfortunately, friends wasn't enough for me. I wanted more. My every sex-filled dream was about that woman, about that sharp as a knife tongue swirling around the head of my cock, about me plunging within her warm depths. It was torture to be around her, to see her walk around the club, watch as she smiled at a customer and flicked her hair over her shoulder, watch her sit in meetings crossing a shapely leg over the other.

The temptation to take home a different woman from the club each evening had been overwhelming, but I recalled Ash's words to me about not shitting where she ate. Apparently she liked to tell all the staff that in the hope they'd avoid working relationships and help her avoid staffing conflicts when the relationships petered out. You could see why they would happen here though, amongst an atmosphere of constant sex, lust, and abandon. Aidan had named the place well.

I'd thought my floor had enough action, but Ash had gone all out to make sure that XL really was about the elite indulging their every desire.

Once again, just like on my floor, there was a bar area with tables and chairs that made the place look like a sophisticated bar. But it was the rooms this bar led to that added the XL. One room had one giant bed in it. It was actually a series of beds that had been put together, mattresses sown to make one large one. The bed could take approximately forty couples and the walls had been hand painted with orgiastic scenes of sexual excess, debauchery, and gluttony. There were a series of smaller rooms all with hand-painted artwork on the walls and the fittings you'd expect from a five star plus hotel. Each even had its own large wetroom. There was one larger BDSM room complete with 'equipment', and a harem room, where one man or one woman could book and choose how many others came into the room with them. The room's rules were one person of one sex and at least three of the opposite, and that everyone had to receive the ultimate pleasure; no one should be left unsatisfied. Ash had said reverse harems had been the latest trend in ebooks. I'd been surprised when she'd told me she read the titles appearing in the Amazon Erotica Top 100 often as they gave her an insight into current sexual trends and interests.

The harem room had a switch that meant that everything the occupants did would be played out on a screen in the interconnected small cinema. An intercom ran between the two and the 'actors' could view who was observing and call for participants to their 'movie'. The staff knew how to attend to every demand of the divas and playboys who would book Abandon XL, but most would bring their own staff along with them, ready at any notice to supply condoms, a new set of clothes, or a masseur.

In all the months I'd been working with Ash, to my knowledge she had not had a single date. Her life was indeed the club and she thrived on it. It was as if every success of her work gave her a high, a buzz that had replaced the need for sexual satisfaction and a relationship. I'd never asked her about it outright because yes, I would now say I was a friend, but I was a colleague mostly and I knew I mustn't do anything to jeopardize that. However, it was becoming more and more difficult with every day that passed.

Tonight, I had Jess looking after my floor. She was now deputy manager, as she had outgrown her assistant role. Aidan had met with us a month ago to restructure. Ash was manager of Abandon XL and overall general manager. I was the manager of Abandon. Jess, and a man called Connor who had worked for GoDown Productions, were now deputies, and between the four of us we kept the club running at its best. New assistants had taken Jess and Connor's places and soon there would be even more advancement as Aidan was in the process of buying a club in Miami.

He'd asked me if I wanted to go there as general manager. I'd asked him for time to think about it.

He'd looked at me with confusion on his face but had agreed to give me a couple of weeks and said no more.

I did not want to leave. I wanted to stay where Ash was.

But if there would never be anything between us maybe the best thing I could do was go?

CHAPTER SIX

Ashley

The last few months had been a whirlwind. If I'd thought I'd been busy before, it was nothing at the side of the work undertaken to get the new floor and apartments completed, alongside training new staff and schmoozing prospective clientele. Aidan had insisted on me staying at The Global and I had to say it had been a blessing, being able to relax in luxury when I was eventually able to leave work.

Lucas had proved to be an excellent support and held the reins of Abandon with ease. We'd become firm friends and thank fucking God he had not detected the giant crush I appeared to have developed on him. I was embarrassed at my own behavior, prettying myself up for work, getting into bed at night and replaying every conversation we'd had where he might have smiled at me a little or said something complimentary. He never crossed a line, remaining strictly professional at all times. Unfortunately, the more I knew I couldn't have him, the more I wanted him. I tried to tell myself that it was just the fact I'd had no time for a relationship. Maybe if I just put myself out there again, had someone take me to bed and satisfy my sexual urges, my libido might calm down when I was in Lucas' vicinity.

I knew that there was no way he'd been a saint since he got here. He must have dated or slept with women surely? But he gave nothing away, kept that side of himself private.

I'd dated no one, throwing myself completely into work, and now the fruits of our labor were here. I was stood at the bar in Abandon XL waiting to welcome our first proper client, a rock star called Denver Lomas. Den was the lead singer of F-Higher (pronounced fire), who were setting the charts alight and currently held the top five positions on the American Billboard Chart.

Denver was living a life of excess, in a world where no one currently wanted to say no to him. He'd paid me three times the usual fee to secure the very first use of Abandon XL. We'd donated the extra to Aidan's charity.

I wasn't all that interested in music, but you'd got to be dead not to have heard of Denver or F-Higher, and when he walked in, his charisma hit me with such force I felt I could have flown backward. They say people have the X-factor, this guy had the whole fucking alphabet.

He held out a hand and I reached out my own to shake with his, but he grabbed me and pulled me into a hug. The smell of his musky aftershave mixed with that of cigarette smoke and bourbon. It was a heady mix. He let go of me and gave me a cocky grin.

"I'm about to let loose in your sex club, didn't seem right just shaking your hand."

I guffawed with laughter. "Well I'm certainly not about to shake anything else."

His jaw dropped open. "Oh my god, that's not how I meant..."

I held a hand up. "I'm messing with you. Now we've already talked about all the rules. Just to remind you that no one will be admitted without their invite. If they left it at home, they'll have to return for it. They'll be searched at the door and any electronic equipment will be confiscated. We have signed confidentiality agreements from all participants, so all I have left to say is thank you for choosing Abandon XL for your entertainment and let me know if there's anything else you need."

"I don't suppose your personal cell number is available?" He winked at me.

"Afraid not. I don't mix business and pleasure."

"Shame. Oh well, if you change your mind, you're welcome to come play."

With that he ordered a drink and the evening got underway.

The next few hours passed smoothly, apart from a small drama at reception when someone didn't want to be separated from the narcotics they'd tried to bring in. After some time in the office I decided to walk around the club and witness its first use. I figured it would help me see if any tweaks were needed with the design.

In the orgy room they'd laid fruit out on a model's body and were eating it from her flesh. They were also playing with her, licking her nipples and between her thighs. To me this was so cliché, and I couldn't help but feel bemused that even at this level of VIP there seemed to be a limited number of ideas for enjoyment.

My biggest surprise was in the harem room. There I discovered Denver with three other women. Their scenario was being played out on the movie screen watched by around seven other people. I stood in the shadows and watched.

I didn't know why but I'd imagined Denver letting all the women service his every need, but that wasn't what happened. They were a tangle of arms and legs and everyone was being brought to the dizzy heights of climax. Not one of them was left out or there to put on a show for others. It was the true purpose of the harem room, for multiple people to mutually enjoy themselves, and I was pleasantly surprised to see it being used properly. As a rock star, I'd imagined the cliché of Denver having his cock sucked while he watched the two other women feast on each other. Maybe I shouldn't be so judgmental.

"How's it all going?" A gruff voice appeared beside me and it made me jump and move forward.

I put a hand across my chest.

"Lucas. Jesus, you gave me a heart attack."

"Transfixed were you?" He smirked.

I folded my arms across my chest. "I'm just walking around seeing all the rooms in action. I think it's a success. No one has raised any issues so far."

"With your meticulous planning it couldn't fail to be anything else," Lucas whispered, mindful of the other viewers.

I'd failed to realize that I had moved from the shadows out more into the room until I watched on screen as Denver leaned back and pressed his intercom button.

"Well, Ms. Jenson. I hope you're enjoying the show. You're more than welcome to join us." He beckoned me with his index finger.

I shook my head and pressed the reply intercom button. "Thank you, but I'm still working."

"Pity," Denver replied. "This is what you're missing."

He proceeded to flip one of the women over onto her back and then he pushed her thighs apart, running his thumb over her flesh and nub so we were witness to her glistening pussy, and then he put his head down and feasted there. By the look on the woman's face, Denver had a talented tongue. I felt a little stab between my legs and I swallowed, my throat dry.

"The guy's a dick," Lucas almost growled. "Ignore him. He should respect your professional boundaries. That's the trouble with rock stars, they think they own the world."

"He's harmless. He asked for my number earlier."

I felt Lucas' shoulders stiffen at the side of me. "Did you give it to him?"

I sneered at him. "Don't be stupid. I'm not some schoolgirl with a crush. I'm the general manager."

Lucas shrugged. "He's a good-looking dude. Nothing to stop you dating him outside of the club."

"He's not my type," I snapped, and I turned and left the room.

Annoyingly, Lucas followed me.

"Have you not got your own floor to watch over?" I asked, still abrupt in tone.

"It's fine and I have my cell and pager as you well know. What's bit your ass? I only came to see how your first proper night was going."

I sighed. "I'm sorry. I'm just still a little on edge about tonight being a success. You know how much I've been worrying."

Lucas placed a hand on my arm; I could feel the warmth transmit through my skin. "Look around you, Ash. Does it look like it's not going well?"

"I can't help it," I told him.

"Look. Why don't we take a bottle of wine and go up to my apartment? We have our pagers and the staff are more than capable of doing their jobs. You don't have to be here all the damn night. Let's go have a toast to the first official night of Abandon XL."

I toyed with my lip while looking around. "Hmmmm, I don't know."

Lucas huffed in frustration. "Ash, you're like three minutes walk away; one minute if you run."

"Okay, God, you're such a nag. I'll get a bottle of red."

As soon as I got through the door of Lucas' apartment, I flopped onto the sofa and kicked off my heels. We'd done this for a while now, chilled out in each other's company. It was familiar and nice. "Christ, my feet are killing. New shoes were a mistake. I should have worn them in first."

He passed me a glass of wine. "Here, that'll make it all feel better."

I took a sip and my eyes closed as I took in the flavors. "Mmmm, that is just what I needed." I opened my eyes. "Thank you."

Lucas was looking at me strangely. Like he was a little uncomfortable.

"Is something wrong?"

He shook his head. "No. I was just enjoying watching you enjoying the wine."

My face flushed. "Oh my god, was I that bad?"

He laughed. "I wondered if the wine had been laced with oysters."

I threw a cushion at him. "Jerk."

He threw it back. "You love me really."

I stared at him. There was something different tonight in the air. Had been since we'd been in the room watching Denver. He stared back at me. I saw his eyes flicker over my breasts, back up to my mouth, my eyes. My breathing increased just a fraction and I was aware that I was sprawled across Lucas' sofa, my dress having ridden up my thighs slightly. I'd been too tired to notice.

"You should start dating. You need a life outside the club. Maybe one date with Denver could be fun?" Lucas said, and it was like he'd thrown a bucket of ice-cold water over me.

I sat up abruptly on the sofa, drained the rest of my wine and reached over for my shoes, quickly placing them back on my feet.

"I thought Denver was a dick?"

"Maybe I was being judgmental and stereotypical? I don't actually know the guy. I shouldn't assume."

"Thanks for the drink. I'm going to go make sure everything's okay and then I'm going to head to my own apartment."

"Okay. I've realized how tired I am. Going to call it a night."

I left Lucas' apartment wondering what the hell had caused his sudden change in personality. For a moment there I'd been stupid enough to think he might have actually been a little interested in me. I could have slapped myself in the face. He was my colleague. I needed to stop being an idiot. Perhaps it really was time to start dating again. Was I going to let my last romance be with the douche who went off with my friend? I smacked my purse into the wall, not caring if anything inside broke. I was done being a victim. Lucas was right, the business was running smoothly. It appeared a success. Maybe it was now time to have a little more life myself. I thought back to what Jess had said about Masquerade nights. There was no reason why I couldn't just enjoy some casual sex for a while, or go on dates with rock stars. What was stopping me? It certainly wasn't Lucas Hall.

I stomped back across to the club.

"Hey, pretty lady. I thought you'd *abandon*ed me. Get it?" Denver was sitting on a sofa surrounded by the rest of his group, no sexual exploits in sight.

"Stick to the life of a rock star, and don't try for comedy, will you?" I winked.

"Sit, sit." He tapped the sofa at the side of him and made his bandmate shuffle over. "I like this one," he told his bandmate. "She doesn't take no shit."

I sat alongside him and caught the eye of one of our bartenders. "Can you bring a tray of tequila? We're doing shots," I told them.

I spent the next hour having fun with the band. Denver told me he'd had a great time, but there was only so much sex he had the energy for in one night. He said they'd definitely book the venue again and would also help spread the word amongst their close circle. I couldn't ask for more. I let myself go a little until I was feeling looser. This was so unlike me, to let my mask of professionalism slip, but tonight I just didn't give a damn. I was celebrating the success of the new venture.

I'd thought Aidan might have popped by, but he seemed happy these days to leave things to the team. He and Lori were planning their wedding, so I guess he had his hands full.

We called time on the proceedings and as usual with Abandon it took a while to get people out of the building. As we were leaving, I stayed in the lobby as Denver called the elevator.

"Goodbye, beautiful. I'll book XL every night if it means I get to see your gorgeous face," he slurred.

I laughed. "Maybe one day I'll let you take me on that date."

He grabbed my hand and went on his knees, kissing the back of it. "It'll be the date of a lifetime, I promise," he said. Then his security detail encouraged him into the car and he was gone with a 'call me'.

I wandered back into the club and gathered the staff around. "Tonight has been amazing. Drinks anyone?" We partied for the next hour letting our hair down. We all deserved it.

The best thing about being a little wasted when you leave a club is if your apartment is only a few minutes walk away. The only problem was I couldn't quite get the door open. After a few minutes I decided that I could sleep on the floor with my head against the door and it would be perfectly acceptable, given the hallway had a plush carpet. I even could use my purse as a cushion for my head. I'd just closed my eyes when the door nearby opened.

"What the fuck?"

Footsteps moved nearer to my body, but I didn't open my eyes.

"Ash, why are you on the floor?"

"Jesus, trying to sleep here." I huffed.

"Are you drunk?" Lucas asked me.

"Nope. I'm just a little tired and my door is broken."

He moved my head forward to get to my purse.

"Hey, that's my pillow," I protested.

I finally managed to open my eyes to see Lucas rummaging through my purse before bringing out some keys. He fitted one in the lock and holding my shoulder he opened the door. I was glad he had hold of me because I think I would have just fallen backwards. I didn't see the need to get on my feet, so I turned over and crawled across the floor toward my bedroom. I swear I could hear a chuckle as I did so.

"What've you been drinking?" A voice came from above. I moved to the end of my bed and sat with my back against it.

"Tequila."

"Right. With Denver," he said, his jaw jutting out.

"With Denver and his band, and then after with my staff."

I sat and cackled to myself.

"What?" Lucas said, seemingly getting angrier with every passing second.

"I'm like that one tequila, two tequila, three tequila, floor, because I'm on the floor." I burst into noisy laughter and I found it funnier and funnier. I couldn't stop.

"Jesus."

I closed my eyes.

"Ash, you aren't going to sleep there. I'll get you into bed and then I'll make you some coffee."

"Good luck. No man has got me into bed in a long time," I retorted, before laughing again.

His arms went under mine and he lifted me up and moved me onto my bed where I slumped. It was the comfiest thing ever. I mean I knew we'd purchased the best mattresses and bedding, but right now I really appreciated just how comfortable it was.

"Lucas. Get on this bed, it's so comfy," I demanded, patting the mattress at the side of me while staring at the ceiling.

Lucas dragged me up the bed until I was at the headboard and then he propped me up. I looked down at my legs and saw that my dress had ridden up all the way to my waist and my red lacy panties were currently on full display.

With a strangled groan Lucas threw a robe over my legs.

"I'm not that heavy," I huffed. But he'd already left to get the coffee.

CHAPTER SEVEN

Lucas

The first thing I did when I went into the kitchen was throw cold water in my face. The sight of Ash sprawled out on the bed legs apart showing off those red lacy panties had my cock straining at the leash. I'd had to focus on her drunk face to dampen my ardor, which although cute, wasn't the slightest bit sexy as she pulled weird facial expressions.

Coffee. I set up the machine, thankfully identical to the one in my room and made us both a drink.

As I took them through to Ash's bedroom, I saw that she'd fallen asleep. There was no way I was leaving her in such a state, so I got on the bed at the other side of her and sat there for a while drinking my coffee. Then I drank the one I'd made for her. I'd just sit a while longer and then I'd go back to my own apartment...

I woke to find Ash's face pushed up against my right pec, her leg thrown over mine.

Holy fucking shit! I'd fallen asleep sat up and she must have moved over. I carefully shuffled myself off the edge of the bed. As Ash's head left my body and hit the mattress she woke with a start.

"What the—"

"Hey, you're okay, Ash. You're in your room. You had a lot to drink. I've been making sure you're okay," I told her scrunched-up face.

She put a hand over her face and groaned. "God, my head."

"I'll go get you a glass of water and two Advil." I knew she kept them in a drawer in the kitchen. Rushing out, I took the two coffee mugs with me.

When I returned, she was sat up, but had got under the covers, her dress still on. She took the water and tablets from me. "I vaguely remember not being able to get in my apartment and you lifting me onto the bed but that's about all," she said. "The staff and I celebrated. I'm sorry. It won't happen again."

"Seriously it's fine. You were no trouble."

"But I'm your boss. You shouldn't see me in this state. It's unprofessional and I don't want you to think I'm being untoward."

"Ash, you are not Jo. Never in a million years would I take anything you did as unprofessional. You aren't that kind of woman. To be honest it was nice seeing you let your hair down. You're funny when you're wasted."

"Oh my god. What did I do?" She put her hands over her eyes.

"Just tried to sleep on the floor outside the apartment."

She groaned again and looked at the clock. "Thank goodness it's a day off."

"Yes, Sunday is the day of rest. So get your coffee and then you can either go back to sleep or hit the shower."

"Thanks for looking after me, but you don't have to stay now," she said. "I've already taken up too much of your time."

"But what if I want to stay?" I raised a brow. "I've already been here half the night and fell asleep on that side of the bed."

Her face heated up. "Seriously? Oh God. I really am sorry, how frikkin unprofessional."

"Ash, stop apologizing, right now. Let's find some program on the TV to watch while we enjoy a coffee and then if you're up to it I'll fix us some breakfast. If you want me to scoot, just say so and I'll leave you to your hangover, but I've no plans today, so we can just chill if you like."

"I'm goddamn starving," she said. "I could eat bacon and eggs. There are some in the fridge." She gave me a little smile. "Okay, I can take a hint," I said, and I went to cook the princess her breakfast.

She devoured the food in what seemed like seconds and then consumed another coffee.

"Oh, I feel so much better now. Thanks, Lucas," she said. "I think I'll hit the shower now. You're free to go. Thanks again." She leaned over and kissed my cheek and then she stopped, placing a hand over her mouth. "Lucas, I'm so sorry. I shouldn't have done that."

"Will you calm down. You've hardly molested me, have you?" I reassured her. "You're very welcome. I couldn't let you choke on your own vomit, could I?" I got up from the bed. "Right, I'll let you get your shower and I'll catch you later. I'm meeting Aidan tonight, just for a bite to eat and a cousin catch up. If you see me resting against my door, I'll expect you to put me to bed and take care of me."

She threw a pillow at me. "Get out of here."

I walked toward the door. "Catch you later."

"Thank you, Lucas, for maybe saving my life," she shouted after me. "Sorry about the kiss again."

Was she sorry? It was only a peck on the cheek, but I wasn't sorry she'd done it. Neither was I sorry that I'd woken to find her cuddled against me. In fact, I was headed to my own bed right now to think about that one some more. My cock agreed and I went into my apartment and hit the sack.

Aidan and I met at a steakhouse downtown and got caught up on family stuff and business. "So, you and Lori. You reckon she's the one?"

He nodded. "I do. I'm gonna marry that woman one day. But right now, she's finishing up her studying, so I'm letting her concentrate on that. It means a lot to her, to achieve that."

"Who'd have thought someone would tame the wild beast that is Aidan Hall." I took a pull of my beer.

"Yeah, I swore I wouldn't find a woman. Even had a bet with Henry and Eli about it."

"What the fuck! You didn't?" My eyes were wide.

"Yeah, first time I've been pleased that I lost a

wager. So how about you then, any women in your life?"

"Nah, I'm not ready to settle down just yet."

"You know I see how your eyes follow Ash around like a little puppy dog's, right?"

I startled so much I almost spilled my beer.

"What? Is it that obvious?" I choked out.

"Nah, bro. I was messing with you. I've seen the occasional glance I thought was a bit lust-ridden, but thanks for confessing. Good to know. You going to do anything about your crush on your boss then?" He winked.

"You're such a douche. I can't believe I fell for that. You'd think I'd be aware of all your wind-ups by now." I was seriously pissed that he'd gotten this out of me. It was bad for my job.

"Look, I know you had the drama with that Jo bitch, but Ash isn't like that."

"I can't ask my boss on a date, dude. She said she doesn't date people she works with. Anyhow, even if she did, what if she turned me down? That would do well for future business, when we couldn't even look at each other. What if we dated and split up?"

"What if you were perfect for each other and it all worked out?"

"We'll never know because I won't ask."

"Fine. Well if you were to change your mind, if

things didn't work out you could go manage the club in Miami."

"I won't be changing my mind."

Aidan looked at me with a raised eyebrow but changed the subject to the night before.

"It would appear XL was a success yesterday. I had a call this morning from Denver himself personally to say how fantastic my new venue was, and how efficient my manager."

"Yeah, fucking jerk."

Aidan's brows creased. "Did he do something I'm unaware of?"

"He hit on Ash. I mean come on, he had all those females in the club and he hit on the manager of the establishment. Not very respectful is it?"

"No, it's not. Though I wouldn't expect anything better from him. He's known for his player ways. I take it she declined his offer?"

"She did. Though I might have told her she should go out on a date with him."

Aidan raised a hand to his forehead half covering his eyes. "You did what?"

"Look, she needs to date other guys, then maybe I can get over this teenage boy crush I'm having and we can get on with our jobs. But I see her round the clock and so it's not surprising I've gotten like this. It's like being in the *Big Brother* house or something. It amplifies your feelings when you're spending so much time together."

"Lucas. You work on different floors, have different shift patterns, and although your apartments are next door you don't have to spend time together. So why do you think you both are? Please don't do an Eli and lust after your assistant for years without doing anything."

"Me and Ash have a platonic friendship. That. Is. All," I snapped.

"You keep telling yourself that," Aidan replied.

I wanted to punch that smug grin off his face.

CHAPTER EIGHT

Ashley

The door closed behind Lucas and I slid down under the comforter, pulling it over my head. Fuck, I'd acted crazy last night. Drinking tequila with the band and then drinking with the staff? So across the lines of professionalism. Lucas had found me sat outside my own door? I vaguely remembered not being able to get my key to work. My cheeks were hot with embarrassment. I just kissed Lucas on the cheek. It seemed right at the time, a friendly thank you, except for when my lips hit his cheek, I kinda wanted my whole body to follow and push him back onto the bed.

This would not do, and anyway, before my

drunken behavior last night in his apartment, he'd encouraged me to date Denver. That I *did* remember.

I dragged myself out of bed and into the shower, grateful for the warm water that cascaded down my face. I really did need to get back to my life. I was thirty-four years old and life was going to pass me by if I wasn't careful. It would be so easy to stay immersed in work. I loved it and got such a sense of achievement from it, but what happened when I was older? Would I regret not having a partner, children? I knew deep down inside I would.

As the shower rained down on me, it was like a dam had burst as the walls I'd built up around me to protect myself from further hurt began to collapse. I sat on the floor of the stall as large, wracking sobs came from me. All the pain caused by my ex and best friend rose to the surface and I mourned my past relationships and let myself feel the hurt finally that had happened all those years before.

When I eventually stopped, I washed myself, dried off, crawled back into bed and slept for hours. When I finally woke, I felt calmer than I had in years, and hopeful for the future.

I'd not expected to see Lucas again, given that he'd said he was going for drinks with Aidan, but I heard him return at 9pm and was surprised that he didn't call around to see how I was. Surprised or disappointed, I asked myself. I really needed to expand my horizons and I knew exactly what I was going to do first. I was going to Masquerade night on Friday. I knew Aidan wasn't working Friday evening, Jess was covering, and so it was the perfect time for me to go to explore. I didn't think I'd have the confidence to join in anything, but at least I would have pushed myself out of my comfort zone.

"Can you tell it's me?" I asked Jess, the only person I'd confided in that I was going.

"No. You're dressed in hot pants, a bandage top, and PVC boots that aren't designer. With the heavy makeup I've put on you plus the blonde wig, no one is going to know this is you. You're worlds apart from the sophisticated designer-clad brunette that walks around the club."

"Tell me I'm not making a huge mistake, Jess." I looked in the mirror. Who was that woman with the crimson glossed mouth and fake mole? Jess had used contouring makeup and even my face shape looked different.

"You're only looking. Oh, I got it! Pretend you're a mystery shopper! In fact, if you're recognized, which you won't be..." She saw the panic in the tensing of my body. "That's what you say. That you've gone undercover to check they are doing their jobs properly."

"I can work with that," I told her, handing over my cell phone. "Okay, you keep that. It's my night off so no one would expect to see me anyway, but I don't want that ringing and identifying me."

Jess took it from me. "Right, gorgeous, I'm off downstairs and if you don't arrive within the next hour, I'm coming back up here to drag your ass down. We clear?"

"Crystal."

Walking into my club as a customer instead of the manager was enough to stop my heart. The fake ID I'd created had obviously worked straightaway, but I just had visions of being recognized instantly. It took an hour of drinking wine (which Jess brought over to me, so I didn't have to speak at the bar) before I relaxed, realizing that in fact no one here gave a damn who I was. I was wearing the wristband that showed I was just 'looking' and not participating, so no one had approached me. I took a deep breath. It was time to walk around the club and enjoy myself. Time to see what turned me on and try to relight the fire in me that my ex had extinguished.

I was envious seeing people who had totally given

in to their lust and desire. People came to our club because there was no judgment. As long as things were legal and consensual then any fantasies could be acted out here. One man in a room was wearing a giant nappy and was sat on a domme's knee. In another room two couples were enjoying what I presumed were the other one's partners. Yet none of it appealed to me. I'd seen it so many times I was immune. Great, I was broken.

Finally, I walked down a corridor to our playroom. This was a room I didn't come down to often as it was right at the end of the hall. I stood at the viewing window and watched as a man took his partner's hand, guiding her until she was against the wall, her arms outstretched. She was completely at his mercy secured by her wrists and ankles. I watched as he tormented her to the cusp of orgasm with his fingers and with a vibrator. Then I watched him fuck her. She encompassed the name of the club as she gave into him and pleasure with abandon and I felt between my legs get wet. I'd found the key to my locked-up self. I wanted to be entirely at someone else's mercy, free for them to do what they wanted to me.

I took a deep breath and started to push open the door.

CHAPTER NINE

Lucas

I had the night off. I'd been to the gym and when I came back, I knocked on Ash's door. After largely avoiding her all week, I decided I was being stupid and so thought I'd see if she wanted to share takeout. There was no answer. I called her cell and was surprised when Jess answered.

"What are you doing with Ash's cell?"
"She's in a meeting and can't take calls right now?"
"What meeting? With who?"
"Sorry, Lucas, it's all strictly confidential."
"Not if it's to do with the club it's not."
A sigh came down the line. "It's not to do with the

club. Calm your briefs, Lucas. Ash is fine, she just needed me to hold her cell for an hour or so."

"This sounds shady."

"What it is, Lucas, is none of your business. Now I'm working, so if you don't mind, I need to get back to it."

She ended the call and I began pacing around my apartment.

Where was she?

A meeting, but with no cell phone. What sort of meeting would that be?

Then clarity came to my mind. Oh God. Was she with Denver? I'd bet he wouldn't allow cell phones or electronic equipment on dates for security reasons, so nothing got recorded to be sold to gossip magazines. I'd done it. I'd pushed her into Denver's arms. What a dick I was.

I slipped my shoes back on. I was going down to the club. I was no use here pacing around. I'd try to get the details out of Jess, then I'd go to wherever they were.

And do what?
If she's on a date what business of yours is it?
What if she's in bed with him?

That thought was one too many for my brain and I slammed my apartment door behind me and stormed downstairs.

"Hey, Jess."

"What are you doing here?" Her face said what her words didn't because up until then I'd thought Ash was out somewhere, but as Jess' eyes darted around the club, I knew without a doubt that Ashley was somewhere in this club, and if she didn't have her phone, what was she doing?

Keep calm, Lucas.

"I was bored. You know what it's like. This place gets under your skin. I'm going to head to the office and do a little paperwork. You're sure Ash is safe wherever she is with no cell?"

"Yes, I'm sure."

"That's good enough for me then. Sorry, I went a bit alpha. It's no business of mine what Ash does in her spare time, but she's a friend."

Jess looked at me with the same kind of expression I got from Aidan, a look of bemusement. I ignored her and went to the office.

On our system was the same video access to the rooms that security had. We had monitors and could look around the club. I sat down and painstakingly started to look from monitor to monitor. I couldn't find her. The trouble was it was masquerade night and many of the customers were wearing masks and wigs.

Is that what Ash was doing? I started again from the first monitor trying to find a clue, a giveaway body shape, a hair flick, anything that would give her away. And then in front of my eyes there she was. I watched as a slim female dressed in hot pants walked across the playroom. She was so hesitant, it made me look twice. I switched on the sound as she sauntered halfway across the room.

"S- sorry, I made a mistake." Her voice was unmistakable. It was definitely Ash.

"There's no need to be shy," the male spoke. "It takes courage to come into a room with another couple. You must have been intrigued."

A tongue flicked around dark painted lips. "I was. I enjoyed watching you together. My reaction was to come in and see if I could join you, but I've changed my mind. I realized I only want to do this with someone I'm seeing. I'm sorry for the interruption."

The woman against the wall had said nothing throughout and I guessed she had to be given permission to speak. The man continued to talk. "I would have declined your offer. I'm here with my wife and we're exclusive. But we enjoy when people watch. Stay."

"Thank you. But I've found what I came for. I wanted to know what interested me and it's this. How your wife gave herself up to you completely. You've helped me answer some questions I had about myself tonight. Thank you. Enjoy the rest of your evening."

With that Ash walked back out of the room and I followed her from monitor to monitor. Unfortunately, the bar was an area we were unable to listen in to, so I had no idea what Jess said to Ash about my being here. I just saw a flicker of panic in Ash's eyes and then she left the club—quickly.

I didn't know what to do with myself. Did I rush after her?

What if she told me to get lost?

I decided I'd wait ten minutes and then I'd knock at her door on the pretense of not being able to get hold of her. The woman was driving me fucking crazy. The sight of her in hot pants and high-heeled boots sending me out of my mind.

In fact, fuck ten minutes. I was going up there now.

I banged on the door. "Ash, it's me. Open up."

My cell rang. It was her. "I've got a headache, Lucas. Is everything okay? Only I'm in bed."

"Don't lie to me, Ash. I saw you on the monitor."

There was a silence and a sigh. Then the door unlocked.

She stood in the doorway. Her wig gone, her long

brunette hair fell messily; her makeup made her look like a movie star, and she stood there in a tight top that showed the outline of her perfect breasts, and hot pants that displayed her willowy legs.

It was like being an alcoholic on a boat in a sea of liquor. I knew if I fell, I could drown—but what a way to die.

"What do you want, Lucas?" she said haughtily.

"You," I croaked out.

Her jaw dropped open and I came to my senses.

Fuck, I'd blown it now.

"I'm sorry. God, I'm sorry, Ash. I should nev—"

But I didn't get to finish my sentence because Ash had pulled me toward her and our mouths met in a frenzy of need.

I picked her up, her legs going around my waist and I carried her to her bedroom.

I broke off long enough to say to her, "Are you sure?"

The breathy reply of, "Kiss me," was all I needed to hear in return.

We feasted on each other, tongues tangling and when I finally broke off, Ash's lips were puffy.

"I watched you," I told her. "I saw what you need. Now I can give you that. Do you want it?"

"Yes," she almost mewled.

Working down her body, I pulled the hot pants from her. She was bare underneath and it almost was my undoing right then. Her pussy was bare apart from a thin line of hair. I pushed her hips apart and licked up her seam. She gasped and her fingers held onto my head. "Oh God, yes."

But I'd seen that what she'd hankered after had been to not have control, so I moved away and undid my tie. Ash's hooded gaze watched me. I helped her shed her top, then I said, "Hold out your wrists. Together."

I bound her with my tie and then I flipped her onto her front. I gasped as I saw the tattoos that covered her back—a hidden secret of the true Ash—a large skull with snakes running through it led to another pattern that covered her left hip, buttock, and the top of her thigh. I traced the snakes with my fingers and my tongue and then ran my tongue down through the crease between her buttocks. I pushed her up onto her knees and entered her pussy with my tongue. Her juices coated my face, she was so fucking wet. Reaching underneath her, I cupped her breast, tweaking her nipple.

Her breast pushed into my hand and I could detect

just how hard she was breathing, how heavy her heart thudded. After taking my fill of her honey, I moved back and freed my cock, dropping my pants and briefs to the floor. I lifted Ash off the bed and pushed her up against her bedroom wall, her bound arms above her head. Legs parted, I placed my raging hard dick next to her entrance and then pushed inside. Her warmth accepted me straightaway. She was so wet I was welcome immediately. I withdrew and then pushed in again, reveling in how it felt to be inside Ash's pussy. She gasped as I entered her and pushed back against me trying to take me deeper inside her.

"Oh my god, Lucas, I'm going to come," she said and so I quickly found her clit with my fingers and I strummed that nub while I felt her come apart on my cock. I stilled for a moment letting her recover, but I wasn't done. Not by a long shot. I threw her down on the bed on her back and undid her hands. Those perfect breasts displayed before my eyes and I had to taste them, had to capture a hardened bud in my mouth and lick it, before nipping with the edge of my teeth. I looped my tie around one of her wrists and then secured it to the headboard. Looking around the room I saw Ash's robe and I slipped the tie from that and secured her other wrist.

"Now what shall I do with you while you are completely at my mercy?" I asked her. I saw she was about to talk, and I held a finger against my lips.

"Ssh. Just close your eyes and enjoy."

Ash's gaze met mine and then she nodded and closed her eyes, giving me permission to play with her body as I pleased. I ran a finger into her slippery wetness and fucked her with my digits, curving my fingers to find her g-spot as I licked at her clit.

She groaned, her hips moving up to meet my mouth. I wondered what Ash would keep in her nightstand drawer and with a wicked thought I moved closer to open it. I took out the vibrator as Ash opened her eyes and they went wide when she guessed my intentions.

"Trust me. Now close your eyes," I told her.

I switched on the vibrator and as it hummed I held it against Ash's clit. At the same time I entered her pussy with my tongue. "Lucas, I can hardly bear it," she yelled, trying to lift her hips up and away. It just made me press it against her harder. I switched it around, letting it buzz at her entrance while I sucked on her clit. "I'm gonna... I'm gonna..." she screamed and I threw the vibrator to one side. My arms positioned either side of her, I thrust inside her hard. I gave her no mercy, plunging inside her again and again. She lifted her hips to meet every thrust and as I spilled my seed inside her, she came hard, her pussy walls clamping around my cock, her shudders milking me of every last drop.

I collapsed at the side of her on the bed. Our heartbeats thudding in tandem as we got our breath back. I lifted up and untied her arms and took them one by one and rubbed them. Ash was silent throughout, so I went to gather her into the crook of my arms.

She flinched at my touch and said in a whisper, "What the fuck have we done?"

CHAPTER TEN

Ashley

I'd let lust take over and obliterate any common sense.

Now I turned to look at the hot, naked man in my bed and an overwhelming sense of panic overtook me.

What had we done?

What had I done?

"Fuck, Ash. You can't be regretting that just happened. It was amazing. Surely you feel the same?"

"But I'm your boss. How is this going to affect our working relationship? I'm supposed to manage you. I've seen workplace relationships where they fondle each other when they think no one is looking. The focus moves away from work, the couples get distracted. I've ruined our working relationship by allowing this to happen." I bit my lip and sat up, leaning against the headboard, running a hand through my hair.

Lucas sat up at the side of me, dragging the comforter up his body as he did so.

"Ash, we fucked, not fucked things up. If you want to regret it go right ahead but I'm not going to."

I let out a large exhale and turned to look at him.

"I don't regret it. They're not the right words. I'm just... I'm scared, Lucas. Work has been my world for years, my one constant, and now I could have done something to jeopardize that."

"And what if you haven't? I can still be entirely professional at work. If things go wrong, I'll accept the job in Miami and leave. You wouldn't need to see me again." He reached over and touched my cheek. "Please don't end this before it's even started, Ash. I want you."

I leaned back once more and closed my eyes and let my mind and body tell me what they wanted.

My pussy was soaked, my clit pulsing and ready for more.

My nipples were stiff peaks.

My breathing was erratic.

Butterflies flitted around my stomach.

My body craved more of his touch.

"Give me your fears, Ash. I'll blow them all away," he said and I was done for.

I molded myself into his body, my curves fitting in perfect alignment against his warm skin. His mouth caught mine and we kissed for what felt like forever, until curled up together we fell asleep.

The next morning, he took me back to dizzying heights before I hit the shower and he went back to his own apartment. We had work to do. God knows what happened from now on. I welcomed the warmth from the shower and felt the telltale tingles of a body that had sought and found pleasure. Maybe Lucas could vanquish the ghosts my ex had left? I knew I had to try.

True to his word, at work Lucas was the consummate professional and no one would have known what was going on between us. Abandon XL was now booked two years out and Aidan was taking us out for a meal in celebration. I was sitting in the office catching up on some paperwork when Andrea, one of the secretaries walked in carrying a huge bouquet of flowers.

"Someone's popular today," she said. "There are nine more bouquets outside to bring in."

"Say what?"

"Ten bouquets delivered for you this morning and here's the card." She handed me over an envelope with my name scrawled on the front. Stupidly, disappointment that it wasn't Lucas' writing flashed over me.

I opened the envelope and withdrew the card.

Thanks for a great night.
Den.
I'll call you.

I sighed. "Do rock stars ever get told no, do you think?" I said to Andrea who looked at me in puzzlement.

"They're from Denver from F-Higher. You know, we hosted them for XL's first night?"

She nodded. "Oh that man is hot. And he's sending you ten flower bouquets? He must be interested."

I laughed. "That man could drop a thousand bouquets and not feel a slight pinch to his wallet, and his assistant will have arranged all this. It's all show and doesn't interest me at all."

"Well, when he calls can you pass on my number?" She giggled. "What do you want me to do with the others?"

"Give them out to whoever wants some. We all have offices and homes that can use flowers, right?

Helps brighten the place up. Just make sure there are no more cards."

I pushed the card onto the corner of my desk. Later I'd think of a way to let Denver down without upsetting his ego.

There was another knock to the door and I sighed. It was going to be one of those days; constant interruptions put me off my stride. At this rate I'd be hitting the espresso by ten thirty.

Lucas walked in and my day suddenly got a lot brighter.

"Hey, you."

"Good morning, Ashley."

I laughed at him behaving so officially when only a few hours ago he'd been devouring my pussy like a starving man.

"How can I help you, Mr. Hall?"

He caught sight of the massive bouquet. "Nice. I'm not missing your birthday, am I?"

"No, just a satisfied customer," I replied. "What did you need me for?"

"Three members of staff have called in sick. Any chance of me stealing one or two of yours?"

"Shouldn't be a problem. I'll check the roster. You could have telephoned me about that. You didn't need to come up to see me."

"I didn't *need* to, but I *wanted* to," he said, and I smiled.

Despite our best intentions, our developing feelings for each other were beginning to invade the workplace and there wasn't a damn thing either of us could do to stop it.

One evening the day staff left at six and by one minute past six Lucas was in my office.

"Do you have much more work to do?"

"Yes, Lucas, I do, and then I'm working all night, which you already know."

"I can't be without you tonight. It's too hard." He ran a hand over the bulge in his pants showing me just how hard it was.

"I have break time. If I take it now, we have thirty minutes," I told him. "I'll meet you at your apartment."

He strode over to me. "I want you now, here. I can't wait another second."

The hunger in his voice and the lust in his eyes danced with my own desires and the voice in my head who said *no, not at work*, was pushed out of my mind. Instead, I turned to him and said, "Where?"

Locking the door first, he was on me in seconds, pushing up my skirt and pulling off my panties. He lifted me, placing my bare ass against the cool glass of my desk, moving papers aside. Then he stilled.

"What's wrong?" I asked.

He held the note from Denver in his hand, his knuckles whitening as he snarled out. "What the fuck is this?"

I felt stupid and vulnerable, my bottom half naked, my juices running onto the desk beneath me and I made to move and pull down my skirt. His free hand grabbed mine and held my thigh, gently, but with intention.

"'This man makes me want to kill him with my bare hands."

"He just sent flowers as a thank you for the night he enjoyed at Abandon."

"If you truly believe that, you're naïve," he said.

He threw the note back on the desk and ran a hand between my thighs, trailing his fingertips through my wetness and flicking on my clit. "He wants this, Ash. He's a man used to getting what he wants, but do you know what?"

I looked up at him and in a breathy whisper said, "What?"

He leaned in toward my ear. "He can't have you because you're mine."

His finger entered my heat and I groaned, my legs parting wider to allow him to get even closer. He tilted my head with his other hand and lowered his mouth to my neck, nibbling and licking, causing goose bumps to rise across my flesh. His tongue licked the edge of my earlobe, making me shiver.

Lucas added another digit and I was bucking against his fingers frantically. Then he stilled and dropped his pants and briefs, his erection springing free. He grabbed my ass and pulled me towards him right onto his rock-hard cock and I gasped as he filled me with one solid thrust.

"Fuck," I groaned.

"That's right, baby. I'm fucking you. Open your eyes. Look. Watch my cock as it slams inside you. Who do you belong to right now, Ash? You want to give yourself up to me, baby?"

"Yes," I mewled.

"Give me everything, Ash. I want you to come apart on my cock. Don't hold back."

He thrust faster and faster and my body started climbing. My pussy was soaking wet and I could feel my tension building and then I soared.

"Oh my god," I shrieked as I came hard around his cock. Lucas thrust inside me a few more times until he came with a groan.

I rested my head against his chest while we allowed time for our breathing to slow. Then I felt Lucas reach over for something. I watched as he got the card from

Denver and swept it across my pussy juices mingled with his spunk.

"Send him that back." He threw the card on the floor and took my mouth again.

I should have been shouting 'who the hell do you think you are', but I didn't want to. I loved how possessive he was being, acting like he owned me. It made me feel like I was wanted, not discarded like yesterday's papers.

"Enjoy the rest of your working day. Text me when you get back to your apartment," he said. It wasn't a command, more of a plea, and it showed me that his possessive behavior was only part of our bedroom play and he wasn't a control freak.

"It'll be late, and I'll be tired," I told him, though a smirk curled the edge of my lip with the thought of more sex after my shift.

"So, we'll be exhausted," he said. "It'll be worth it. Text me."

"Okay."

We used the restroom and then with a kiss he was gone. I sat in my chair for ten minutes after he'd left, touching my mouth and replaying what had just happened in my mind over and over. I was becoming addicted... Lucas my drug.

CHAPTER ELEVEN

Lucas

When I'd seen the card from that fucker Denver, I'd just seen red. If he'd have been in front of me, I'd have thrown a punch. Ash might have said it was a thank you for the work, but I wasn't stupid. He'd better back off. We'd been seeing each other for a couple of months now and although I understood Ash's hesitancy, I was getting tired of all the secrecy and didn't see why we just couldn't let people know we were in a relationship. It took the times I found myself in my apartment alone, for me to kick back and realize that not everyone was made the same way and that Ash's past romantic history and the betrayal from her best friend meant she needed to proceed with caution. I just had to show her I wasn't going anywhere.

A text came in from her at 4am and I opened my door to her tired features. Scooping her into my arms I took her to my bed, stripping her and cocooning her until she fell asleep right next to me. As I stared down at her, I realized I was falling hard and deep for this woman. I just hoped she started feeling the same way.

She stirred in my arms at just after 9am.

"Aren't you supposed to be at work?" she asked.

"I told them I had an early morning meeting." I smirked.

She stretched. "I'm gonna tell."

"Really?" I raised an eyebrow. "I have a feeling you won't."

After breakfast, coffee, and a shower, I got Ash to follow me down the private back elevators that were used by customers who didn't want to be seen coming in the main entrance. Security didn't run cameras beyond the front desk until the evening and so when I sneaked her into the room right at the end of the hall, I was already hard.

"What's going on? What did you want to show me?" Ash asked I led her toward the wall. "I can't see anything wrong."

"I may have got you down here on false pretenses," I confessed. "The thing that's wrong with that wall is that you're not fastened with your ankles astride against it."

Ash's breath caught.

"I saw you that night. You wanted this. I heard you say so. But you didn't want it with that couple. I do believe you want it with me."

"What if someone comes in? We'd lose our jobs, our dignity." Ash shook her head. "This is too much, Lucas. I can't."

I looked at the floor and sighed. "You're right. I just wanted this, with you."

"There are other clubs, Lucas." She grinned. "I have an amazing blonde wig."

I found somewhere and a couple of days later when our evenings off coincided, we found ourselves in the playroom of Diablo, a new on the scene club. It was a lot smaller than Abandon and catered more for the BDSM scene.

I led Ash up to a set of restraints that were suspended in the middle of the room. "Hold up your arms," I commanded.

"What if someone comes in?" she asked me, staring past me to the door.

"Then they're going to see you coming over and over, Ash."

She nodded. "Okay." Then she held up her arms.

I fastened her into the restraints and then I unzipped the strapless top she was wearing and let it fall to the ground. Her breasts were exposed to the cool air. I reached over and captured a nipple in my mouth, sucking and then swapping for the other. The restraints rattled as she shivered under my ministrations.

I dipped a hand under her short mini skirt and slid a finger under the leg of her panties, fingerfucking her until she was chasing an orgasm. "I'm so close. Please?" she begged.

The door opened and another couple came in.

"Can we watch?" The guy asked.

Checking Ash's expression, I saw her nod. "Of course," I told them.

Ash's face was filled with lust. Her lips were red and swollen and her eyes hooded.

"I'm going to make you come now while this couple watch us," I told her. "What do you want me to do next?"

"Take off my skirt and panties," she begged, "and then lick me until I come all over your face."

I did exactly as instructed and kneeled down as she

hung there suspended. I placed her legs over my shoulders and fucked her with my tongue and fingers.

"Oh my god. Yes. More, please, yes, more. Oh, I'm gonna come."

I held her butt firmly while I continued to eat her out and she bucked frantically against my mouth until she screamed as she came all over my face. By this stage the couple who had been watching were now fucking over a chair.

"My turn." I freed her arms. "On your knees and take my cock in your mouth," I ordered.

She fell down to her knees and it took all of my willpower not to just fuck her there and then. She stripped me of my pants and boxer briefs and then fastening a hand around the base of my cock she took me in her mouth, her soft warmth enveloping me, and she began to suck. It was the first time she'd gone down on me and I softly rocked my hips back and forth as she continued to suck, breaking off occasionally to run a tongue around my mushroom head. As the tension mounted, I began to thrust a little harder, holding onto the back of her head, taking care not to disturb the wig she had fastened with pins. Her head bobbed up and down as she took me deeper into her throat and her eyes fixed on mine. Seeing her taking my cock was magnificent and as I came, she kept her mouth around me, swallowing my cum.

I led her to the wall where I fastened her arms to cuffs and used a spreader bar to separate her legs. Taking a whip and feather teaser, I used the feather end first to stroke across her nipples and over the rest of her silky flesh. Goose bumps erupted on her arms. Next, I turned it to the whip end and gently thrashed her nipples with the soft tassels until they were hard as rocks. I ran the tassels down her flesh, over her stomach and then teased her between her thighs.

"Ooooooohhh," she groaned.

Trailing it down her thighs, I lashed her lightly with it, then I struck her pussy with it gently.

"Yessss," she gasped, pushing her pussy out toward me.

"You like that? Do you want it, bad girl?"

"Yes."

"Yes, what? Tell me."

"Yes, Lucas. I want it. I want you to hit me with the tassels harder.

I ran the whip back up her pussy and then flicked it, this time with more power behind it so it whipped across her clit.

"Oh my fucking god."

Again and again, I did it until she came. I stood back watching as she shuddered, her body shaking with her climax. Just as the final little tremors were leaving her body, I grabbed the base of my cock and thrust inside her.

"Oh yes, oh yes, fuck me, Lucas, please?"

I thundered into her, lost in her warmth, lost in her.

Afterward, I took her down from the restraints. We bid goodnight to the staff at the club, plus a few of the members such as the ones that had watched us, and then I hailed a cab. I ran a bath and tenderly washed Ash from head to toe.

"I loved tonight," she confessed. "I want to buy one of those whip things."

"I'm going to order so many toys for us to play with," I told her. "Expect me to be inside you every spare moment we have together."

In bed I took her a final time, before exhausted, we collapsed in each other's arms and slept.

Two nights later it was the celebratory meal that Aidan had insisted on. There was me, Ash, Connor, and Jess, and the club was being left to the other staff for a few hours while we ate.

"So, all the staff have a bonus in their paycheck this

month as thanks for their hard work in getting the two clubs running so smoothly." Aidan said as we sat in the luxurious PlayKing's bar. PlayKing's was owned by Aidan's friend, Eli, and had an excellent restaurant to the rear.

He handed an envelope to each of us. We looked at each other, frown lines appearing on our faces. "Well, open them," he said.

We'd each been given $3000 dollars of travel vouchers.

"This is too much," scolded Ash. "How many times have I said you are far too generous?"

"Well you aren't my assistant now, so I don't have to listen to you." Aidan laughed and winked at her. "Just take it in the spirit that it's been given. It's a reward for all your hard work so that you can have a break." He cleared his throat. "Now, I got Andrea to check the roster and we can have two of you off at a time, so Jess and Connor, you can schedule your vacations for anytime in the next month and your vacations can overlap if needed, as Ash and Lucas will provide cover and then vice versa for the month after."

I noticed that Connor blushed a little and then I realized. Him and Jess? Well, me and Ash had been so busy with each other that we hadn't noticed what was going on right under our nose.

Aidan looked at me and smirked. He'd done this

deliberately. Did he know that me and Ash were an item?

After we'd eaten, Jess and Connor excused themselves, thanking Aidan for a lovely evening.

"If you'll excuse me, I'm just going to use the bathroom," Ash told us.

I watched as she walked away. "You're pussy-whipped. You know that don't you?" Aidan stared at me. "So are going to take her away and bone her half to death so I don't have to look at your puppy-dog eyes and open mouth anymore? It's amazing that you haven't actually drooled yet."

"Fuck you," I said and laughed.

"So how long have you two been an item?"

I rubbed my chin. "A couple months."

"A couple months?" he shouted out. "And you didn't tell me? I'm family. I'm disappointed, Lucas, at the serious lack of gossip."

"We're taking it slow. She's had a rough break up in the past," I explained. "I didn't want to say anything in case it fizzled out or it made you worry about the club."

"I'm not worried about the club. My staff are excellent, but you're all replaceable." He laughed. "I wouldn't be a businessman if I didn't have back-up lined up for if needs be."

"You won't need it. I'm not going anywhere," I said.

Famous last words.

CHAPTER TWELVE

Ashley

I was trying not to smile all the time, because I was so gloriously happy. As I left the bathroom, I looked over to our table, watching Lucas' profile as he chatted to Aidan. His shirt sleeve was rolled up showing me that corded wrist, and his fingers danced as he used them to enunciate whatever words he was saying. Those clever fingers that played me like an instrument, hitting all the right notes. It also appeared that Aidan might know what was going on. Had he really hinted that Lucas and I could vacation together? Perhaps it was indeed time to face the fact that I was in a relationship with this man and go public.

"Ashley, God, you're a hard woman to track down." I spun around to see Denver in front of me. From his eyes he was wasted on either alcohol or booze. He slung an arm around me. "You didn't call me. Why didn't you call me?"

I tried to take a step back because he reeked of alcohol and he was making me uncomfortable. "Because I have no reason to."

He looked and me and snarled. "Oh yeah, you just wanted me for business, right? Had what you wanted so now you don't need me. Just another slut trying to take what she can get. Well this time, I'm taking what I want."

He leaned toward me, his face coming nearer to mine and then he wasn't there anymore.

I watched as Denver hit the wall and then heard a loud crack as Lucas' fist connected with his nose. Blood sprayed out.

And just like that everything fell apart.

Camera flashes went off everywhere.

Aidan rushed over, looking at Lucas in horror. "What have you just done?"

Denver's PR was getting him medical attention.

"I'll deal with this. Get him out of here. I'll call you if I need you," Aidan snapped.

I nodded and dragged Lucas out to a waiting cab,

wading through crowds who were trying to see what happened.

He sat in my apartment as I assessed his sore and bruising knuckles.

"You know you're probably going to get charged with assault, don't you?"

"I don't give a crap. He was being a jackass to you."

"I could have dealt with him myself."

"Yeah? He was about to press you up against the wall. Man's twice the weight of you."

"I didn't need you to come over playing bodyguard."

"Well I did, so it's too fucking late to start giving me shit for looking out for you."

"I think maybe it's better if you go to your own apartment now," I said. "Wait to see what Aidan says."

The look he gave me broke my heart. Hurt and disgust rolled into one. He got up and left, slamming the door behind him.

I sat on my sofa wondering what would happen now.

SEX CLUB WORKER PUNCHES DENVER LOMAS IN BRAWL OVER SEXY BOSS

We'd been called into the office to see Aidan who was pacing around like a caged tiger throwing down the papers and press releases.

"They're making Abandon look like a seedy, brothel type establishment," Aidan spat.

"Luckily for you." He jabbed Lucas in the chest with his fingers. "Denver won't be saying a word or pressing charges."

"How?" I asked.

Aidan laughed, but not in an amused way; it was more of a huff. "He was made aware that I have security tapes of him walking around with a butt plug with a donkey's tail on it, amongst others. I don't like having to use blackmail, but he could have ruined me, and I'm not about to let that happen." He folded his arms across his chest. "Sit down. It's not getting any better," he said and we both took a seat.

"Your ex has sold a story to the press. That he had to seek comfort in your best friend's arms because you were addicted to work. That you spent all your time in Club S at Henry's mercy. He's given them photos of you in lingerie. Photos I guess you trusted him to take at the time."

I gasped and placed my head in my hands. Just when I'd thought my life was getting back on track, it sent me another earthquake to rock my world.

"Let me see," I requested.

He handed me a printout from the internet.

MY EX WAS OBSESSED WITH SEX. JUST NOT WITH ME.

There I was in four photos, clad in sexy lingerie and pouting at the man who I had at that time loved. Now I looked like a cheap whore.

"Ashley, your shifts are covered. I want you to take a week off until this calms down. Maybe use those vacation vouchers and get away for a while?"

I nodded. I couldn't get on a plane fast enough.

"Lucas. I'm sending you to Miami in a consultant role. Go there and supervise things."

"I'm not going anywhere."

"Yes, you are, Lucas. Listen, I know you were protecting Ash, I get that. The sleazeball was all over her, but I have my club to fix. Half my life savings are in this. What you've done could affect my future, my plans for my wedding, for my future family. So I'm not asking you, I'm telling you, until I get this all sorted and PR on it to smooth things out, you get your ass to Miami. Am I clear?"

Lucas' jaw was tight, but he nodded his head, "Yes, Boss."

"Get out of here, both of you," Aidan said. "I'll be in touch, we'll sort this."

I packed and booked a flight and a few hours later I was on my way to Hawaii. A week to myself to try to relax and regroup and once again close down all my feelings into that locked box where my heart should be.

CHAPTER THIRTEEN

Aidan

Goddamn cousins with alpha tendencies.

I knew if that had been Lori, I would have also been over there pummeling Denver Lomas into the wall. I couldn't blame him, but I needed to do some PR repair work.

If only he and Ash had had the confidence to go public, this probably wouldn't have happened, but hindsight was a wonderful thing and Denver was a prick, so there was no saying he wouldn't have tried it anyway.

Now I had work to do.

The first thing was to arrange for someone to visit

Ashley's ex. A large sum of money and a legal document soon made him disappear from the public eye.

Next, I got my assistant to arrange an interview for me on prime-time television. It helped when the chat show host frequented your club. By the time I'd finished, Abandon would be even more on the map. Even negative publicity could be good publicity dealt with in the right way.

Denver was to make a public apology stating that he had been drunk and had meant to cause no offense. His PR were sending him to 'rehab' for a week to sort out his alcohol dependence issues. In real terms he was off on vacation for a week, but his bad boy status would rise, giving the band another chart boost.

I'd made it clear that he was no longer welcome in Abandon.

So all that was left now was to get my cousin back from Miami, my club manager back from her vacation, and to hope to God they finally got their shit together.

Sometimes fate needed a helping hand, so I'd arranged a little something while they were gone.

I just hoped it didn't blow up in my face.

CHAPTER FOURTEEN

Ashley

My vacation had proved one thing to me. I couldn't suppress my feelings for Lucas. He'd got into my very marrow, into my head and my heart. I loved him. No matter how much I tried, I couldn't stay mad that he'd tried to protect me against that sleazebag, Denver Lomas.

I topped up my tan and got ready to return home. No matter if I lost my job, no matter if my name was dragged all over the press, it was worth it.

For Lucas.

Lucas

I'd gone through the motions in Miami, but my heart belonged in New York with Ash. I couldn't wait to get back. When I got Aidan's call, telling me he'd sorted everything out, that I was a pain in the ass, but I was family and he loved me, and to get on back to the club; well, I couldn't get back fast enough.

It was time to lay out to Ash exactly how I felt.

To tell her that I loved her.

CHAPTER FIFTEEN

Ashley

I got back to my apartment to find tape across both mine and Lucas' apartment doors with *out of bounds* across it.

A note with my name on was taped to the door. I took it down and opened it, sliding the paper out of the envelope.

Had to close the apartments for urgent maintenance work. Suite booked for you at The Global. Room 1218, key card within this envelope. You're not required at work

until Monday, so you have the weekend to relax and unwind. Call Andrea if you need anything. The hotel will launder your vacation wear, so you have some clothes. Aidan.

Yeah? Did he expect me to spend the weekend in my bikini?

Ignoring the note, I tried my key in the lock. It didn't work, the locks had been changed.

Goddamn it. I smacked the door with my hand. I just wanted to sleep. I turned around and made my way across to The Global.

Finally getting to the floor of my apartment, I dragged my case to the door and put my key card in the slot. Pushing it open, I entered the room to find Lucas sitting in a chair, nursing a beer.

"What the fuck?" I yelled.

Lucas placed his beer down and walked toward me.

"It would appear that we've been set up, by my cousin. By our boss."

He stood facing me.

"I need to apologize for what I did. I was acting like

some stupid, immature, jealous Neanderthal man. I'm sorry." He took my chin in his hand and tilted my head up toward his.

"What I won't apologize for is why I did it," he said, his steely eyes fixing on mine. "I love you, Ashley Jenson."

I swallowed, my mouth having gone dry.

"You don't need to apologize. You were looking out for me. I understand. Denver was a jerk. He had it coming. I only wish I'd managed to get a punch in first." I smiled up at him. "I love you too, Lucas Hall."

He leaned toward me, his mouth capturing mine. Then he broke the kiss and looked at me.

"You look tired."

"I am tired."

"Well, do you want to sleep? We don't have to be at work until Monday?"

I moved my hand to his neck and began unfastening his tie, sliding it away and holding it out to him.

Then I shimmied out of my clothes and stood before him naked. I turned around and held my wrists together behind my back.

"We can sleep later," I told him over my shoulder.

I was his.

He was mine.

Everything else was abandoned as we gave into love.

EPILOGUE

Lucas

Five years later

The familiar sound of gravel crunching under tires caused Delia to jump up and down in excitement. "Mommy's home, Mommy's home," she repeated, wriggling off of my knee and starting her escape from the living room towards the front door.

Smiling to myself, I followed her little footsteps, watching as the door opened. Ashley's purse and laptop bag were abandoned in the doorway, and our three-year-old daughter suddenly scooped up and twirled in her mother's arms.

"Baby girl, did you grow again?" Ashley teased.

"I think I did, Mommy, because I reached up and took a cookie and Daddy got cross."

"Did you now?" Ashley grinned at me as she listened to our daughter's recollection of the day.

"Uh-huh, but I won't do it again. I have to ask nicely, Mommy, but s'okay because Daddy will say yes anyway."

She squirmed in her mother's arms to be put down and stood up straight, demonstrating how far she could reach. "Carlie can't do that," she said.

Carlie was our eight-month-old daughter. In the past few years everything had changed in mine and Ashley's world.

Two years after getting together we had tied the knot, holding the wedding in *The Global* seeing as it had been such a part of our lives. Abandon and Abandon XL had gone from strength to strength and then one day, shortly after our wedding, Aidan had called us into a meeting...

"I have news. Big news, and I'm hoping I've done the right thing, but as I'm the boss, you'll just have to suck it the fuck up anyway."

"What did you do, cous?"

"I've sold Abandon and Abandon XL, GoDown Productions, everything."

Our mouths dropped open. "What?"

"And as they'd rather have their own management team, they want to make you a financial settlement for you to walk away, which means a win-win."

"We're losing our jobs and that's somehow a win-win," I yelled.

Ashley patted my wrist. "This is Aidan. He's not finished, so shut up and let the man talk."

"While owning sex clubs and an adult movie business has brought things more mainstream as I had hoped, now that my wife and I are about to have a baby..." Lori was due to give birth shortly. *"I want a more family friendly business portfolio. So it's gone. And..."* He paused for effect. *"I bought The Global."*

Ashley spluttered the mouthful of water she'd been drinking, out over her lap. "You bought The Global. Just like that. I mean, it's just like pocket money really isn't it," she added with a heavy dose of sarcasm.

"I've spent enough money in the place, so thought what the hell, I'll run a luxury hotel next and might just open a few more in time. To that end, it would seem I need staff to manage the place. Can you think of anyone suitable? Comes with an amazing financial package and a part-ownership in the business."

Ashley looked at me and I nodded.

"There's just a little complication," she said, announcing she was pregnant.

"What did I just say about family friendly?" Aidan stated. "Congratulations. Lori will be ecstatic that our baby will have a little cousin not much younger than ours."

Ashley had worked as far along her pregnancy as she could and then had gone on maternity leave. But I could see that while she loved our daughter unconditionally, she missed work. It was in her blood. I, however, no longer had the same hunger for it. I suggested I become a stay-at-home dad. We could afford it, and so that's what I'd done. Ashley settled into her role as general manager and part-owner of The Global and I became a silent partner and stay-at-home parent.

It was the best decision I ever made. Home with my two daughters, and with a happy wife, I had to chuckle to myself when I thought back to how resistant I'd been to having a female boss.

Because now I had three.

And I wouldn't have it any other way.

THE END

Brianna King's story is next.
Brianna first appears in *The Billionaire and the Assistant*: The Billionaires, Book Two, but *Exception* can be read as a standalone.

EXCEPTION

BOOK TWO

EXCEPTION
DEFINITION

A person or thing that is excluded from a general statement or does not follow a rule.

CHAPTER ONE

Toby

New Years' Eve, 2020

I'd been invited to Eli King's new year's celebrations after sealing the deal and moving in to one of King Enterprises' most luxurious residences. Life was a challenge at present as my star had ascended to such a point that I'd had to go off-grid for a while. Eli had reassured me that security would be tight. I guess it had to be when you were a billionaire.

Eli had known my father from before I was born, and it was when my dad had visited New York and seen how burned out I was that he'd got in touch with his old buddy to ask if he could help me.

And so here I was. About to walk into a room where there would be barely anyone I knew, yet feeling like I could breathe for the first time in a long, long while.

Well, until *she* crashed into me, taking my breath away.

The blonde in front of me looked up, giving an annoyed huff as if it were my fault we'd collided. I took in her long, straight hair; the black silk evening gown, slit right to her navel, tit-tape working its magic to reveal only a tantalizing sliver of the creamy orbs below the fabric. Black winged eyeliner accentuated those green eyes, and a slash of red lipstick meant her haughty pout was delivered in style.

My appraisal of her was interrupted by a pat on my back. I turned to see Eli appearing at my side.

"Ah, Brianna. I see you met Toby. Toby has recently moved into one of the condos on Park Avenue. Please don't mention that to any of your friends. He's trying to stay a little off-grid, even though that's damn near impossible."

"Yes, bloody paparazzi follow me everywhere." I sighed. In some ways it made me homesick. Back in London the paps didn't give much of a shit what I did. There, they were only interested in *who* I did. The rest of the time I was left alone. If I wanted to jog, I could run the equivalent of a marathon undisturbed. If I wanted to date, well, then they were in my face, finding out all about the object of my affections. Whereas here in the US, my every breath seemed to be reported on. That's why I needed some time away from filming, to get my head straight and work out if the movie roles were worth the life that went along with them, or whether to go home to the U.K. and settle for less. However, right now, in front of me was this gorgeous blonde and not a pap in sight. "So, Brianna, right?" I said, putting what I hoped was a winning smile on my face. "How do you know the bride and groom?"

My smile faltered as her eyes narrowed and her nostrils flared. "Eli is my bastard of a father. Now if you'll excuse me, I've had enough of this shit show already." She pushed past me, and I turned and watched as she stormed out of the room. I couldn't help but notice how the dress molded around the curves of that perfect arse.

Eli had a grown up daughter? I didn't know him well, but I'd thought he might have mentioned her, given she appeared around my age. Mind you, given the attitude she'd just shown toward him, it looked like there might be some issues between them.

Keep away and don't get involved, my inner thoughts chided. *You want peace and quiet, not a dramatic, sassy blonde in your life.* Unfortunately, my eyes weren't listening, and they kept looking for her throughout the night.

I didn't think she was going to re-appear, but *oh boy* did she make a re-entrance... It was a quarter to midnight, and I'd spent the evening largely alone nursing glasses of scotch, although I'd passed easy conversation with a few other attendees. Some of the realtor staff who'd handled the purchase of my condo were here and had introduced me to their significant others. It showed me most people here tonight were in happy couples, all loved up and waiting for the new year to come in, no doubt hoping for that perfect year ahead. Looked like myself and Eli were among the rare group of singletons here.

Or so I'd thought.

Brianna crashed back through the doors. And I mean crashed. The force in which she'd pushed through had made them bang into the walls at either side. She teetered on her heels, looking unsteady and extremely drunk, no doubt courtesy of the large bottle in her hand. Should I go see if she was okay? I noticed her father following her as she headed toward the microphone, set up I imagined for Eli to wish us all a happy new year. Brianna grabbed the microphone. "Is it new year yet? Only I don't have a watch." She waved the bottle in the air. "Though I do have my dad's best scotch."

Looking at the crowd of people around me, some were laughing, clearly thinking this was part of the evening celebrations, while others, in particular the realtors from Green's, and Eli's assistant, Alex, looked uncomfortable. Troubled almost. Eli whispered in his daughter's ear.

"Oh yes, yes, yes. Go to your room, Brianna. Fuck off out of my life, Brianna. You're an embarrassment, Brianna. Here have some money and leave me the fuck alone. Fine, Father. Fine," she hollered. "You win. You carry on here with your new wife." She pointed at Alex. As gasps sounded around the crowd, clearly this was a huge surprise to all. "And your new perfect life. While you're at it, why don't you plant your seed in her, if you haven't already, and have a replacement Brianna? One that's not a fucking embarrassment. Or, maybe you'll realize that you are the most fucking pathetic father ever as you screw up the life of baby number two." She raised up the bottle and then took a huge gulp. "To the bride and groom, everyone."

Storming off the stage, she pushed her way through people and came right past me. I tried to grab her arm, to see if I could help her in any way.

Those narrowed eyes landed on me for a second. "You can go fuck yourself too." She shrugged off my hand and was gone. I should have been insulted, but her haughty attitude had just made my dick hard.

Eli picked up the microphone and asked for everyone's attention.

"Right, well, that wasn't quite the way we'd planned to announce things. But if you'd like to raise your glasses." He beckoned to Alex. "Alex and I eloped on December 18th. So we please ask that you celebrate our marriage as we bring in the new year."

People cheered, but Alex went off after Brianna instead of joining Eli on stage. The party continued for about another hour and then it came to an abrupt halt. As I left, returning in a private car to my new condo, I couldn't help but wonder what had gone on between Eli and his daughter to cause her to make a scene and to act with such hostility.

I spent the early hours of the new year looking on the internet for any information on Brianna King, discovering not much more than her being the only daughter of Eli and his ex-wife. It seemed she lived with her mother, and so must have been here visiting over the holiday season. Reminding myself I was enjoying some time of solitude and reflection, I tried my best to push away all thoughts of her and the trouble that clearly surrounded her.

Over the following weeks I enjoyed spending time alone in my new condo. I had time to read over scripts, to chill out, and to decide that I wanted to stay in the US, but I'd pick less movies to film, and build in more time for living. I'd up my security presence when I went anywhere and try to find all the anonymous places where celebrities could relax.

I knew that Eli had been to his ex-wife's wedding and then had stayed out there for a few weeks. Alex was handling the business and the rumors were that all wasn't well between the couple. It wasn't my concern. And yet I couldn't help but be interested, because I still couldn't forget the woman who'd almost literally knocked me off my feet.

Then Eli was back. I bumped into him at the Park Avenue development where I lived. He said goodbye to the man he'd been speaking to and then walked toward me.

"Toby! How are things? You still loving the condo?"

"It's perfect. Best move I ever made. How are you?" I

cleared my throat. "Polite question only. I've heard things haven't been easy. I'm not expecting you to explain." *Shut up, Toby, you fool*, I scolded myself. Why didn't I just come out and ask him how Brianna was and have done with it?

"I'm getting there. Things have been tricky of late, I'm not going to lie." I realized then just how tired Eli looked up close with dark circles under his eyes. "But I think it might all work out in the end. I must apologize for that evening. Hopefully, now my daughter and I are working on things, she might not provide the entertainment at any future parties."

"That's good, that you're working on things. Is Brianna back here in New York then?"

He shook his head. "Not at the moment. She needs to figure out where she belongs and that's her decision to make."

Taking a deep breath, I made my move. "Could I have her number? Only she's around my age and I thought we might be able to hang sometime if she comes back to Manhattan."

A genuine smile lit up his face. "That'd be fantastic, Toby. The girl could use some more friends."

He gave me her number and then received a call, said his goodbyes, and left. I went back to my condo and sitting on the couch began composing a text.

. . .

Brianna 'Brat' King. No one has told me to go fuck myself in a long time. Everyone likes to say yes to me. In fact, it's amazing what people will do for a movie star. Except you. I have a feeling you'd make me work for it. You've been on my mind since you left. So what do you say, want to play?

TL.

Then I pressed send and waited.

CHAPTER TWO

Brianna

The text couldn't have arrived at a better time. After being back in Pacific Palisades the past few months while we went to family counselling, my father had now returned to Manhattan and my mother and her new husband, Roger, had gone on their long awaited and postponed honeymoon.

And after exhausting all the spas, and shopping until I dropped, there was another word beginning with S that I sorely needed and had been missing in my life for quite some time... *sex*.

I wasn't about to lament on quite how long it had

been since my most intimate parts had been seen by anyone other than the woman who waxed my pussy. Therapy had taught me it was time to focus on moving forward in life and not to dwell on the past. That could now encompass the dearth of bedroom action.

And now Toby London wanted to play. Not only that, but he seemed quite happy if I still behaved like a brat. Which was good because while I was doing my best to be a reformed character, miracles didn't happen overnight.

I began my reply.

Brianna: TL? Who is this?

Laughing, I clicked send. It wasn't long before a replied beeped.

Toby: Like you don't know who this is. But I'll play along. Tobias London, 29, lives in a prestigious condo on Park Avenue, Manhattan. Has a big cock. Also has your number and I don't mean the cell phone one. I said I wanted to play though, so do continue to keep me entertained.

. . .

Well, well, well. My pussy was wet just from a text message, so who the heck knew what the big cock might do.

I typed in the reply box.

Brianna: I'll arrive sometime tomorrow. Need to organize the plane and a hotel.

Toby: No hotel. Waste of time when you'll be in my bed.

Brianna: So presumptuous.

Toby: Tell me I'm wrong.

Brianna: I would, but I feel I'd be lying.

Throwing my phone down onto the thick carpet, I stretched out my limbs, and smiled while I laid on the couch staring up at the ceiling. I'd also spent the last few months studying event management online and while I was in Manhattan I intended to get in touch with Alex, my dad's significant other, and see if I could begin organizing some events so that I could get some hands-on experience. If things didn't work out with Toby, then I'd use the money I had in the bank to rent a place for a while. I still had three million in there for my own home that Roger and my mother had gifted me, but it had been agreed that while we were doing the therapy, I'd stay with them. Now, I was more than ready to make moves to be the adult I was.

I wasn't proud of my brattish behavior of the past, but therapy had helped us all as a family work out where it had come from. Individual therapy had helped me with guidance on how to move past using tantrums etc as a defense mechanism and how to now embrace the fact I was twenty-five and should be standing on my own two Louboutin-ed feet. It was scary, thinking about revealing my 'true self' and in reality, I didn't know who I really was. I'd never been independent, just petulant and demanding. It had been Alex who had begun to unpick my defense mechanisms and who ultimately had started the whole process.

But Alex had her own crap to deal with. She and my father had married in haste after she'd been his assistant for years. It was clear they were made for each other, but they'd agreed to start from the beginning and to date again. I could only hope that it would all work out between them because she made my dad happy, and I know he made her happy too.

My stomach fizzed as I thought about what I was about to do. Was I really going to go stay at a virtual stranger's house based on an invite to 'play?' This might be the stupidest thing I'd ever done.

I sent another text.

Brianna: Are you sure about this?

His reply came a couple of minutes later.

Toby: Are you getting cold feet? Because I can warm them up no problem. With my mouth...

That was all I needed for me to throw caution to the wind.

Brianna: No cold feet although I might pretend to have them now... just about to book my plane that's all. See you soon.

About to call for the private plane, I changed my mind. I'd sort out my own transport and fly, first class of course, to Manhattan. Not only was it independence, but then my mother wouldn't be alerted to my movements and start questioning me on what I was up to.

I discovered there was a flight from LAX to JFK at 2:30 pm the following day that arrived at 10:30 pm Eastern time. If things went to plan, I'd be in Toby's bed by late tomorrow evening.

I sat up and swung my legs off the couch. It was time to pack and see if I could get an early morning appointment for a blow dry and a last-minute wax.

By the time I was sitting on the airplane the following day, my stomach was fizzing as much as the champagne I'd just been served. I'd let Toby know my flight details and he was sending a driver to the airport to greet me and bring me to his condo.

What the hell are you doing, Brianna? My mind began to doubt my hasty decisions. *You don't know this guy at all beyond what's in the press and the brief interactions you had with him at the party. This is crazy!*

I drank the rest of my champagne and got a refill until I began to calm down. My father knew his father. This man was not a complete stranger. He'd bought one of my dad's properties. It wasn't like he was going to be a serial killer who banged me then butchered me. I knew the guy himself was taking some time-out and that's why he was in Manhattan in the first place. His career had gone crazy and it had all proved too much so he'd gone to ground for a while. His team had done well to keep his whereabouts other than 'Manhattan' out of the press and so my being there was extremely unlikely to be discovered.

In other words, it sounded absolutely perfect.

Fun with a man who by his own admission had a big cock. Let's hope he knew how to use it.

"Welcome to Manhattan, Miss King," the driver said as I approached him, having spotted his sign with my name on.

"Thank you."

He took my luggage from me and placed it on a cart.

"If you'd like to follow me."

I was escorted through to where the limo awaited, and the driver opened the door for me to climb inside, before placing my luggage in the trunk. The back of the car was furnished with light refreshments, and the driver asked me what music I'd like streaming.

"Just sit back and relax and I'll get you to Park Avenue," he said and then we were on our way.

Relax. Hmm, that was pretty impossible knowing that this car journey was the only thing left before I reacquainted myself with Mr. London.

I distracted myself by taking in the sights. It didn't matter how many times I came to Manhattan, I loved looking at the city and its bright lights. Eventually, we entered a private parking lot and after taking out my luggage and opening the door for me, the driver used a special key to open a large elevator. He placed my luggage inside and gestured for me to step inside also. Then he took his cell phone from his pocket and dialed.

"Mr. London. Miss King is in the elevator." There was a pause. "Thank you, sir, you too."

He pressed the button for Toby's condo.

"I wish you a pleasant stay, Miss King. Mr. London

will meet you as you exit the elevator." With that he nodded his head and turned away. The doors closed and the elevator began to rise. Holy shit, this was really happening.

I had only a brief moment to check out my reflection in the elevator mirror before the cab ground to a halt and the doors opened to reveal Toby in all his glory.

And the moment his cheeky smile met my, no doubt, nervous gaze, all my concerns melted away.

He was everything I'd remembered and more.

"It's been less than twenty-four hours, so why does it feel like I've been waiting for years?" he said as he gestured for me to step out of the elevator. I did so and he brushed past me to reach in for my suitcase and duffle. I felt like an electric shock had passed through me as his body met mine. His arm had briefly come into contact with my right breast and in closing the space between us, it was as if my body just wanted to let him completely in.

When we'd met so briefly at my father's new year party, I'd been so angry at my dad. So furious at his new life with Alex and his continual ignoring of the life he'd already created—*mine*—that I'd only briefly acknowledged how attractive Toby was, before I'd remembered why I was there, to cause a scene, and had dismissed Toby.

The man before me now looked slightly different. Still with his blue eyes and his charming smile, but his hair was now brown.

"Your hair." Of all the first things to say to him that was the one I'd gone with.

He lifted a hand to his scalp. "Oh yeah. The blond had been for one of my movie roles. This is me: brown hair and blue eyes."

"An intriguing pairing. Unusual. But I like."

His brows raised. "I'm glad you like. Now, come with me and let's get you settled in my condo. I don't have staff, because when I wanted to be alone, I meant completely alone," he explained.

"But if I'm there, you're not completely alone, are you?" I teased.

"Oh, Brianna. With you I'm making an exception," he said.

As I followed him through the entrance of his condo, I very much liked the sound of that.

Toby's condo was huge. I'd not seen my dad's building before. I'd never taken an interest in his business beyond accepting money from it. However, it was impressive, and given I'd lived among the elite —my stepfather was a billionaire—I recognized luxury when I saw it. My father had developed his Park Avenue condominiums to perfection, or his team had.

Large windows around the open-plan room let in vast amounts of light and the views were stunning. The interior design was all clean lines, and whites and taupe's including a white marble fire surround and two huge taupe couches that faced each other. The couches were placed perfectly in front of one of the vast windows, a coffee table that looked more like a sculpture set between them. Thick white rugs laid under the couches upon the wooden floors. But even with its obvious luxury, it didn't look like Roger's where there were some rooms you were scared to move in, just in case you broke an antique vase. It looked comfortable here, like you could relax.

"The place is beautiful," I finally said, as I turned to Toby.

"Not as beautiful as you," he replied, moving closer to me. "Let me take your jacket, and then do you want a drink or anything to eat?"

I passed him my jacket. Underneath I was wearing a tight cream dress that molded to my curves and I watched as Toby's eyes raked hungrily down my body.

"A girl could use a glass of wine," I said. "But other than that, I think I'd just like to see our bedroom."

"So you're happy to share my bed?" he queried, followed by a nervous smile.

"I'm counting on it." I grinned.

"I'll just hang up your jacket and get that drink," he said. "In the meantime, make yourself comfortable." He explained where the bedroom was and that there was an en suite attached to it. I didn't need any further encouragement. While Toby did his tasks, I found his bedroom: another huge space, with a huge bed. I took a minute or two to splash water on my face and quickly brushed my teeth and then I headed back to the bedroom where I stripped off my clothes, down to the pale lilac lingerie set I'd chosen to wear that day.

By the time Toby entered the room wheeling in a hostess trolley carrying a bottle of red and a bottle of white, wine glasses, and a carafe of water and tumblers, I was sitting on a chair near the window waiting. I was trembling slightly, more I think from the anticipation hanging in the air than the slight chill of the air-conditioning.

"Which wine would you like?" he asked me, his voice thick as he took in my appearance.

"Red please."

He poured a glass and brought it over to me. I took

a sip and then placed it on the small, circular coffee table next to the window.

"Can I get you anything else?" he almost growled.

"The only thing I want now is you, deep inside me," I said, standing up.

Toby closed the distance between us in record time.

CHAPTER THREE

Toby

Not putting my hands straight on her body and my cock straight in her pussy had been a mammoth feat of endurance, but I didn't want to scare her off. I needed to let Brianna dictate the pace. So her words were everything I'd wanted to hear. I think I'd have died via blue balls if she hadn't given me permission to fuck her at that moment, given how she looked like the perfect present to unwrap in that purple lace bra that gave a hint of rosy-pink nipple and the g-string that clearly showed me her pussy was bare.

Closing the gap between us as she stood up from the chair, I took her chin in my hand and tilted her face up toward mine. Her green eyes flashed with lust. There was no hesitancy there as our mouths moved toward the other's. My mouth landed on her full, soft lips; gently at first as I got used to the feel of mine brushing against hers. Then I deepened the kiss and Brianna parted her lips. My tongue sought entrance, weaving against her own. With a groan, I picked her up and carried her toward my bed.

She was the first woman I'd ever brought here. Like I'd said, I'd chosen to be alone up until this point. The only people I'd been in contact with were members of my team and I'd kept them to video calls and regular calls. My body rejoiced in the contact between it and a soft, warm, willing body.

I placed Brianna down on the bed carefully and climbed alongside her, pulling her onto her own side facing me. Trailing my fingers down her face and across the bud of her lower lip, she made me gasp when she sucked one of them into her mouth, her hand now holding my wrist in place as my digit entered the warm heat beyond her teeth. All I could think of was getting my dick inside her other warm place, but I had to wait. Had to take care of Brianna first.

But Brianna had other ideas. She pushed me onto my back. "You're fully clothed. This will not do at all," she announced. She sat astride me and slowly unbuttoned my shirt, placing kisses down my chest as she undid each one. It was agony, my cock straining against my pants just below where she sat.

I soon realized I didn't know the meaning of the word agony as she unfastened my lower buttons and rearranged her arse so she was sat directly on top of my cock. And she fucking well knew it, grinding her hips around before undoing the last button of my shirt. With my shirt gone, she paused for a moment looking down at me, her blonde hair falling over her face slightly. I ran my hand through it.

"You're killing me here, Bree."

"But what a way to go," she whispered.

Lifting up, she moved to the side of me, and I had to help her with unfastening my pants and zipper. She then moved off the bed altogether, walking to the rear of it. "Raise your hips," she directed.

"So bossy," I said, doing as she asked.

"I'm a brat, remember? I demand things and I get what I want."

"We'll see about that," I challenged, but I already knew I was a lost cause and Brianna King could demand of me whatever she wanted right now. I was powerless to resist.

My boxers followed my pants onto the floor and then I was commanded to close my eyes. I did as asked. I felt the bed depress and then a soft breath blew across the head of my cock.

Oh my.

A warm hand lifted my dick and then a hot, wet mouth enveloped it.

"Oh fuck," I groaned, wondering if I was going to last long given how amazing it felt. Her small hand gripped the base of me, and Brianna took me in completely, right to the back of her throat. I began to move my hips slowly, working with the rhythm she dictated. My eyes being closed meant I was deeply focused on the sensations: on the sucks, the flick of her tongue around my glans, the cool air against my wet skin when it met the room's air-conditioning, the feel of the roof of her mouth against me when I slid back in. Her other hand began stroking at my balls.

"Jesus Christ," I uttered. "What are you bloody doing to me?"

Brianna let me slide out of her mouth and giggled. "I'm giving you a *bloody* blow job," she said attempting my British accent. Then she took me in her mouth once more and upped her pace and the strength of her sucking. I bucked against her, riding her mouth, until I felt my balls tighten and then I shot my load inside her mouth, Brianna not letting me pull out, but swallowing every last drop.

As she gently placed my cock back on my stomach, I watched through heavy-lidded eyes as she ran her tongue around her lips. "Mmm, delicious," she boasted, coming back to my side.

"Okay, bossy boots." I winked. "What do you demand happens next?" I wanted to take care of her, even though I felt like I'd just enjoyed a six-hour massage.

"I demand you return the favor," she ordered, spreading her thighs wide.

"Oh that will be both my pleasure *and* yours," I informed her. "Now close your eyes because it makes it all the sweeter."

"Now who's being bossy?" she sassed. But she closed her eyes.

I slipped a bra strap off one shoulder and then the other. It was a front fastener and so I flicked it open. Brianna helped me remove it, and then her gorgeous creamy orbs were revealed in all their perky glory. I suckled on one nipple and then the other, teasing her areole with my tongue and slightly biting down. I knew where she wanted me most, but I intended to enjoy my descent down the slope of Brianna's body. I gave my attention to every inch of her flesh, fondling and kissing, licking and nipping, every bit but her pussy. Brianna was plainly aroused as she whimpered as I nibbled the top of her thigh, getting closer to where she craved me. Finally, I brushed my fingers over the top of her panties. She was soaked and writhed to attempt to get extra friction for her clit from my fingers. I pulled off her panties and then I pinched her clit. Her face was a picture of intense longing, and I couldn't help but study her. I was as hooked on her facial expressions and the sounds she made as I was in playing with her pussy in that moment. Brianna was simply intoxicating.

As my fingers probed her wet heat, she raised her thighs.

"I'm so fucking horny right now," she confessed. That was my cue to begin to dine on her pussy. Pushing her knees up and apart, her pink folds were revealed to me. The view was spectacular, her juices glistening and running down her slit. Her cunt accepted my tongue, darting inside her although she jerked slightly as I brushed against her clit. She tasted like the finest honey, and I couldn't get enough. Alternating between entering her pussy with my tongue and flicking it over her clit, as I felt Brianna start to buck more wildly against me, I focused on sucking on her nub and pushed three digits inside her.

Breaking off for a brief moment, I cajoled her, "Come for me, Bree. Fuck my face."

Just a couple more sucks and Brianna writhed wildly against me. I moved from her clit back to feasting on her juices and I felt the tremors as they dispersed from her.

Her breath rose and fell in sharp bursts as she laid on the bed in what looked to me like a wanton heap. But I wasn't finished with her. I needed to be inside that pussy. Climbing over her, I lined my cock up against her entrance, then hooked her leg around my arse and sank deep inside her.

"Fuck that feels so good," I moaned, and I started a steady rhythm. Brianna met me thrust for thrust, finding her second wind. She brought her other leg up so that her feet rested against my arse cheeks, and she pressed them down giving me a hint to go harder.

That hot pussy sheathed me tight and worked me good, milking my cock until the familiar tingles started at the base of my spine. I pulled out of her to grab a condom, and she hissed, "I was about to fucking come."

"Sorry," I whispered. "I should have done this earlier, but you make me forget my own name."

I pulled the condom onto my dick and turned her over so she was on all fours. That peachy arse was all on display, and unable to resist, I brought my hand down on her arse cheek, not too hard, but enough for it to tingle. The slap resonated in the air. "That's for being a naughty girl, almost making me forget to be safe."

For a moment, I wondered if I'd just fucked up in doing it, but instead that butt was wiggled in front of my eyes.

"Well doing that isn't going to make me behave any better because I rather like it. Do it again," she demanded.

So I did.

I kept slapping her arse cheeks, one then the other, and then rubbing my hand over the slight pink marks that appeared. Brianna's wetness was dripping onto the duvet she was so turned on. Grabbing her hips, I thrust my now sheathed cock inside her.

"God, yes. Fuck me hard now, Toby. Don't hold back."

I withdrew and then slammed inside her.

"More. Harder," she yelled.

I gave her my all, plunging inside her roughly, while pinching her clit until she collapsed against me with a shriek as she came, her pulsing pussy taking me over the edge as I spilled my seed into the condom.

It was without a doubt the best sex I had ever had, and it had only been our first time.

She'd only got here just over an hour ago and I was already wondering how I'd ever let her leave.

I removed the condom, taking it into the bathroom, and used the bidet to wash myself. Running a washcloth under the warm water before returning to the bed, I ran it gently between Brianna's thighs.

"I should go freshen up myself, but I don't think I have bones anymore," she announced before yawning.

"You've had a long day with the flight and neither of us have anywhere to go tomorrow, so why not just close your eyes for now? The bathroom will still be there when you wake up, as will the wine."

"As long as you'll be there when I wake up," she said languidly.

"I'm not going anywhere." I pulled her into my arms, wrapping my right arm over her breasts and I gently kissed the top of her head. We fit together perfectly and before I knew it Brianna's breathing had slowed, and she was asleep.

I was a little in shock at what had happened. When I'd texted Brianna to come here, I hadn't really expected us to fall straight into the bedroom. I thought face-to-face there'd be an awkwardness around each other, and we'd start with dinner and get to know each other better. Instead, there'd just been this amazing connection that had set the bedsheets alight. I didn't know what the morning would bring, whether in the cold light of day she'd regret her impulsivity or thank me and leave, but for tonight, I'd make the most of the smoking hot body currently nestled against me.

Not long after that, my own eyes closed and that

was it until morning broke, light flooding the room. I opened my eyes, finding myself alone in the bed. There was no one in my arms and an empty space at my side.

Sitting up, the wine still laid on the nightstand untouched beyond that first taste, and there was no sign of Brianna.

Had she bolted? If she had, I knew I would be in hot pursuit.

CHAPTER FOUR

Brianna

As my eyes opened, the first thing that struck me was the heat. Used to a vast bed all to myself, I couldn't understand why I felt so warm. But all was quickly remembered as I felt the arm loosely wrapped around my body. I was in Manhattan! I carefully lifted Toby's arm and moved over to a cooler part of the bed. The room was light enough for me to see that Toby was still sound asleep, his mouth parted. He looked so peaceful. It gave me time to study his features. There was what looked like a slight scar right at the edge of his left brow. His cheekbones were sculptured, and his jaw defined, a slight scruff now starting to appear under his nose and around his chin. My fingers begged to trail over the stubble, to unite the smooth pad of my fingertips with the rough texture, but I didn't want to disturb him. He'd escaped to find some peace and right now he was enjoying some, so I would leave him be.

Having always slept in sleep shorts or pajamas, I didn't feel altogether comfortable being naked. Now fully awake, I noted my dry mouth and full bladder. Creeping slowly to the edge of the bed, I carefully lowered my feet to the carpet and then I stood, quietly heading to my luggage. I managed to grab my wash bag without disturbing Toby at all—he really was in a deep slumber—and exited the room, going in search of the master bathroom.

Having found it, I took in a few mouthfuls of water from the faucet at the basin to appease my dry mouth, before turning on the shower. There were toiletries in a basket next to the basin and towels in a heated rack. I took what I needed and then I stepped under the hot spray. I'd not realized how tense I'd become until the heat and firmness of the jets began to ease the tight muscles in my shoulders. Having made the trip here and being brave, I was now experiencing what I recognized as vulnerability, and I didn't like it. Being vulnerable in my past had always led to crushing disappointment and rejection, and no matter the therapy I'd been having, I just wasn't ready to put myself out there like that at present. Not yet. Having time to think while the water cascaded over my body, I knew I needed to keep my guard up because hadn't Alex and my father gone too fast and look what had happened to them. I made a promise to myself there and then that I'd enjoy the sex, and enjoy getting to know Toby, but I would keep a distance, at least until a decent amount of time had passed and I believed he wouldn't hurt me. Because I knew I already liked him a lot, and that just made the thought of his rejection worse.

Pushing down my burgeoning feelings deep inside, I washed myself, noting the tenderness between my thighs. I hoped it wouldn't be long before I was ready to go another round because the sex with Toby had been off-the-charts incredible. It was like he'd been given a map to my erogenous zones.

I was reluctant to leave the comforting embrace of the shower water, but my stomach began to gurgle, and my throat craved its morning warm beverage, so I quickly washed my hair before turning off the faucet. Stepping from the stall onto a bathmat, I pulled a bath sheet from the towel rail and wrapped it around my body, sighing in bliss as the heat of it sunk into my skin. I placed another heated towel turban-style around my head.

Then I left the bathroom and went in search of coffee.

I was sitting on a couch, enjoying my coffee and a warmed croissant when I heard footsteps and a sleepy Toby entered the space. He rubbed at his eyes. If his hair hadn't been so short, I reckoned he'd have had cute, mussed bedhead. The thought made me smile and I watched as Toby returned my smile.

"I thought for a moment you might have left already. Used me for my body and then gone home."

I placed a hand on the top of my arm and rubbed it in what I knew was a self-soothing gesture. *It's okay, Brianna.*

"I guess we didn't clarify when you asked me to come play, for how long the invitation extended, and well, I'm far from bored with you yet. There's still plenty for us to play with." I wiggled my brows at him.

"Cool. I'd have been disappointed if you'd left already."

Disappointed to lose the pussy, not you, I warned myself. *Don't fall for the guy, it's too soon.*

"I see you found how to work the coffee machine. I'm in need of one of those myself. Had quite the workout last night." He arched a brow at me. "I am right in assuming that the sex was stellar, right?"

"Much as it pains me to admit anything that might make your head bigger, yes, it was incredible."

"It's not my head that's growing bigger. However, as tempting as it is to ravish you right where you are, I want you to know I am actually a gentleman, and I thought today we could enjoy a date."

"I thought you were lying low so as to keep away from paparazzi?"

"I am, but I'm also learning from people like your father, in that if I want privacy, I can get it. Just leave it to me. We can go out, with no one any the wiser." He tapped the side of his nose and moved to the coffee machine. "I want to get to know you better, Bree King." He paused for a moment. "Am I okay to call you that? Bree?"

"Sure. No one else does."

"Not your parents?"

"You must be joking. Up until the past few months, I'd been Brianna, *Briiiaannnna*, and spoiled brat, and that's on the few occasions I wasn't entirely invisible to them." I couldn't help the bitterness in my voice even though my parents had repeatedly apologized of late. It had been many years of their toxicity and few of their love.

"I don't know how anyone could ignore you," he

said, coming to sit on the couch opposite me carrying his own coffee and a blueberry muffin. He was in black sleep shorts and a grey tank, and my eyes feasted on his biceps as he took a bite of muffin. I wanted him to take a bite of my ass. My cheeks heated as I thought of it, and I felt a tiny pulse between my thighs.

"Tell me about the party on new year's. It was so confusing. One moment your dad announced his marriage and the next the party was over. But Alex is still helping run the business. When I saw him, your father said he hoped things would work out in the end?"

"My dad and Alex had crushed on each other for years apparently. Then my father decided to make a move having lost a bet with his friends which forced his hand. Next thing they were in Vegas and married. I came to stay with my father and found I had a new stepmom who my father was clearly besotted with. Even more clearly, he didn't want me around. Long story short, my parents were so focused on themselves that I became an inconvenience and I soon learned that the only way I could get any attention at all was if I behaved atrociously. So I did. I'm not proud of how I acted on new year's eve. I took to the stage pretending to be drunk in order to spoil my father's announcement. I mean, you didn't even know he had a daughter, yet he couldn't wait to tell people he had a new wife."

"Fuck, I had no idea."

"Alex told him he needed to sort things out. That he and my mother needed to sort things out, with me. So Dad came back to Pacific Palisades while we had therapy and worked on our relationships. It's not going to erase the past, but it means I might get a future reasonable relationship with my father, so there's that. Anyhow, I sent him back. I know he and Alex can work things out. I saw them together. They just went too fast. They do say 'marry in haste, repent in leisure', don't they?"

I noted the curl to Toby's lip and watched as he slowly, but forcibly exhaled.

"What's wrong?" I asked, feeling a crease form between my brow.

"What's wrong? I'm hearing that the beautiful woman in front of me, has only just been recognized for what I clearly saw the first time I met her. It pains me to know that you've endured that for..." he paused. "How old are you?"

"Twenty-five now."

"Twenty-five years. Twenty-five fucking years of treating you like crap. I don't know how I won't punch your father in the face the next time I see him."

"I recently had a birthday and things were okay for the first few years of my life, but yeah, 'father of the year' he hasn't been. But he's trying now, and I'm not looking back, because there's nothing to be gained in doing so."

"Listen." Toby's gaze on mine was intense, those blues like a stormy ocean. "I know we didn't clarify how long you were going to be here for, but while you are, I intend to make sure you know just how amazing you are."

I wanted to believe him. I really did. But I didn't have trust. Not yet.

"I don't know how long I'm staying. I'm going to get in touch with my stepmonster. That's what I call Alex now. It's a nickname, she's cool with it," I said as he frowned. "To catch up with her and also about some business stuff, which I'll get to explaining at some point. I feel I've already talked quite enough for one morning. But you let me know if I outstay my welcome and I'll go check into a hotel. Though I don't think that would be half as much fun as being here."

"You can stay as long as you like."

"You say that, but we have no idea how this is going to go. You might get bored of me, just like my parents did. I'm a work-in-progress. A challenge."

"I'm up for a challenge."

"Toby, you're here by your own admission to have a break from the drama that comes with your career. I hope I can help relieve some of your *tension*." I winked. "But we both know this is only temporary. You'll be back to filming movies before long, and I intend to concentrate on myself for a while, find out who Brianna King really is, and start my new business."

He looked pissed again, and opened his mouth to say something, so I swiftly changed the subject.

"I want to hear about you now anyway. I'm bored of myself. It's time I got to know you a little better, Tobias London." I took a drink of my now cooling coffee. "Tell me something about yourself."

I noted the flare to his nostrils, but he composed himself and said, "Okay, well for a start my name isn't Tobias London."

CHAPTER FIVE

Toby

Brianna had said so many things I wanted to process. How her parents had treated her. About her therapy. Her new job. But all I could hear in my mind was her, *'This is only temporary.'*

Yet before I could think on this and about why it made me feel so incensed, she'd started to ask me about myself. I didn't want to talk about me, but I quickly saw in her expression that she needed it. Her green eyes held a plea for me to change the subject, one she clearly found challenging.

And it came to me then. She couldn't give me her all right away, because she'd yet to learn who she was and what she had to give. Also, she was correct. I would be moving on at some point to film, wouldn't I?

The fact was my heart was all in with Brianna King. I'd had an instant and irrevocable heart-on for the woman. But Brianna and my head were now reminding me that there were outside influences and extenuating circumstances that suggested I pull back and take this one moment at a time. Especially when I saw the fear in her eyes. The clear fear that she couldn't commit as so many people had let her down, and that she couldn't promise she could offer anything beyond right now.

So I composed myself and did what she wanted me to do. I talked about myself.

"Then what is your name?" she asked as I informed her Tobias London wasn't it.

"Christopher Tobias Smith. Chris Smith isn't very glamorous and movie star sounding, is it? My agent suggested I went with my middle name and the surname of London given I was a British born actor hoping to make a name for himself across the pond."

"Hmm, so do I call you Toby or Chris?"

"As long as you're shouting out my name in ecstasy, I don't care which you use."

She rolled her eyes at me. "I'm going to stick with Toby. That's the name you were introduced to me as. It would feel weird calling you anything else now."

"Makes sense. Okay, so once we've finished these drinks and this spot of breakfast, would you like to go out on our first official date, Miss King?"

"I graciously accept, but provisionally. I reserve the right to change my mind if I don't like where you take me."

I grinned and took a mouthful of my coffee. She wouldn't be changing her mind once she saw where we were going.

I'd planned ahead for once. When Brianna had said she was coming to Manhattan, I had made arrangements to hire a space. My personal assistant knew to ask no questions and just make whatever bookings I requested. Her iron-clad non-disclosure agreement and contract of employment covered all bases.

And so that's how I was able to get my driver to pull up at the private entrance of a prestigious hotel knowing we could spend the next few hours disturbed only when we requested and only then by the staff of the hotel.

"An iconic and luxurious hotel," Bree said as staff escorted us to a private elevator. "Are we having lunch... or dessert?"

"Lunch," I confirmed.

The Symphony Hotel's porter, John, currently standing in the elevator with us, kept an expressionless face. I'm sure he'd heard much more exciting things in the past than the flirtations of a movie star and his date.

John opened the door for us. Taking Bree's hand, I pulled her outside.

"Oh *wow*," she exclaimed as she stood and took in the view.

It was the hotel's private rooftop terrace. Enclosed, it held a fake lawn, elaborate statues, and a fountain. Usually catering for events, I'd had all but one table removed and a swing seat added, plus two sun loungers. I'd also requested a portable jacuzzi.

"I don't have a costume," Bree said.

"We have staff and we're near Fifth Avenue," was my only reply.

I'd not dropped her hand and I tugged on it again. "Let's take in the views across the city and then how about we lounge for a while?"

Bree nodded and we walked over to the edge of the rooftop and gazed at Central Park.

"How long do we have this for?" Bree asked.

"Until eleven pm if we wish, so we can have lunch, afternoon tea, and dinner out here. I pointed to the end of the space. "Over there is access to a private suite, should you want to siesta and take a break from the sun."

"Thank you, Toby. This is amazing. Could you request some sunblock for me and a costume? I think we should move onto the loungers and enjoy a nice, chilled glass of champagne and maybe some strawberries."

Her wish was my command and I called through to the staff who were taking care of us today.

"So tell me about this business of yours," I requested once we were comfortable on the loungers. Though to be honest I wasn't that comfortable given Bree was now wearing a red bikini which had given me a boner.

"I've been training to be an event planner for the past few months. I'm ready now to take on a few engagements and see how it goes. That's why I want to see Alex. My father always has something he's throwing an event for. I figured while I'm here I could make myself useful and show him I'm capable of more than being petulant."

"But you're doing this because you want to, right? Not just to prove a point to your father?"

She nodded. "I'm really into it. I've been to enough parties in enough places that I know a good party/event and a terrible one. My knowledge of venues across Manhattan and LA is exemplary. I just have a really good feeling about it all. My mentor thinks I'm a natural and ready to take my first fledgling steps."

"That's fantastic."

Bree beamed at me. All the tension she'd been carrying since this morning had now melted away.

"If it's okay with you, I'd like to arrange to go see Alex tomorrow."

"Of course it's okay with me. You're not imprisoned with me. Although." I tapped at my chin. "There's an idea. Maybe I could rent a dungeon next."

Bree picked up a strawberry and sucked on it. "Maybe you could," she said.

And once more my cock hardened.

"You know I can see exactly what I'm doing to you, don't you?" Bree took the strawberry and dipped it in her glass of champagne and then licked the liquid off it. I groaned.

"We're supposed to be getting to know one another," I protested.

She ate the strawberry and then peeled off her bikini top. Picking up the champagne she tipped some over each nipple.

"We are. Inside and out." Brianna beckoned me with her little finger. "Come tell me which tastes better in your mouth: the strawberries, the champagne, or my erect nipples."

"Do you want to take this inside?" I nodded my head in the direction of the room we had available.

"No one can see us and even if the staff do, they aren't allowed to say anything are they?"

"True."

"Then I'd like to stay right here for the *tasting* session." Her eyes moved right to my groin, and she licked around her top lip.

I was done asking questions and delaying the inevitable.

Moving from my own lounger, I pulled Bree's lounger more upright before sitting myself at the side of her. I cupped a breast and lowered my head, taking her nipple in my mouth. The champagne had already dried under the heat of the day, but I flicked my tongue over the hardening bud, biting down slightly. My left hand headed south, my fingers dancing across the skin of her stomach, the material of her bikini bottoms, and then pulling the ties at the side of them apart so that the material fell away, allowing me entrance to her pussy.

My fingertips brushed her nub and then I ran them through her slick folds. I let her breast fall from my mouth.

"So wet for me, and I know you'll already taste so sweet, but let's add some more."

I moved myself off the lounger and picked up my

glass of champagne and then I came around to the front of the seat and knelt down, pushing Bree's legs wider apart so I could nestle between. I poured the champagne so it ran from her belly button and down into her cunt, and then leaning forward I let my tongue follow the trail. Dipping into her belly button, down the soft skin that led to her shaved pussy and further down still, dipping and tasting, licking and sucking.

I broke off to look up at her. Her eyes were languid pools, her pupils lust blown.

"Just as I thought. So fucking sweet."

Grabbing a strawberry, I ran it through her pussy and then sucked and ate it.

Bree's thighs tightened.

"Don't stop. I need to come so bad," she begged.

Bree being desperate for my touch was my new favorite thing.

My head returned to between her legs. I dug my fingers in below her arse, so I could lift her up to me like a ripe peach, and then I dived right in, concentrating on sucking on her clit and then pushing my tongue deep inside her.

"My clit, please, back to my clit," she whimpered, and I knew she was close. I did as requested, and Bree's movements become more fervent as she rode my mouth, sitting up, her hands fixing around the back of my head, directing me to move exactly as she needed.

She came with a squeal of, "Oh fuck, yes," and I didn't let her back away, the waves of her climax echoing over my lips and tongue until she sank against the back of the lounger, spent.

"Fucking hell, that was *intense*," she acknowledged before closing her eyes.

I just watched her. The serene expression of deep relaxation she now wore. Her mouth parted as she breathed deeply. The rise and fall of her breasts as her breathing began to return to normal.

I barely knew her, but I'd already decided that this woman should be at the center of Toby London's world. That with her in my life, I knew everything would just work out. I tried to talk myself out of my feelings. That it was just lust. That getting my cock wet was addling my brain, but deep down I knew it wasn't. It was like fairy tales had reversed and I'd just found my Princess Charming.

I knew fake feelings and lust from filming movies. 'Falling in love' with your co-star to make the chemistry on screen sizzle. Sometimes you fell into bed together, but once the movie was over, so were you. And I knew this: me and Brianna, was something very different to all that.

"Penny for them." Bree was staring at me, a question in her gaze. "You seemed far, far away then."

"Honestly? I was thinking about how very beautiful you are, inside and out." I repeated her words of earlier.

"You're not bad yourself," she said, sitting up. "Now lie back on your lounger because I have a champagne popsicle I'm looking forward to tasting."

I didn't need asking twice.

CHAPTER SIX

Brianna

This was hard and I didn't mean the cock I was currently blowing. Toby looked at me like I was a feast and he was starving. Like he'd been missing a piece of jigsaw and I was it. But was this him acting? A couple of days wasn't long enough to know someone well enough to let yourself fall, and yet I felt like I was on the edge of a cloud and one gust of wind would push me over.

And this was why tomorrow I would go to see Alex and find something else to do other than spend time with Toby. My mother had depended on men for her needs all her life. I had depended on my parents for my financial needs and no-one but myself for anything else. My guards were still very much up. I had something to prove. My dependence on my parents was a thorn in my side I needed to extract. To plant my own roses and watch them bloom.

Toby and I spent the afternoon talking, making out, and feasting on the culinary delights from the hotel kitchen. We finally left at around ten forty-five, sitting in the back of the car hand-in-hand. The evening was spent with us fucking for half the night. It was like we couldn't get enough.

When I finally fell asleep, once more wrapped in Toby's arms, I felt like I never wanted to be anywhere else. And that scared me half to death.

In fact, when I woke early the next morning and found once more Toby was sound asleep, this time I showered, changed and wrote Toby a note to let him know I'd gone to see Alex before leaving the condo. He'd told me last night that I could find a spare keycard in the living room dresser drawer and use it while I was here to come and go, but this morning it felt a lot like running away. I'd not even called Alex to see if I could chat with her. I made sure to exit the condo wearing a black cap pulled over my head while dressed in skinny jeans and a plain white tee with a lightweight beige jacket, but I couldn't see anyone around anyway. Toby seemed to have found a place to stay where the paps hadn't found him, and hopefully, I didn't look anything special even though my clothes were still designer. We were in Park Avenue after all.

I caught a cab over to near my father's offices and then found a coffee shop nearby. I hadn't been in a normal everyday coffee shop in my whole life. I didn't know whether to be nervous or ashamed as I pushed the door open.

You could feel the buzz of the place in the atmosphere. There was a queue and as I joined it, I watched people as they chatted to friends; or tapped their feet, some clearly in a hurry and hating the wait. The staff had smiles on their faces, but looked tired, no doubt hoping for a break in the rush of the morning crowd.

To me it was all so novel and new. Standing in a queue having to wait my turn, instead of barking orders at someone to get me what I wanted. And there came the shame. It poured over me in such huge waves I thought I might fall to my knees right there. My behavior had come from a place of hurt, but a lot of the people I'd treated like shit hadn't deserved it.

I had no money of my own. My bank account was full and my closets fuller, but it was all thanks to my mom's choice in boyfriends and husbands. I'd not earned a dime of it myself. Well, that was all about to change.

"What can I get you?" the barista asked, followed by a large smile in greeting.

"An Americano and I'll have one of those muffins please." I pointed to a lemon muffin that looked delicious.

"Name?"

"Bree." I spelled it out for her, "B, R, E, E." Crazily, I needed to see that name on the side of my paper cup. The barista wrote it on and told me how much I owed her. I asked her to repeat the price. Not because I'd not heard what she'd said, but because I couldn't believe it.

"Four bucks, fifty, ma'am," she repeated.

I handed her a twenty-dollar bill. "Keep the change."

"Are you sure, ma'am?" The barista stared at me.

I nodded.

"Well, bless your kindness, and you make sure to have a really good day."

"Thanks, you too." I went to stand and wait with the other patrons, and the barista moved on to the next customer in line. Once my drink was ready, I took my tray to a window seat and gazed out to people watch. Turning my cup around, I looked at the name *Bree* scrawled on it.

I liked being Bree. Bree didn't have the baggage of her complicated past. Bree was free.

Picking up my cell, I called Alex.

"Hi, Brianna. Everything okay?"

Fuck, and here was the baggage. Alex was only used to hearing from me when I needed something. I sighed because ironically it was still the case, even though it was to help me eventually stand on my own two feet.

"Everything is fine, but I'm here, in Manhattan, and close to your office. I wanted to come talk to you about event planning, if you have some time. I'll be here for a few more days at least, so whenever you can see me."

"My stepbrat is here. I can make time for her whenever."

"Stepbrat?" I laughed down the line.

"You call me stepmonster. It's only fair."

"I like it. Better than Brianna, any day. I'm just enjoying a coffee and madeleines at Starbucks, but I won't be long. Thirty minutes tops."

"Run that past me again. You're in a Starbucks?"

I laughed again. "I know. Hell froze over. I broke Satan."

She laughed back. I ended the call and went back to people watching and enjoying my change of scenery and first forays into a truly independent life.

Alex enveloped me in a hug. "It's good to see you in the flesh, stepbrat. I've been wondering how you were. Talking on phones isn't the same as seeing you in real life."

"If it's okay with you, I'd like to be called Bree from now on. I'm having a fresh start. I don't mean you can't call me stepbrat; I shall for sure still call you stepmonster at times, but instead of Brianna. I want to put Brianna in the past."

She raised a brow. "Bree. I like it. Should I change my own name, given I'm having a fresh start of my own?"

She indicated for me to take a seat on the leather couch in her office.

"Dad's out, I take it?" His office door was open.

"Yeah, he's at a meeting. He might get back before you leave though. Depends if it finishes on time, and on how long you'll be here."

"I came to see you anyway. I've seen enough of him lately. He and my mother."

Alex grinned. "I can imagine. Do you want another drink or are you full?"

"Could I trouble you for a water?"

Alex looked bemused.

"I know, it's a novelty being met by politeness

instead of demands, isn't it? It's all your fault. You were the one who got to the root of my problems."

"You'd have got there yourself at some point, Bree. You couldn't sustain that forever. You'd have taken your parents' money and run, and eventually met someone who loved you for the real you."

My mind flitted back to thoughts of Toby.

"Ohhhh *my*," Alex exclaimed.

"What?"

"You totally met someone. Your expression went dreamy, and you had a little smile to yourself."

"I did not," I protested.

"Oh yes you did, and I'm not discussing one bit of business with you until you confess to all."

I ran my tongue over my teeth while I considered. "As long as you don't tell my father."

"Not a word shall pass my lips." She mimed zipping across them.

"Okay, I'm here staying with Tobias London. We're hooking up."

Her jaw dropped.

"You're sleeping with Tobias London? He's hot as fuck. Wow. How did that happen?"

I filled her in on all the details. On how we'd met at 'the party' and how he'd asked me to come over.

"It's all just a bit of fun though. I've learned from you and dad not to rush into things."

Alex tilted her head at me. "It's good to be sensible, but just because me and your father didn't work out after rushing things, doesn't mean you wouldn't. I've had friends who have married after whirlwind romances and who are still together. And I'm quietly confident that your father and I will be fine. It's just working together and living together; it's going to take some adjustments that I'd rather we squared up while we live apart. We're still 'together' for the most part."

"For now, it's fun."

"Oh, I'm sure it is, but see that look on your face? I've worn that myself for years, Bree, so don't think you're fooling me."

I sighed. "I do really like him, but it's been thirty-six hours or thereabouts. I'm not committing myself to anyone when I need to find my own independence."

"Okay, I'll get you that water now." Alex stood up and picked up a tumbler and then went into a small refrigerator and took out a bottle, handing both over to me. "How can I help you with this independence then?"

Having brought Alex up to speed with my training, and my need for real life clients, she sat back and clapped her hands.

"I have the perfect job for you. Last minute and needs to be the kind of event talked about everywhere."

"Tell me more," I said, reaching into my purse for my iPad.

"Who are you and what the fuck did you do with Brianna King?" Alex giggled. "I definitely believe in alien invasion and demon possession now. Knew I should keep holy water in that fridge beside bottled."

I stuck out my tongue at her. "Sit down and tell me about this job."

"Now there's my bossy stepbrat after all."

I gave her my middle finger as a response this time, but she just carried on giggling.

"So, Aidan Hall, who you know, just sold his publishing company because he wanted to put his investment into something more aligned with Abandon."

Abandon was a member's only sex club in the city.

"Your father bought the company, but immediately made the CEO an offer of 45% of the company if the CEO ran it and only consulted with him when he needed to. Barnett accepted straight away because after two recent-ish takeovers he was beginning to fear for his role, and also that the place may change and go in a direction he didn't agree with."

"So what would I be needed for? What's the event?"

"They're about to launch a new author and there's been a lot of hype about them. Her name's Giovanna Amore. They need an event that will have this author's career cemented. Inviting the main reviewers, celebrities who will stand with the book in their hand, that kind of thing."

I felt butterflies dancing in my stomach, along with a general feeling of excitement. "Let me do this, please? I promise I will be amazing at it."

"It's yours. Don't let me down. Keep me informed of your plans though because we can't afford for this to not be a success."

I nodded vehemently. It would truly be a disaster for my father's relationship with Alex, and my relationship with him if I fucked up.

But I had no intention of doing so.

"Okay, you tell me more of what my father has in mind, and then can you give me Barnett's details so that I can arrange to go see him?"

"I can feel your determination from here. I have a good feeling about this," Alex told me.

"Me too," I said.

After filling me in on all the other information I needed, I was just ready to leave when my dad returned. He did a double take as he walked in. "Brianna! Is everything okay?"

"Yes, it's fine. I'm in Manhattan on business and called to see Alex. I'm going to plan the Book-ish event if that's okay with you."

I saw my father look to Alex for his answer. I couldn't blame him. I'd not exactly been trustworthy or reliable before, so the slight pained expression was forgivable on this occasion.

"I'm overseeing, with it being her first event," Alex confirmed.

Dad turned back to me. "Then this should be celebrated. Your first event. Dinner this evening. You choose where."

"Erm..." Fuck, I wanted to spend my evening with Toby.

"I'll arrange something," Alex said. "For around eight. Why don't you ask your friend to come too, Bree?"

I was going to kill her.

Dad turned back to me. "Friend?"

"Yes, you remember giving my number to Toby? He said he'd be happy to meet up with me if I ever came to Manhattan. He's letting me stay in his guest room."

"Such a lovely boy. His dad's always been a great

guy. That's very kind of him. Don't you abuse his good nature."

I sighed. "I won't. That's why I'm wanting to start work as soon as possible. So I'm not under his feet all day," I lied.

"Yes, he's currently enjoying a break, isn't he? Why didn't you book into a hotel?"

"Because I think as much as Toby wants a rest from the chaotic life of movies and fame, he could use a friend. He insisted I stayed with him."

"See, he knows you're trustworthy being my daughter and also you know about the bad side of being rich."

"Exactly," Alex said, giving me a sneaky wink. "They're becoming firm friends."

I said my goodbyes, as Alex told me she would text me the dinner details. Now I just had to return to Toby's after my disappearing act and hope he fancied dinner with my dad and kind-of stepmom. On day two no less of us having hooked up.

I'd only got as far as the elevator when my phone pinged.

Stepmonster: Your father is still as clueless as ever when it comes to signs of attraction. You'll probably be able to make out beneath the table and him be completely unaware.

Bree: For an acute businessman he is blind. There's no wonder it took him years to notice you were squirming in your seat for him.

Stepmonster: Looking forward to dinner. Won't be me squirming then.

I sent her a tongue out emoji.

CHAPTER SEVEN

Toby

Once more finding an empty bed, I found myself disappointed. My second morning of waking up and instead of being snuggled into the warm, hot body of Brianna, there was a cold space where she should be. I got out of bed, pushed my feet in my sliders, grabbed my robe, and went in search of her.

But all I found was a note. She'd gone to see Alex.

I exhaled loudly, and shuffled over to the coffee machine, my sliders tapping on the floor. Having attempted to take a drink of too hot coffee, I swore loudly. This morning I was a grumpy bastard for sure. Slumping onto my couch, I let out a large exhale. Why was I so pissed? Brianna had said she planned to do some work while she was here.

Because it's only your second morning and you're wondering if she's already bored of you, my bruised ego stated. *Or maybe you're coming on too strong and she's just come over for a bit of fun?*

I would make sure to encourage her in all her business pursuits, but also make sure that she was so satisfied in the bedroom, she hung around. This time when I took a sip of my coffee it was just the right temperature, and I took that as a sign that my plan was a sound one.

My cell phone tone rang out and I picked it up to see my agent was on the line. Chris Inkler wasn't happy with my break but was tolerating it as long as I took his calls. Then he could manage my contracts and sponsorships, keep the offers coming in, and the 'customers happy.'

"Hey, Chris."

"Toby, my man. You all rested up yet?"

"I'm getting there."

"Good, because they're bringing production of *Night Vision* forward and you're needed on set Monday."

"What? No, Chris. They'll have to wait. That's scheduled for next month."

"They've told me clearly that you get there for the

new date, or they look around for a new lead. It's in your contract to be flexible around your other commitments, and, my friend, you don't have any, do you?"

"I have a commitment to my mental health," I complained.

"This role is likely to get you an Oscar nomination. You need to decide whether you'll be there Monday in LA, or whether you're walking away. You've got twenty-four hours to think about it."

"Fine," I snapped, but Chris had already ended the call.

I leaned back against the couch and began massaging my fingertips through my scalp. I could feel the tension building.

Back to filming Monday, and not just any filming. For this: an intense dark suspense, I had to gain weight, lose weight, and then get ripped as part of the role, to show the man's suffering from happy and content father and husband, to prisoner, and then trained assassin. If I pulled this off, there was no doubt this could be *a*, if not *the*, highlight of my career. I'd be able to pick and choose roles afterwards and ultimately wasn't that my aim? To be able to do a movie when I wanted, a movie I believed in, and also command a huge fee for it. Sometimes you had to make sacrifices and it looked like the remainder of my respite period was it.

Bree returned to my place later that afternoon beaming from ear to ear and talking ten to the dozen.

As she paced my living room, catching me up on her meeting with Alex, I walked up and placed my arms around her shoulders and looked down into her eyes. "Breathe, Bree. You're going to pass out if you don't take a breath."

She laughed. "I'm just so excited. I have so many ideas."

"Hold those thoughts and take a seat," I gestured at one of the couches. Then I went over to my chiller and took out a bottle of champagne. "Time to celebrate," I said as I walked back over to the couch, armed with two glasses as well.

Popping the cork with a loud bang, I poured us both a glass and we raised them. "To Bree King, and her new career as an event planner. May all your events be a huge success."

We toasted and she took a sip of her drink.

"Now for my other news," she said.

"You have more? Goodness, it has been a busy day," I exclaimed.

"My father returned to the office just as I was leaving, and he insisted on us having dinner with him tonight."

My mouth dropped open, and I paused with my glass halfway to my mouth.

"Us?" I panicked.

I saw Bree's expression sullen and immediately regretted what I'd said and how I'd said it, but I was envisaging Eli having a quiet word with me, seeing as I'd gone from asking for his daughter's number as a friend, to putting her in my condo like some kind of concubine.

"Don't panic. I told him I was staying in your guest room as a friend. And given he's so gullible and naïve when it comes to anything like attraction, he bought the whole thing. Alex, however, knows we're hooking up but will keep it to herself."

Hooking up. That's how she'd described it to Alex? It was just sex then, nothing more. At least I knew now where we stood. *Of course, it's hooking up, it's been forty-eight hours, you idiot.*

"What time is dinner?"

"Eight," she said, naming a popular restaurant downtown.

"Plenty of time for you to tell me more about the event you'll be planning then," I said, and Bree's expression cheered once more as she gulped her fizz and told me all the ideas she'd had.

"So I'll be out for quite a bit of the day and maybe

even some evenings now. Is that okay, or would you rather I looked for a hotel?"

"It's fine," I said. "Actually, I have some news of my own."

"Oh?"

"Filming of my next movie has been brought forward. It starts Monday. I'll be leaving on Saturday to get over there in time."

"S-Saturday?" I could have sworn she looked disappointed for a moment, but if I had seen it, it wasn't there now.

"Yes, so if you'd like to stay on here while I'm away, you'd be more than welcome. You know it's a private and quiet place, and you'd be doing me a favor keeping an eye on it."

She paused for a moment, chewing slightly on the side of her top lip. "You sure that would be okay?" She checked. "I honestly don't know how long I'll be here for, but I want to manage a few events before I decide where I go next."

"Where you go next?" I didn't understand what she was saying. She'd not mentioned traveling on to anywhere else.

She nodded. "My mom and new stepdad are ready for some time to themselves. I need to think about where I want to live, whether it's near to them in Pacific Palisades, or whether I stay in Manhattan, or, well, I could go anywhere. I'm finally free of the label of Brianna King: ungrateful and spoiled daughter. The world is my oyster."

"It is. You can go wherever you want. Travel the whole world, putting events on everywhere."

Her eyes lit up. "I really could." She took a drink of her champagne. "How long is your filming?"

"Three months minimum, but these things usually always overrun."

"Wow. Three months. I didn't realize." She fidgeted with the stem of her glass.

"Yeah, on average it takes an hour to shoot one minute's worth of movie."

"And where are you shooting?"

"In LA."

"Oh, maybe we could meet up if I get back there before you finish?"

I shook my head. "It's a closed set."

Understanding filled her gaze. "So we have just five more nights together?"

I nodded. "I guess all good things come to an end, right?"

We both took sips of our drinks and said no more about it. When Bree finished her drink, she excused herself to go and get ready for dinner.

Once I was alone, I wanted to hurl my glass at the window in frustration.

"Tobias. So good to see you again." Eli tapped my back and grinned at me as if genuinely pleased to see me. He seemed to view me like some nephew he only got to spend time with occasionally.

Alex held her hand out to me to shake. "Good to meet you, Toby. Sorry I didn't get a chance to introduce myself at the party."

"That's okay. You were busy," I replied.

Looking over, I could see Eli's face clouding over, no doubt at the recollection of the last time I was there, so I swept my gaze around the opulent restaurant and did some of the fine acting I was known for.

"This place is *amazing*. I've never been able to get a table in here before," I lied, having been here on a couple of occasions in the past.

"Yes, being a billionaire does have its perks. Alex married me just for my money you know."

Alex pushed him in the shoulder. "Eli, behave," she scolded, looking at Bree and I and rolling her eyes.

Brianna was hugged by both of them and finally we were seated and had placed our drinks and food orders.

"It's so good of you to have allowed Brianna use of your guest room," Eli said, while he shook out his napkin and placed it on his lap. "She could have stayed with me of course, but at least I know she's somewhere safe. I'd have worried about her in a hotel, no matter how good its reputation. You hear about people breaking into other's rooms, don't you? It reassures me to know that Brianna is safe in hers."

Alex's gaze met mine, her top lip rising in a slight smirk. I suddenly became very interested in how clean my silverware was.

"There's no way I was staying with you, Dad. Not with Alex no doubt coming over and you two 'working on things,' Bree stated.

"I think you're much better off staying with Toby. I'm sure you're enjoying the peace and quiet of having the guest room all to yourself," Alex shot back.

I quickly warmed to Alex and could see just how besotted with her Eli was. She was friendly and chatty and kept the conversation flowing. Eventually, I relaxed, knowing that I wasn't going to be outed as his daughter's fuck buddy this evening and so wouldn't be strung up by my balls.

"Did Barnett get back to you?" Alex asked Bree.

Bree nodded while finishing the mouthful of food she was eating. "I'm meeting him tomorrow for lunch at *Gatsby's*. I do have a few ideas, but I want his take on things before I really get to planning."

"Just make sure to not fall for Barnett's bullshit," Eli said. "He's a fantastic asset to the business, but word on the street." He lowered his voice. "The word from the staff who work there, is that he's a manwhore. So make sure he knows you don't mix business with pleasure."

"Eli, Bree can date who she wants to date. You can't warn her off people. And how can you say not to mix business with pleasure? You married your assistant!" Alex teased.

"Nope. It's been annulled. That means it never happened."

"Potato-potahto." Alex shook her head while laughing.

"I've no intention of flirting with or dating this Barnett man," Bree huffed, and I had to confess it made me want to punch the air in joy.

Eli stared at her. "That's great news, but he's rich and you're…"

"Not my mother." Bree's nostrils flared.

"I was going to say pretty and single. He's bound to be interested."

"Well, I'm not."

Eli scratched his chin. "Are you… seeing anyone? You can tell me, you know. Once they pass my private investigator's checks, I'll be happy to approve." He chuckled.

"I'm not convinced you're joking, Daddy," she replied. "But in answer to your question, I'm concentrating on my career right now. There'll be time for romance later. That's my hope anyway."

She didn't meet my eyes.

She didn't need to. The message was loud and clear. First saying we were 'hooking up' and now more talk of her career and 'romance later.' I needed to enjoy this for what it was, a friends-with-benefits situation, and get on with my life.

Eli arranged for a driver to take us home. The journey back had been quiet in the main after we'd passed polite chit chat about how nice the meal was. I don't think either of us was comfortable saying much in case the driver had been told to report back to his boss.

As we walked into my condo, Bree kicked off her shoes. "Oh, thank goodness. My poor feet can have a rest now."

I laughed. "Why do you wear footwear that makes your feet hurt?"

"Have you seen these shoes? They're a thing of beauty. A creative delight. It's only after the first couple of hours they make my toes ache. It's worth the pain, to be able to stare at them all night."

"Are you telling me you'd rather look at your shoes than at me?" I quipped.

"In the restaurant, absolutely," she teased. "Back here at home..." She bit her lower lip. "You can clearly see the shoes have already been discarded and you have my full attention." She began to pull her satin top over her head revealing a black lacy bra. After unzipping her skirt and it falling to her feet, she stepped out of it.

I took a step closer, but Bree held up a hand. "I'll say when."

She then unhooked her bra and cast it off to one side, and finally stepped out of her panties. She stood there, completely bare to me, revealing those luscious tits and her bare pussy. I was hard as a rock and needed in her immediately.

So I was surprised when she began walking away from me and into the living room. She walked around the back of the couch and bent over it, her glistening pink folds revealed to me as I dropped to my knees behind her. I didn't touch her though. Not until she said, "When."

And then I dove into that pussy like a man starved when the man had actually just enjoyed a six-course dinner. None of it had tasted as good as Bree's pussy though. As I noted her tells that she was about to come, I stood, pulled down my pants and briefs, quickly rolled on a condom I'd had in my pants pocket and thrust deep inside her.

"Fuck, you feel so good."

Bree pushed back against me.

"I love you fucking me. Being deep inside me. Fuck me harder, Toby."

I did as requested, my hand holding her waist as I bucked and rutted against her. She made me feel wild. I just couldn't get enough. I hated having to use birth control because I wanted my seed to spill inside her; not to get her pregnant, but like in some kind of a claim, an imprint. God, I was turning into a fucking caveman, I thought as I felt my balls tighten. I fucked her as hard as I could, coming with a loud grunt of, "Oh God, Bree."

I pulled her down to the carpet with me and wondered how I was supposed to walk away from this woman. But I had no choice. Not unless I wanted to be sued for breach of contract and risk never getting a decent role again. Where I might have thought 'Fuck it all' for a woman who was telling me they felt the same way, that wasn't the case. So for now, I would lose myself in Bree as much as I could, before I lost her, probably for good.

After managing to get carpet burns from our escapades, we finally made it into bed, and as the dawn broke through on another day, this time when I woke up, Bree was still beside me in the bed. Curled up right next to my body, her back to my chest. She fitted there so well. Her breathing was soft and rhythmic. She seemed blissfully asleep.

But as my fantasies of waking up with her were realized, I was still aware of the reality that our time together was running out.

This time when Bree awoke, it would be to that empty bed. Because I couldn't lie there any longer tormenting myself. Instead, I got up and began to prepare breakfast, and sent out for the morning papers.

CHAPTER EIGHT

Brianna

I woke and felt sad and happy within the same minute. Sad I was alone in bed, with no Toby at my side, and sad that he was leaving to film his movie. But then I remembered my first proper business meeting for my event planning career and that gave me a huge buzz and a fizz of excitement deep in my belly.

Shoot! I needed to get ready. It was already ten am. Seemed I'd slept in. I couldn't say it was a huge surprise that I'd slept well given I'd had a busy day, followed by a large meal, and then an evening with a sizeable amount of 'aerobic activity.' I stretched out the kinks in my body and then went and ran a hot shower, sluicing off the sex scent and sleepiness.

When I walked through to the kitchen and living space, Toby was sitting at his kitchen island nursing a large mug of what I guessed from the aroma was coffee, with the day's papers in front of him.

"Please tell me there's more of that delicious smelling nectar left in the pot."

He looked up, startled. "Morning, gorgeous. Yes, take a seat and I'll get you a cup."

"You been up long?"

"A couple of hours. You were sleeping so soundly, I didn't want to disturb you, so I decided to have a relax and read."

"Anything exciting happening in the world?"

"Afraid not. Just the usual: politics, natural disasters, terrorism."

"Sounds like a cheery way to start the day." I raised my brows.

"I know it seems crazy, but it grounds me reading or watching the news. Part of what I wanted to escape from was the false reality that happens in showbiz, where no one tells you no, and the tragic things that happen in the world are used as excuses to party, as fundraisers while the celebs give away a week on a yacht."

I didn't say anything for a moment, and Toby's brow creased.

"What's wrong?"

"Your description of 'showbiz'... that's been my whole life. Money beyond what anyone could dream of; nothing out of reach; no one telling me no, or rather if they had, I'd have a tantrum until they said yes. It wasn't a 'false reality' to me, Toby, it was very, very real." I gestured at his newspaper. "You're reading the paper while sitting in a condo on Park Avenue. If you think that's grounding you, you're mistaken."

"I just meant it reminds me of everything else that's happening out there."

"I get why you came here to have a break from it all. Fame and fortune do reveal a whole other world, but it's not necessarily a bad one. It's just different. There are good people and bad people in all walks of life."

"I wasn't saying it was bad. I think you're being defensive because what I had a break from was the life you've come from." He bristled.

"No. I know what I've come from, and I've learned how it's shaped me. Not only the money and lifestyle, but also how my parents treated me. I'm on my own journey because of it, and I see you're on yours but in reverse."

"I've not come from nothing. My father is an astute businessman."

"I know, but like you've said, Hollywood is a whole other ballgame, and it's threatening your identity, right? You want to hold on to being the man you know, the one with his head firmly on his shoulders, but that life can lead you to stray, to indulge in the excess."

He nodded. "I want to act, but I don't want to turn into someone who tries to outdo their contemporaries in throwing the best parties, or compete for a limited-edition car, and it would just be so easy." He huff-laughed. "Because I really like cars and I have room in the private lot for many of them."

"You'll get there," I said, softening my tone. "You'll adjust. I don't think you'll lose yourself over there. You're a sensible guy at heart, but there's a place between the two I'm sure, a happy medium. It's what I'm trying to find. We're from different walks of life, but we're not so different, you and I."

"Both trying to find our way in the world. Maybe that's why we get along so well?" he said. His eyes felt like they were burning through me; not with desire, but with a desperation for something. Like I held the answers to his questions. But I didn't. I was as lost as he was.

"Maybe so," I answered. "But my answers lie in

finding out how I manage some independence and yours lie in finding how to act and cope with the life that comes with the trappings of success."

"It's not our time, is it?" Toby said, my heart beating faster at his words before a feeling like ice-cold water ran through my veins.

"You feel it too?" I asked.

"Completely. You?"

"Absolutely." I felt the tears forming at my lashes with the tragicness of the fact that we both knew we had something special happening between us, but we had to let it go.

Toby came around the island and standing close, his body fitting next to mine, he wiped the wet from beneath my eyes.

"No tears. My mother always says, 'If it's meant to be it'll find a way.'"

"I hope so," I whispered. "I can't believe I have to walk away, but I can't do 'this.'" I pointed between us. "Until I know who I am. Not until I've pursued some things for myself."

"Ditto." Leaning down he brushed his lips over my own, softly, before lifting his head back up.

"I could fall in love with you, Bree King, if I haven't already."

"I think I'm already in love with you," I replied. "But I need to learn to love myself."

He swept me up in his arms, took me back to bed and we made love. This wasn't lust blown, dirty sex. It was heartfelt, tender lovemaking. Afterward, we laid in each other's arms for a while before I had to climb out of bed and get ready for my meeting with Barnett. As I kissed him goodbye, I wondered how I would manage to kiss him when I knew it was the last one. Time was running out for us and there was nothing we could do to stop it. Not without sacrificing ourselves.

Gatsby's was everything I'd imagined, with its 1920's themed décor. It was a bar and bistro. A waitress greeted me.

"Hi, I'm here to meet Barnett Ford? He booked us a table for two."

"Right this way, please. He's already arrived."

She escorted me over to a booth where a tall, dark, and handsome man in a suit shuffled out of the booth, giving me a winning smile.

"Bree?"

I nodded and held out a hand. "Nice to meet you, Barnett."

His handshake was firm, his hand warm and large. It dwarfed my own. It held with my first impressions of him. He had a beefy build like he played sports. I could see him hurling a ball down a field. His eyes were so dark-brown you could barely discern his pupils and his chin was fighting to grow a beard back despite the fact he'd clearly shaved that day. He was hugely attractive and yet he didn't call to me at all. No, my heart was firmly held in Toby's hands.

We ordered drinks and then I pulled out my tablet, jotter, and a pen.

"I've blocked off plenty of time for this lunch. Look at your menu and we'll get to the business part after the *pleasure*."

It was such a line. My dad seemed to have hit the nail on the head when he said Barnett was known as a manwhore. I'd barely been in his company five minutes and he was already flirting.

"I haven't blocked off plenty of time for this lunch, so we need to order and work," I told him, having decided that once business was concluded I'd get straight back to the condo. While my career was important, it didn't mean I'd spend the afternoon wining and dining Barnett when I could be home with Toby.

I realized I'd called it home. I guessed it was at the moment. And probably it was the first place where I'd felt myself.

"So you do business, but not pleasure?" Barnett looked bemused.

"Oh I do both, but they're strictly separate. No

mixing of business with my personal and private life. I want my reputation to be about the events I hold, not about how good in bed I am."

Barnett nodded. "Message received and understood."

I picked up my menu, and quickly chose. He waved over the waitress, and we placed our orders.

From then on Barnett the businessman was in play: friendly, but the sleaze factor had disappeared. A fact for which I was extremely thankful as it made my forthcoming job a hell of a lot easier if I wasn't dodging his flirtations.

"So what are you thinking for the event? Goody bags including the book? A reading? Maybe a cake that looks like the book?" he asked me.

"Absolutely... not."

"No?" He pressed his lips in a fine line.

"This is your first event as partner in the business, correct?"

Barnett nodded.

"And it's my first event as a planner."

"Really? A virgin occasion for us both." He arched a brow and I couldn't help but break into a smile.

"We're gonna pop that cherry and it's landing in a large bottle of champagne, my friend. Go big or go home. We need this event talked about for months."

He sat back and relaxed. "Tell me more."

Firstly, I checked some facts about the book with him, making sure the information I'd researched was correct. I double-checked his budget, and what he hoped to achieve from the event.

"So, off the top of my head, I'm thinking we have some actors actually act out some scenes from the book, in place of the reading you'd expect from the author. The attendees would have their focus held much more that way than by a dry read, and Giovanna comes across as an author who'd rather stay behind the scenes than in front."

"It's the curse of the author. That they need to market themselves when really they wish to hide in their caves writing their next bestseller."

"She said something similar in an interview I read while I was doing my research. This way, Giovanna can be around to chat, but doesn't have to have all eyes on her. I mean, if she did a reading and didn't emote the words, it would be a car crash. Whereas actors will show that books intentions and emotions perfectly. We'll set up a small stage."

"I'm sold. What else?"

I realized I did completely hold Barnett's attention now, and not because he thought I was attractive, but because he saw I could benefit the business. After we'd chatted further and begun to pull together the components of the event, I realized he'd not once mentioned my dad, his boss. That was weird. Also, come to think of it, would he have flirted with me if he knew who my father was? I pushed it to the back of my mind and carried on planning. I was loving this and could only hope that I could pull off these plans.

"So where are we holding this? I assumed one of the main bookstores, but having now spoken with you, I'm second guessing all my thoughts."

"We want to make all the interested parties happy. So we hire a venue, and make it look like a bookstore. But while we want to launch Giovanna's book with aplomb, the main aim to me is to launch Book-ish's name so that you become a major player. In our fake bookstore we can feature all your current and upcoming writers, put info about their books and bios there. We'll have all the promotional copies of Giovanna's book on the shelves and people can go help themselves. We'll have a fake counter and attendees can come to 'buy' their book and that's when they can be handed the goody bag. Giovanna can be there to sign the book, then the 'cashier' will place it in the goody bag and hand it back. If you stand near the counter, you can grab people as they move away."

The meal finished, we enjoyed a coffee, and then parted company, with a plan for me to finalize my proposals.

"Do you have a final say, or do you have to run it by anyone else?" I asked him.

"I have the final say. The other partner trusts me with the day-to-day running of things."

"Great, so I can just communicate with you directly and we won't have to wait on things being signed off."

He nodded. "It's such a relief, I have to tell you. My employers before this didn't give me much of a voice, which is why the business stayed small. It's great to be believed in."

"I understand and I'm thankful you haven't demanded someone more experienced with event planning. It's also made me feel believed in."

I could see flirting with me again was on the tip of his tongue, to see if we could 'understand' each other under the sheets as well, but he refrained. I breathed an inner sigh of relief because I needed Barnett firmly in business mode so this event was a resounding success, not to be dodging innuendo and invitations.

"Well, it's been a pleasure, Miss London."

I startled.

"Are you okay?"

"Y-yes, just a tickle in my throat." I was going to kill Alex. That was why she'd told me she'd spoken to Barnett, and he was expecting my call and to just introduce myself as Bree, the event planner. It also revealed why he'd not asked me about my father. I guess she'd done me a favor. I'd been able to be myself, not Eli's daughter. Who would I have met today if Barnett had known? A man who probably wouldn't have wanted to debate any of my ideas about his event, figuring I'd just run to daddy.

My inner teenager liked thinking of the name Bree London. And now, I just wanted to leave and get back to the man himself.

We said our goodbyes, and I caught a cab to the condo, letting myself in with the keycard Toby had told me to take as my own.

"Toby?" I called out, but there was no response. He was no doubt busy making arrangements for leaving.

I was disappointed he wasn't around, but decided I'd plan a lovely intimate dinner together for the evening with candlelight and mood music. I headed towards the refrigerator so I could see what items I needed to buy to make the only meal I could manage myself: a carbonara. As I passed the island, I saw the folded note with *Bree* scrawled across it.

My heart thudding through my chest, I willed for it to just be telling me he'd had to go out for some reason, but deep inside, as the feeling of a stone weighed heavy in my gut, I knew what I was about to read. I picked up and opened the note.

I'm sorry.
I didn't want to say goodbye… couldn't say goodbye.
If it's meant to be it'll find a way, right?
Toby.

CHAPTER NINE

Brianna

August 2023

I'd thrown myself into my new career. My first event for Book-ish had been a huge success and gained us a lot of press attention. It meant within a month, I'd had to hire assistants and *BK Events* was launched. The highlight of the year though had been that December when I'd helped my father with his second proposal to Alex. The following year I'd helped arrange their wedding. And now...

. . .

"Push, lovely. Just one more push and I think we'll be there."

They'd been right. One more push and the most beautiful baby ever was born.

My little brother.

My father had been caught in a traffic jam and so I'd accompanied Alex into the birthing suite. Thankfully, Dad had arrived on time, but they'd asked me to stay. I would never forget the experience, it was everything. My heart, that I'd locked deep down inside and forgotten about, burst out of my chest with love. So much love as I watched Dad and Alex greet their newborn son.

"I'll leave you two now," I said, thinking my jaw might break from the smile on my face that just seemed to get wider.

"Not until you've held him," Alex ordered, and she beckoned me over.

She placed the tiny bundle in my arms and said, "Bree, this is your brother, Damian Alexander."

I gazed down at him. "Hey, Damian, I'm your big sister and I'm going to be the best big sister a guy ever had, okay?"

And I'd meant it.

A few days later...

"How are you feeling about all this?" Alex asked me.

"I'm okay. Dad said he did all this kind of shit with me. It was when I was around eight the shit show started. I'll book a therapy session for when Damian's eight and dad still likes him," I joked.

She stroked my arm. "Thank you for being here; you were a great help at the birth."

I smiled at Alex. "It was my pleasure. What an amazing thing to watch my baby brother being born. I'm planning on moving to Manhattan. Work is bringing me here most of the time now and I want to see as much as I can of my brother."

"Well, you're more than welcome to stay here."

"No, I'll leave you lovebirds to it. I'm going to get myself another place on my own."

All that time ago, after I'd returned to Toby's empty condo, I'd decided I couldn't stay there alone. It hurt too much. Instead, I'd rented a place for a few months while I'd worked on the Book-ish event and then set up my business. Once I'd had a team in place, I'd done what I'd said I'd do and I'd traveled the world. Alone. Occasionally, I'd hooked up with a random guy, but feelings had never been involved. I'd been in search of orgasms, not love.

My path hadn't crossed with Toby's again. Last year he'd won an Oscar and a Bafta for the role that he'd left to film and his fame had shot to new levels. I'd sent him some champagne and a card via his PR company, but he'd never responded. Hopefully he'd found a way to cope with his success, but it was no longer my concern. Firstly, he'd not responded to my card and gift, then as time passed, I'd stupidly expected him to get in touch with me when he'd 'found himself.' Figured if he'd had huge feelings for me then he'd have come and swept me off my feet, but it hadn't happened.

The nail in the coffin had come in January this year when he'd married his co-star, Liza Ordach. He'd moved on. At some point so would I, but for now, only this little guy in my arms was my priority.

"Work and home in Manhattan. You'll never look back," Alex said.

"I don't intend to," I replied. "It's time to look to the future and my own happiness."

It was time for me to put down some roots now I'd found career happiness, family happiness, and inner peace. Now I was finally ready for love.

December 2023

. . .

"Bree, my client is being an asshole now and is insisting you take over. The event is next Friday. I mean, why didn't he book with you in the first place?" Bay said.

I sighed. We were a week away from Christmas and had enough stress without clients becoming demanding. It came with the territory though. We organized events for the elite, and many were expectant and spoiled. Luckily, my staff had been trained to deal with them in the main, I mean who had been a better trainer than someone who herself had been expectant and spoiled? At least I could laugh at myself now.

"Give me their details. Usually, I'd argue with them, but we don't have the time. I'm working on a Book-ish event that night. Barnett will be fine with me handing the reins over to you."

Barnett had become a good friend over the years. I'd never forget the time we'd spoken after he'd found out who my father was. Dad had asked him about the event and Barnett had said something to the effect of that I'd been an amazing planner with fabulous ideas, and it was a shame with my rocking body that I had a no mixing business with pleasure rule.

Apparently, my father's gaze had Barnett withering in place, (and he'd said another part withering away too), as daddy dearest had explained the event planner was his daughter. It had been the first time I'd laughed in days.

"Great. So, the client is Tobias London."

I had to grab the edge of the desk as I heard his name.

"T-Tobias London?" I double-checked, even though I'd clearly heard Bay say it the first time.

"Yes, what a coup, right? But he's insisting on now dealing with you. He signed off on the event so none of what I arranged needs changing, but he wants you overseeing the final set up. I'll email you all the details over.

"Thanks, and it's fine. I'd expect little else from a Hollywood superstar. I'll do the same and send you the details of the Book-ish event."

"Thanks, Bree. Catch you later."

Having ended the call, I sat back in my chair, trying to come to terms with the fact I was going to see Toby again and wondering if it was too early for wine.

CHAPTER TEN

Toby

Leaving Bree behind was one of the hardest things I'd ever done. It seemed crazy to me seeing as I'd only spent a few days with her. As I'd thrown myself into the movie role which required me to lose myself in the character and I became Axel Daniels, ruthless assassin, thoughts of Bree had faded to the back of my mind as I spent my days and nights filming, learning lines, sleeping, eating, and little else.

After finally emerging from my 'filming coma,' I'd retired to my penthouse condominium rental in LA and thoughts of Bree had returned. Surely, my feelings couldn't have been that strong? Anyhow, I'd not had so much as a text message from her, so clearly she'd moved on. My curiosity got the better of me and I hired a private detective to find out what he could about Bree and let me know how her life was.

He told me how her business had exploded, celebrity clients rushing to book in with BK *Events*, that she had a team in place, and that she'd just travelled to Paris. Over the next month he reported all the different places she'd gone to, how she was clearly enjoying life, going on dates with different men and then onto her next destination, hosting events in between.

She was living her dream, and not looking back, and now I needed to do the same thing. It took me some time, but I moved on too.

The next movie I filmed was a story of an intense love affair and my leading lady was Liza Ordach. She reminded me so much of Bree it hurt. Same long blonde hair, similar green eyes, similar pout. And although I knew she wasn't Bree, I went along with the character I'd now become and tried to make myself fall in love with her. But I couldn't because Liza wasn't the woman I really wanted.

I won the Oscar, and it finally gave me what I'd craved. The ability to choose the roles I wanted, the cream of the crop, and at the pace I chose. And even though the celebrity side of things rose to crazy levels, I learned to create a larger support team to bear the brunt of PR and a large security team to keep people away when I needed time to myself.

I'd thought that if Bree was going to contact me at any time, it would have been when I won the Oscar. But there was nothing. Not so much as a text. That was when I'd decided that my feelings clearly hadn't been reciprocated and I questioned whether it had just been lust, not love over those few days we'd spent together.

I threw myself into the relationship with Liza and proposed. We married in January in a glitzy affair covered by *Hello* magazine. Our relationship had been fine while wrapped around filming commitments, but the moment we ended up both living together in my condo, the cracks soon started to show. We were nothing alike. And the final straw had come when one day I'd called her Bree.

It seemed I hadn't been able to get the woman out of my head after all.

Liza and I had split up by April but neither of us needed negative publicity at that time and so we stayed in the condo together when we weren't filming. We worked out fine as roommates, just not bedmates.

And last month, Liza had asked me about Bree. My mind wandered back.

Liza had got back from completing a movie the day before, had left her belongings and luggage on the floor and had gone straight to bed. I'd arranged for the clothes in the case to be freshly laundered and left everything else near her bedroom door.

Eventually, she surfaced.

"Hey, stranger. How was the journey home?"

"Good. Smooth flight." She went to the refrigerator and fixed herself a glass of orange juice which she drank down greedily. "God, that's better."

I smiled. "Want me to order breakfast?"

She nodded. "Order me everything."

It was as we were enjoying breakfast that she dropped her bombshell.

"I've met someone, Tobes. It's serious. So, I—"

"Want a divorce?" I finished for her.

"Yes."

She told me excitedly how she'd fallen for the director of her latest movie. Whether it was true love, or a new passing movie fling would remain to be seen, but while we sat there we acknowledged that our own nuptials had been a mistake, though we wished each other well.

"Who's Bree?" she asked me, quietly.

I sighed, and I told her about the woman I'd had a brief dalliance with, who I'd thought I was in love with, and who I'd never seen again.

"That name sounds familiar," she said. "I thought that when you said it before, but I'm not sure where I know it from."

"She's a top events planner, so that's probably why."

"Oh, yes." Her brow wrinkled. "That doesn't feel like it though. It'll come to me."

"It doesn't really matter," I said. "She obviously didn't feel the same way as she never made contact with me, not even when I won an Academy award."

"Fuck! That's it." Liza's eyes went wide.

"That's what?"

"I'm ninety-nine percent positive that when we were filming, some flowers and champagne came for you, with a card. The staff gave them to me, and I opened the card, not noticing it wasn't for me. I remember that her name on the card made me think of cheese and I'd immediately sent the runner out for a cheese board."

I sat up like I'd been shot with adrenaline. "Ninety-nine percent? What did the card say?"

"I don't remember. I'm sorry. All I remember is her name made me think of cheese."

"But you didn't think of this when I accidentally called it you?"

"No, sorry. Back then I was more focused on being pissed that my husband had called me by another woman's name."

"Sorry," I said, but Liza just shrugged. We were past that now. "She had contacted me. Fuck. I never knew." I slumped back on the couch. "It's like we were never meant to be."

Liza rolled her eyes at me. "Don't be a dick, Toby. She could be feeling the same way, and there's only one way you're going to know that, and that's by going to see her."

And that was when I'd decided to book a party.

I made all the arrangements via her assistant, and I got Bay on board, swearing her to secrecy. She would make out it was for my thirtieth birthday, which it was on that day, and almost three years since we'd first met, I'd be reunited with Bree once more. I could only hope she'd not completely moved on, and that there was still a chance for us.

I received a phone call from Bay. "Hey, Toby. It's all done. She switched clients with me, and so she'll be there at the venue on Friday afternoon where she thinks she'll be setting up, but of course, I'll have already done it."

"You're a star, Bay. I just hope she doesn't hit me with one of the candlesticks."

"I'm rooting for you. She's always been closed off to romance and I've wondered why. Just put it down to her being an extremely focused and determined career woman, but now I wonder if it's because of you."

"Soon I'll find out," I said.

"Good luck." She ended the call.

CHAPTER ELEVEN

Brianna

I'd slept fitfully that night, because every time I closed my eyes, I thought back to the few sweet days Toby and I had spent together three years ago. My body had never forgotten him and as the morning broke, my heart thudded so hard in my chest I thought I might need a physician.

Why had he booked a party with my company? And worse, was I going to meet his wife this morning? Would I have to wear a fake smile on my face and tell them how wonderful they looked together? I'd moved on from being the person who threw a tantrum when she didn't get what she wanted, and yet I pictured myself doing exactly that, screaming at Toby for marrying another woman. Asking why he gave up on us when he'd told me he was falling for me. His bullshit about if it was meant to be it would find a way. He'd found a way to forget me. That was what had happened. I was sure this booking was no more than a pathetic idea he'd had to show his support for what I'd achieved.

The time seemed to pass so very slowly, like I was trapped in this cycle of just sitting on my couch and reminiscing one minute and trying to imagine our reuniting the next. I always turned up primped and polished to my events, but even I recognized the carefully chosen perfume I sprayed on my body, the one I'd worn back *then* and had never worn since. Pathetically, when he'd first left I'd purchased a bottle of the cologne he'd worn and spritzed my pillow with it every night. It had both helped me to sleep and tormented me.

Come on, Bree, I told myself. *Fix that smile on your face and put on a show.* It was what I'd done when either of my parents had requested my presence at any of the parties they attended in the past, but it made my hands curl into fists because I'd sworn I'd never do that again. Never be that fake.

Eventually, ready as I'd ever be, I got in my car and drove to the venue, a function room in a swanky hotel.

I'd been here many times before, but not like this.

Standing outside of the door, and taking a deep breath, I got ready to greet suppliers, get the room set up, and see the man who'd stolen and then broken my heart.

But instead, as I pushed open the door, I gasped. Because inside, the room was already completely transformed. A replica of The Symphony Hotel's private rooftop terrace appeared in front of me, every detail there down to the fake lawn and statues, and then there was Toby. Looking even better than my memory had let me believe. He was dressed in a pair of beige slacks and a white shirt that accentuated the healthy tan his skin wore. A huge smile broke out across his face, and he rushed toward me, sweeping me up in his arms in a loving embrace.

"Bree, you look every bit as fucking incredible as I remember," he said softly against my ear.

I froze. And then as my feet touched the floor again, I got mad.

I pushed him away from me. "Don't touch me," I gritted out, and I felt him tense up before he moved back to give me some space.

"I'm sorry. I'm just so happy to see you."

"I'm your event planner. I'd appreciate it if you'd keep this professional." I gestured around the room. "Although I'm booked to put on an event I'm clearly not required for."

"I just wanted to recreate the past," he said, his expression now downcast.

"I'll create the past for you," I snarled. "Go fuck yourself."

Turning to storm out of the door, a hand caught my wrist and pulled me back.

My now narrowed gaze fixed upon his face. His expression was downcast. "I'm sorry, but please, come and sit at the table and let's talk."

"I have nothing to say to you," I spat.

"Bullshit, Bree. If you really didn't give a crap, you wouldn't be being such a fucking brat right now. You forget though that I know that behavior comes from a place of hurt. It kills me that I've done this to you, so please sit for a while and let me speak. Then if you still want to leave, I won't stop you. I promise."

My nostrils flared as I tried to calm myself down. I swallowed; my mouth so dry I could really use a drink. What would one coffee hurt? Fuck, in spite of everything, I still wanted to spend time with him. But I had to keep myself protected.

"I would usually spend a couple of hours here setting up, so you have me booked for that time. I'm willing to sit and enjoy a coffee, but I need to be clear about something. I have a strict rule of *never* mixing business with pleasure. By hiring my company that means I am here in my professional capacity. Not only that, but I don't want married men hugging me. Do you know what it could do to my business if a pap snapped me wrapped around the Oscar winning actor Toby London?"

He nodded seriously, but then gave me a slow smile, which infuriated me because I still found him so fucking attractive it hurt.

"Brunch it is." He gestured to the one table in the room, and we both walked toward it. As I took my seat, he picked up a phone and requested a breakfast platter from the hotel's kitchen.

Taking the seat opposite me, his eyes had a hesitancy to them.

"I just want you to know that my marriage is over. We split up back in April, but just haven't announced it yet."

The butterflies in my stomach were overridden by my annoyance. "So... what? You thought 'Oh, I'll pop back to Manhattan and see if Bree wants to hook up for a few more days? It's been three years but fuck it?"

He sighed. "I didn't know you sent me congratulations for winning the Oscar until very recently, Bree. I thought you'd put us behind you. Forged on with your career. I know you took lovers."

"You don't know that. You presume."

"No, Bree. I *know*. I paid someone to find out, and

do you know what? It killed me. Killed me to know that they had their hands on what I felt was mine."

My eyes widened. "You had me watched? That's low. A complete invasion of my privacy from someone who always made a fuss about his o-own." My voice shook with disbelief and annoyance. How dare he? "You could have just called me and asked how I was and about what I was doing, Toby, but you didn't. You never fucking called me at all. Not one text, zero. I figured we were a five-day fling, that I'd meant nothing after all, and I got on with my life. And you certainly got on with yours. You married another woman."

"Who looked almost identical to you," he yelled.

I blinked rapidly, not believing what I'd just heard, and then a loud knock came to the door and hotel staff wheeled in our breakfast.

The air felt thick and tense, as if in the shadows of the room, monsters waited to pounce, to tear me apart with their claws until I bled out where I sat. He'd married someone who'd reminded him of me? That was some fucked up shit if it was true. And what did that do to how I felt about him? Did it change things? I was so confused and angry.

Finally, the staff left the room, leaving the two of us; a breakfast I couldn't now touch, my appetite completely gone; and an awkward silence.

"Is there anything you want to ask me about your event?" I queried.

"Huh?" he replied. "I don't understand."

"You booked me to host a party for you, and here I am." I reached into my purse and began to take out my tablet.

"Bree, stop this."

"If you have no further need for me, then I have other clients to get to," I stated coldly. My walls had come firmly down to protect myself. I couldn't do this. Couldn't let him in again, because if he mended my heart and then broke it again, I wouldn't survive.

He knew I was done at that moment. He scrubbed a hand through his hair, tugging it in frustration. "I'm back at my condo, Bree, and I'm not going anywhere until I've had a chance to properly talk to you about this, about us."

"There is no us. It was great sex and then we both moved on."

His mouth curled into a sneer. "You can say those words but we both know it's not the truth. It's far from the truth. I l—"

"Don't you dare," I screamed, sweeping my cup off the table, coffee and ceramic shattering all across the floor. Picking up my belongings, I ran from the room.

Thank God, I'd been here so many times I knew where the restrooms were. I dashed inside and into a stall where I sat and quietly sobbed. My brain couldn't take everything in. It was too much. He'd been about to tell me he loved me. Picking up my cell, I dialed the number of the only person I knew would understand.

"Hey, Bree."

"Can I come round? Is it convenient?"

"What's wrong?"

"I d-don't want to say on the phone."

"Sure. Come straight over. Coffee or cognac?"

"I'm going to say coffee, but I reserve the right to change my mind."

"I'll put a dash in the coffee. Okay, come get your ass here."

"Thanks, Alex," I said, then ending the call I exited the stall, cleaned up my appearance and drove straight to my father and stepmom's house.

CHAPTER TWELVE

Toby

I looked around at the room, at my grand plan to win her back. *Stupid, stupid motherfucker*, I berated myself. Of course, Bree didn't know my marriage had been average at best, that it was over. Did I really think she'd give me a chance to explain?

I was a fool. A fool surrounded by a re-enactment of one of the best days of my damn life. Then I'd thrown it all away for my career. To win a trophy that was now in a safe in my condo. I didn't even have it on display because while I was proud of the achievement, my home in Manhattan was my space away from the glitzy glamor of Hollywood.

Had it been worth it?

If I'd have known. If I'd had the hindsight to know that Bree really was it for me, would I still have walked away?

But then she'd just as easily walked away too.

With a text to Bay that I was done with the room, I walked out of the hotel and into the nearest bar, where I ordered a scotch on the rocks and told the bartender to keep them coming.

"Think you should slow down, buddy? Do you want me to call you a cab? Maybe you're better off going home and grabbing some coffee?"

I turned to the blurry figure at the side of me.

"Maybe you're better off minding your own fucking goddamn business," I snapped.

"Ah, woman trouble," he said. "Same reason I'm here." He beckoned the bartender. "I'll have the same as him but cut him off now."

"Fuck you think you are?" I slurred.

"Someone who knows it's never worth it. They're never worth it."

"She's worth it. She's everything to me," I said, more to myself than to the guy.

I heard the guy scoff. "Yeah, and that's why you're wasted in a bar at one in the afternoon."

"I fucked up, all right. It was me." I thumped myself in the chest hard. "Married the wrong woman, but the right one doesn't want me." I'd attempted to turn around to face the guy, but attempting that at the same time as thumping my own chest like a caveman had me almost toppling off the seat. The man steadied me.

"Sounds like you need a shoulder to lean on, literally and figuratively," the guy said.

"Tell me about your woman. Why you're sitting here too."

I did and he really did get it, so I told him about Bree and asked his advice.

I woke up and looked around me. I was in a booth in the bar. Somehow, I'd migrated from the counter to here, and then I'd clearly passed out.

A bartender walked over. "Well, hey there, sleepyhead. You want a strong coffee, or a cab after you've settled your tab?"

"Coffee and the tab, thanks. And my apologies. I don't usually act like this."

"Oh I know, you usually act on movies. If I could

trouble you for an autograph when I bring over your coffee?"

"Sure."

"I didn't recognize you at first, you changed your hair again," the bartender said. I had. I'd gone back to the style I'd had when I'd met Bree, the style of off-duty actor.

"Did anyone else recognize me?" I asked, thinking getting drunk in a bar hadn't been my best idea.

"No, we were quiet when you first arrived and then the dude you were with asked for me to move you to this booth out of the way."

I vaguely recollected chatting to someone. Seemed a good Samaritan had had my back.

"Anyway, I'll get you that coffee now, you really look like you could use it."

He wasn't kidding. My mouth felt like a garbage disposal and my head throbbed. Coffee and a cab home to sleep this off, and then I would think about how I could get Bree to hear me out.

The bartender came over with my coffee and the tab.

"Jesus Christ, how much did I drink?"

"Well, it's not just yours. You put away a fair bit, but then you agreed to pay for your friend's drinks too and treated him to a bottle of Krug."

"I'm never drinking again," I declared.

"If I had a dollar for everyone who told me that, I'd be a very rich man, and not working here." The bartender grinned. "Let me know when you want that cab," he added, and then he left me to drink my coffee and try to feel even halfway alive.

CHAPTER THIRTEEN

Brianna

Alex answered the door, her brows furrowed. "Come in. Damian's asleep so we can talk."

I gave her a half-smile as I followed her inside the house. "Thanks."

I took a seat on the familiar couch and decided I'd better explain myself because Alex didn't know my meltdown was just because of a man.

"Toby London is back in town," I said.

"And?"

"And he hired my firm for his 'thirtieth birthday.' I air-quoted the words. "When I got to the venue, I found he'd already had Bay there and recreated The

Symphony Hotel's rooftop terrace. We spent a day there during the short time we spent together."

"But he's a married man. Why would he do that? Has he decided he made a mistake?" She absent-mindedly tapped her lips with her fingers, and I couldn't help but laugh.

"Look at you. You're loving this, aren't you?"

She blushed. "I have conversations with a baby all day. Sorry, but this is so exciting to me. I want to know *everything*."

It was all I'd needed. I burst into noisy, and slightly hysterical laughter, but it had broken my anxiety over it all. The stepmonster who'd proved to be the person I'd needed all along in pursuit of the real Brianna King was here and more than ready to listen. I tormented her by holding out until she'd made us coffee and then I told her everything.

"But, Bree, he's not married anymore, and he just recreated your date which clearly must have meant a lot to him. Go get your man, you crazy woman."

"No." I pulled in and then released a slow breath.

Alex's eyes wore a sad look. "You need more than a re-creation of the past, right?"

I nodded. "It brought it all back. All my feelings for him back then, and to be honest they've never completely gone away. But having an event company recreate the past like that, is not an indication that he wants me. How do I know this isn't just a rebound thing from his split from his wife? I throw myself all in again like before, and then what? He gets a call from Liza and goes running back? Or he gets a movie offer he can't refuse again and leaves."

"But maybe that won't happen and instead the two of you can live a happy ever after?" Alex suggested, her voice soft and warm.

"I know life isn't simple, and I know what you and my father went through to get where you are, and how things all worked out. But my business… I don't want my company trashed because I'm being portrayed as the woman who broke up Hollywood's loved up starlets."

Alex leaned over and patted my hand. "Only you can decide what to do about things, but you wouldn't have come here if you didn't want my advice. Toby's back in his condo, in the place where the two of you managed to spend five days undetected. You can go see him and talk more. See if there is still the possibility of something worth salvaging between you. Don't put up walls to avoid getting hurt, because you'll get hurt anyway."

"I don't want to see him again today. I need time to think."

"Then do that. Do whatever you need to do to get

your head straight. Make him wait. Just don't let him leave if he is the one you still want."

I nodded. "Thanks, Alex. I don't know what I want with Toby yet, but I know what I need today."

"Yeah?"

"Cuddles with my little brother. Do you reckon he'll wake up soon?"

CHAPTER FOURTEEN

Hollywood Reporter

EXCLUSIVE
"The only woman I've ever really loved."
Tobias London's drunken confessions about a New York event planner, as his marriage falls apart.
By Geraint Granger

There are things you don't expect to see and one of them is an Oscar-winning Hollywood actor propped up at a small bar in Manhattan, blind drunk.

But that's the sight that greeted me as I wandered into a bar, the *Reporter* having been given a tip-off that he was there.

Toby seemed happy to chat about his current situation to me, buying me a drink, and suggesting we move to a table in the corner, him becoming aware of his very public seat, and that was where he told me everything about his marriage to Liza Ordach…

CHAPTER FIFTEEN

Toby

I'd woken with more than a sore head. I'd woken to my cell phone ringing off the hook. A stern text from my agent had me dialing him first.

"Get online and read what the Hollywood Reporter just released about you exclusively."

I tapped in on my phone and my face paled.

I never loved Liza. She was a pale imitation of Bree.

Liza has met the love of her life. Now I want mine back.

"Oh fuck."

"'Oh fuck' indeed. I've scheduled an online

meeting with your PR in thirty minutes. Get cleaned up, and a coffee down you. There's damage limitation to do."

After ending the call, I sat and re-read the words again. Fuck. It was all there. All my true feelings about Bree. Splashed all over a celebrity tabloid's online pages. Which meant that when she woke this morning, Brianna would no longer be famous for her great event planning, but as the true love of a movie star.

I quickly sent her a text.

I am so very sorry. I didn't want this to happen. It's all my fault and I'm working to deal with the fallout.

Then I did as advised by my agent, and got myself showered, and caffeinated to the hilt, ready to do whatever needed to be done. But first, I needed to call my wife.

As I picked up my cell, I saw a text message come up from Geraint Granger. Motherfucker must have put his details in my phone while I was wasted. There was a video of the bottle of Krug on his table. I saw the cork popped and it poured into a glass.

It burned like indigestion in my chest that he'd put that on my tab as he scored his career making exclusive.

But right now, I had more important things to think about.

"So *Hollywood Daily* have booted off today's guests for an exclusive with the two of you," my lead public relations manager, Dolores stated on a Zoom call an hour later. "So, get your ass over here, Liza. Because there's no such thing as bad publicity and we're going to turn this around by tonight so that your fans will be rooting for the two of you to get your happy ever after's... with other people."

CHAPTER SIXTEEN

Brianna

I was back at my father's house. Basically, a prisoner while pandemonium reined. After talking to Alex, I'd spent the evening thinking over and over about those five days from three years ago, about seeing Toby in the flesh again, and trying to figure out my next moves.

And then my phone had gone crazy and I had paparazzi surrounding my building. My father had called to say he was sending security around to get me out of there, and as they protected me, my head covered by a blanket, the press shouted at me.

"Brianna, what do you think about the fact Tobias declared his love for you?"

"Bree, what did you think when he married Liza?"

The questions fired at me like shrapnel, each one making me wince as I wondered what in the hell had happened while I'd slept.

My father and Alex filled me in when I finally got to their house. Sitting reading the article I couldn't believe my eyes.

It had only ever been me, he'd said.

"I think you got your answer about how he truly feels about you," Alex said.

"How did I not know about this?" My father spluttered. "All that time I'd thought he was being a good friend to you."

"You are so blind when it comes to love, that you need it spelling out to you." Alex laughed at him. "And there it is in black and white. Spelled out for you. Now go to work and leave us ladies to it."

He kissed her cheek and then came to me and kissed mine. "I can hire a hitman if needs be. There'd be no trace."

"Dad!"

He shrugged. "You wanted a father who showed you he cared. Here he is. Deal with it."

He wandered over to the crib and then looked at Alex.

"Go on. Pick him up."

He lifted Damian from his crib and snuggled him

and kissed him. "See you later, son. Sorry you have to listen to these two gossip all day."

Damian grouched at having been disturbed and so I leapt up, happy to take him off my father and resettle him. Alex looked happy at being able to carry on and enjoy the rest of her morning pancakes.

"So what are you going to do? I mean there it is in black and white. He has always loved you."

"So says a reporter, and Toby was drunk out of his brains at the time. What I'm going to do is wait and see what Toby does. If he's as madly in love with me as he says he is, then he'll come find me, won't he, and so far…"

My phone beeped.

Toby: I am so very sorry. I didn't want this to happen. It's all my fault and I'm working to deal with the fallout.

"Oh, well there you go." I read out the text to Alex. "He didn't want this to happen. What does that mean?"

"You two need to talk, Bree. It's the only way," Alex said. "Text him."

I sighed, but she was right. I had to know how he

truly felt about me and decide where we went from here. I typed a text back.

Brianna: We need to talk. Let me know when you are able.

It was a whole hour before I got a text back.

Toby: I will. Right now, Liza and I are set to appear on Hollywood Daily tonight. I know what you're thinking. My career first. But it's not true. Just watch and wait. Please.

I sighed and passed Alex my phone so she could read. I couldn't bring myself to say his words. I didn't want to get my hopes up only for them to be cruelly dashed again. My phone rang out as she was passing it back to me. It was Bay.

"Hey, how's it going? Did you let Talia know that everything is in place for tonight's party?"

"I did, but that's not why I'm calling."

"No?"

"The amount of calls I'm fielding about events is off the charts, Bree. I'm calling to ask if I can quickly bring in a couple of temps to take all the enquiries, because otherwise I'm going to struggle to get any work done."

That was so New York. The rumor mill was fueling business.

"Of course you can. I won't forget how you're stepping up either. I think a promotion is in order. When all this quietens down let's see how you feel about becoming my deputy."

"I can already tell you I'm very interested. I'll handle things here, don't worry. You just stay safely away until it's old news."

I ended the call. "So the business has gone insane with people wanting to book my company's services. Funny that." I arched a brow.

"You just got some free publicity from an Oscar winning movie star. You'd better start thinking of that deputy and taking on more staff, because your business is about to explode beyond your wildest dreams."

I pursed my lips. "I don't want it becoming a success because of Toby."

Alex came to sit beside me, placing her hand over mine. "Your business was already a success, you idiot. What you need to remember is that even if this thing with Toby brings you more bookings, it's still BK Events that will bring them the best event they ever held."

"I honestly don't know what I'd do without you," I told her, leaning over to give her a hug. "I'm always here in return if needed."

"Oh I'll get you to pay me back in babysitting," she said, and we both stared at Damian.

"Anytime," I replied, knowing Mummy wouldn't be parted from her baby anytime soon, but I was happy to step in whenever she was.

CHAPTER SEVENTEEN

Toby

Liza walked into the green room. "Tobias London. Drunk in a bar? Really?"

"I'm so sorry, Liza. I've made a mess of everything."

"No you haven't. Bo is ecstatic. There's a new buzz around the movie now, and interest from people wanting to get in on the project. It's all good." She plonked herself down on the couch. "Now all we need to do is to put on an amazing performance for the cameras, then you can go get your woman."

"If she'll have me after all this drama," I said, sighing.

"She will." Liza smiled. "If she didn't want drama, she shouldn't have hooked up with an actor."

Hollywood Daily had been forewarned on what they could and couldn't ask us. All questions had been pre-approved and Liza and I were camera-ready. Irina DeBekk, the anchor of the show, was a celebrity in her own right. She air-kissed both of us.

"I got you both. Let's make this interview sing. We have lots of eyes on us this evening."

Before I knew it, it was time.

"Tonight's guests have given Hollywood Daily their exclusive. It's the only 'official,'" Irina winked at the camera, "interview, because we can't be too sure if one of the guests might go rogue in a bar again." She laughed. "I have great pleasure in introducing Tobias London and Liza Ordach."

That was our cue, to walk on in front of the live studio audience. We walked on hand in hand as we'd planned, then dropped our linked hands to first wave to the audience and then to shake Irina's. Then we took our seats.

"Welcome. Welcome. So let's get straight to the

questions on everyone's lips right now. Was your marriage a fake arrangement, set up just for publicity? Only there are a lot of people feeling duped right now who had been thinking you two were still very much a happily married couple."

Liza took that question. "No, our marriage was very real. When we first got together, things were great. We met on set, dated for a while, and one night Toby proposed. It was all very spontaneous. We were on the beach at night, enjoying a picnic and looking at the stars." People had heard this before. Liza and I had shared our wedding story in the past many times, but I looked out over the audience to find them enraptured and hanging on to Liza's every word.

"And coming to you now, Toby."

"Yes?"

"Thinking of when you proposed. Looking back at what has happened this week. Did you mean to propose? As Liza said it was spontaneous. Was there something else at the root of it all? You told the reporter that Liza was a 'poor imitation' of the woman you purport to be madly in love with."

"Look, Irina. I was wasted and so I can't know what I said for sure, but even drunk I doubt I called my wife a 'poor imitation.' I proposed because I was in love with Liza and I saw a future together for us. My past was exactly that, my past. We got married, both assuming the future would be bright. What we hadn't realized was that when we spent more time together, away from a movie set, we'd realize we were actually two very different people."

Liza picked up my thread. "I think, and Toby agrees with me, that our movie roles, and having to fall in love on set had, as has happened in the past, bled over into real life. As we began to film separate movies to each other and those roles faded away... when we reunited, it was to a certain extent like we were other people to the ones who had married each other. The more we discovered about the other, and the more our filming commitments separated us, the more we drifted apart. We decided to separate back in April."

"April?" Irina pretended to be shocked. "But we're in December and we're only just finding out this information?"

"We wanted to announce it in our own time," I said.

"But not quite the way Toby did it." Liza rolled her eyes at me.

"No, not quite that way." I made an 'I fucked up' facial expression to the audience, who laughed. "We wanted to be sure. To have time to come to terms with us separating and make sure it was the right decision, because we were both raised in families where you were told you married for life. Sorry, Mum and Dad," I said to the camera. I'd only managed a brief text to my parents to say I'd be in touch when I could. In response I'd just got an 'We're here if needed.'

"We planned to announce it in the New Year," Liza stated. "Our families knew, and to us we wanted to draw a boundary around ourselves until our separation wasn't as raw."

Irina went on to ask Liza about her new love affair with Bo.

"As soon as I met him we clicked, you know? And it made me realize that I wasn't happy with Toby, that I felt our marriage was over. But Toby and I had rushed into the wedding, and I didn't want to rush into anything else, so even more so that's why I've wanted to take my time."

"Did you know about Bree?" Irina asked.

"I had a hunch there'd been someone in his past who had left a mark on him, but Toby has always, well until a couple of days ago, been extremely private. He confided in me about Bree when I told him I'd fallen for Bo, and we both agreed to end the marriage then. There was no anger or betrayal felt over the fact we both loved other people, and that was the most telling thing of all. We were, we *are*, happy the other has the potential for a true happy ever after. We weren't suited in the end, and that happens in many marriages. It's just ours gets played out in the press. We know this. It's part and parcel of the career we chose, although I do wish that the focus would be on our performances on screen, rather than off."

"Well maybe if Toby's performance off screen hadn't been so impressive…"

I groaned. "It's my last alcohol for a while, let's put it that way. Although I don't have anything left to hide."

"So let's talk about the woman you confessed to loving still, Brianna King." They flashed a photo of her up on screen, dressed immaculately and professional. "So the daughter of billionaire Eli King and a successful businesswoman. How did you two meet?"

"I met her at one of her father's parties, three years ago. We dated very briefly, and agreed that the time wasn't right, and to move on." I took a deep breath. "Unfortunately, despite my best efforts, I never did move on. I just buried my feelings down, but found they'll resurface at inappropriate times, especially if you've consumed copious amounts of alcohol." I smiled at the audience again.

"Are you pissed that Geraint pretended to be a friend when actually he spotted the opportunity for an exclusive?"

"No. The guy was just doing his job. I shouldn't have been in a downtown bar in that state. I should have drowned my sorrows at home."

"And I guess it was a major announcement to the woman herself, so has there been any movement on that? Have you been in touch with Bree?"

"I've seen her very briefly in a professional capacity and then this news broke and we've both been fielding press ever since. I'm hoping I can get to speak to her very soon, but as to what happens from here, well, that I can't tell you."

"You can't tell us that, but you can confirm to us your feelings for the woman," Irina pushed.

I looked at the camera. "Bree, if you are watching tonight. I am so sorry for how this came about, but I'm not sorry for loving you. I'll never apologize for that."

Irina made the most of that. "Oh, Bree, how could any of us resist that?" She clutched her chest. "My heart."

She went on to ask us a few more questions about movie roles and other gossip she'd heard and then she brought the interview to a close.

"So there you have it. The exclusive news that Tobias London and Liza Ordach have separated and are seeking a divorce on the grounds of irreconcilable differences, and that they *are* both in love, just not with each other. Thanks so much for joining us here tonight and I wish you both well for the future."

And that was it. The movie star side of me had done his performance and now the real me needed to go and win the heart of the only woman I'd ever truly loved, once and for all.

I left the studio immediately with a quick kiss to Liza's cheek, jumped in a private car, and went back to my condo to think about what I did next.

CHAPTER EIGHTEEN

Brianna

I sat in front of the TV at my father's. Both he and Alex watching alongside me. My dad had told me he was viewing the show and would then decide whether to hire a hitman or not.

He'd said, 'Well this performance should get them both Oscars,' at least twice before Alex told him to shut up.

And then Toby looked directly to camera.

"Bree, if you are watching tonight. I am so sorry for how this came about, but I'm not sorry for loving you. I'll never apologize for that."

Alex's gaze burned through me. "That's not

acting," was all she said.

The interview finished and my father came to sit beside me. I waited for his warning lecture about being taken in by actors.

"Brianna. I will never tell you what to do with your life. It's up to you who you love. But I will tell you that the man I just saw speak to camera is broken hearted and desperately in love with you."

My eyes widened, "What? I thought you'd decided he was giving an award-winning performance?"

"They both were up until that point. I know how these things work to some extent. The stories you peddle out to the press, and some of what they both said I feel was a crock of shit to win over the press. But how he looked at the camera to speak directly to you, I know that was the truth."

"How?" I asked.

His eyes briefly alighted on Alex. "Because it's the look I saw in the mirror when I thought I'd lost Alex and knew I'd do anything and everything to get her back."

Alex reached for his hand, and I felt like I needed to get out of the room before they launched at each other and I saw something no daughter needed to be witness to. But I also wanted out of the room for a very different reason.

I needed to see Toby, right now.

CHAPTER NINETEEN

Toby

I'd returned to my condo, discarded my interview clothes, and headed for the shower. I wanted to be rid of the stage make-up and the feeling of 'ick' the interview had given me. I wasn't convinced that Bree would give me the light of day after Liza and I had made out we'd been happily married before we weren't. We'd made things sound a lot better than they actually had been, but neither of us had wanted to confess that the whole thing had been a mistake, because fans wanted to believe in us, and Liza didn't want to let them down. I was now willing to walk away from all of it for Bree, and didn't care, but Liza was half of our marriage, and after my drunken outburst, I owed it to her to help paint over the cracks.

My stomach rumbled and I thought back and realized I'd not eaten since breakfast apart from a small bite of a sandwich at lunch. I'd order takeout. First, I just needed to get dried and dressed.

Walking out into my bedroom, I stilled in shock.

Bree was sitting on the edge of my bed.

I swallowed. My throat suddenly dry.

"Bree. You came."

"Well, I've not come yet, but I'm sure you'll take care of that. Otherwise, I'll just have a tantrum," she sassed, although I could see from the slight tremble to her tone that she was nervous.

I closed the gap between us, knelt at her feet, and reached up to put my mouth on hers. She lowered her head to meet me.

We kissed like we needed the other for air, putting all our words into that moment. And while I knew we would talk, and talk at length, the time for that was tomorrow. Tonight was about re-connecting.

But before that... I broke off our kiss.

"I love you, Brianna King. It has always been you. But first, I have a question for you?"

She nodded, but I saw the apprehension on her features.

"I know you don't date people you've done business with, but what about marrying them? After they've got divorced that is. Or am I still forbidden, boss?"

"I was your event planner, not your boss, and that was only for about ten minutes."

I waggled my brows. "You'll always be the boss of me, so what do you say? Want to break the rules?"

"For you, I say that I'll make an exception. For you, and only you."

"I'm glad to hear it." All the time we'd been talking it had been between kisses. "And I'll propose properly, one day. When I'm divorced."

"I'm glad to hear it," she sassed back. "Oh, and just for the record, I love you too."

EPILOGUE

Brianna

Eighteen months later.

My father took my arm as I walked down the aisle to meet my soon-to-be husband. We'd never looked back after that night. Hopelessly in love, this time we let ourselves fall and let nothing get in our way.

I still ran my very successful business, but with Bay as my deputy and an expanded team as a whole. The publicity from our getting together had put BK Events on another level entirely, but like Alex had said, it was the feedback from the events themselves that kept the bookings coming and us as sought after as we were.

Toby had decided to film one movie a year. He said that was enough for him to continue his dream, but for him to not resent it for taking him away from me for too long. Where it wasn't a closed set, I'd be able to go out to see him anyway. That was part of my agreement with Bay. That where I needed to, I'd take a step back.

I caught the smiles of people as I walked past, including my staff, some of whom were now dear friends like Bay. I caught the eye of Barnett, who mouthed, 'You look beautiful,' as I walked past. My father also caught that given he whispered, "Even on your wedding day that mutt can't stop himself." I laughed. "Dad," I whispered. "Barnett is a nice guy, but I only have eyes for the one waiting for me at the end of the aisle."

"I know, beautiful."

Dad and I had had a tearful moment back at the house. He'd told me how honored he was to be able to walk me down the aisle and once more started to apologize for the past, but I'd stopped him.

"I'm only looking forward now, Dad."

"Okay." Dad had stroked a finger down my cheek. *"I'm so proud of you, Bree, of the woman you've become. I love you so much, but I know I'm handing you over to a guy who loves you every bit as much. You do still want*

to marry him, don't you? It's not too late to back out. Right up until you say 'I do.'"

And here we were now. Dad stepped back and I stood at my fiancé's side.

And we both said, "I do."

Nine months later.

"Push, lovely. Just one more push and I think we'll be there."

Sweat beaded my brow. This was it, one more push and our baby would be here.

I pushed for all I was worth.

A few minutes later, Saskia London was born and placed on my chest. Toby had changed his name by deedpoll and I'd taken that surname when we'd married.

Right at that moment, as my husband set eyes on our newborn daughter, I was instantly relegated to the second most important woman in Toby's life. But I didn't have a problem with that at all. I was completely and utterly besotted myself.

My father and Alex came in to visit and my father teared up. "I can't believe my baby has had a baby." I handed Saskia over to him and watched as he cooed over her. "Hello, baby girl. I'm your grandpa." For a fleeting moment I pictured that that was how he would have been with me.

"Mom's on her way. She texted to let Toby know they'd chartered the jet," I told my dad before I looked over at Alex who'd sat down in a chair. "Don't you get stuck in there," I warned her. Alex gave me a look of daggers. "I'm not that big." She was due any day now. Seems we'd not been the only ones making babies on mine and Toby's wedding night.

"I'm glad you've given birth," Alex said. "Not only for the joyous and momentous occasion, but because it's also got your father distracted from business matters. I mean I'm about to give birth and he's the one grumpy. That's the first smile I've seen on his face in days. However, you've had that baby long enough now, darling. Hand her over." Dad rolled his eyes at me, but did as Alex asked, walking over to the chair to pass Saskia over.

"So what's happening to annoy you workwise?" I asked.

"Bree. Don't get him started," Alex protested, but then she went back to baby talk.

"It's that bloody Barnett. Years I've put up with

hearing all about his womanizing ways but this time he's gone too far. We had Madeline Sylvester about to sign on the dotted line, and he slept with her. She's gone off to LibreLove. We've lost potentially millions. I'm in two minds as to whether to pay him off, but he is good at his job."

"Give him a final warning and make it clear you mean it," I advised. "You're Eli King. Remind him of that fact. You're too soft with him."

"Yes, I shall. You're right. I will show him exactly who's boss." My father's eyes lit up in the way they did when he had a plan.

But his plans that day were about to change, because as it was time for them to leave, Toby took Saskia and my father took hold of Alex's hand to help her from the chair. As she stood up, her water's broke all over the floor.

Two hours later, I had a little sister, Ellie.

From the spoiled child who'd craved love, I was now surrounded by it. As my husband handed our daughter back to me, I knew I now had everything I'd ever wanted right here in this room.

THE END

Read on for more Barnett in CONFESSION.

CONFESSION

BOOK THREE

CONFESSION
DEFINITION

- Intimate personal revelations, especially as presented in a sensationalized form in a book, newspaper, or film.

- A statement of one's principles.

CHAPTER ONE

Barnett

I'd never seen Eli King furious before.

My majority owning partner at the publishing house had largely left me to my own devices since he'd bought Book-ish.

But that was before I'd lost the company a deal with established and bestselling author Madeline Sylvester and she'd gone off to our main competitor.

Now here I was in my office, but Eli was sat behind my desk and I was in the guest seat, also known as the firing line.

"Do you not think I have better things to do today than to come in here and ride your ass?"

That's what we were calling it was it? I noted the shadows under Eli's eyes and watched as he then performed the hugest yawn I think I'd ever seen.

"I'm not impressed that I've had to leave my wife's side when she's just given birth to our daughter," he added, in case I didn't realize this momentous occasion had happened just twenty-four hours or so before.

I got up and approached the coffee machine in my office. I wasn't asking him if he needed one because it would have been a stupid question.

"Eli, once more I apologize. I made a stupid mistake and I won't make it again. Now let me get you a coffee and after we've discussed upcoming business, please go back to your wife and your paternity leave."

"You're damn right you won't make it again because fraternizing with business colleagues is done, Barnett."

I raised a brow, given Eli had married his own assistant.

"You've cost us potentially millions and the company can't take another blow like this. So though I can't make you do my bidding, I'm asking you, Barnett, to not sleep with any more people in the publishing business and to instead focus on getting us a deal with an author that's going to turn around this company's fortunes. Because right now we're sliding. BookLover is laughing in our faces and I don't like playing second fiddle to anyone. Turn the company's fortunes around, Barnett, or I'll look at selling up my share and you can put someone else's business in the toilet."

That rattled me. Eli was a great boss and not many left you to do what you wanted. For the first couple of years of the business the publishing company had flourished under my direction, but then I guess I had got a little complacent and let things amble on, my focus more on my appetite for sexual satisfaction than signing up the next JK Rowling.

After his coffee, Eli left the office with a final warning that he didn't want to have to come back here before his two week's paternity leave was up and so I was to behave myself. I once more congratulated him on the birth of Ellie and once I'd closed the door on him, I leaned back against it and sighed heavily.

I'd fucked up for sure, in every sense of the word. Madeline Sylvester. She'd pursued me and yet I'd got a reputation as a manwhore. Why? Because I had a healthy sexual appetite? It wasn't like these women had been unwilling and I'd pursued them like a sexual predator. They gave me the come on and I was a guy with a large libido. If two people were willing to enjoy each other carnally, I didn't see the problem. Everything had been fine until that fucking woman played me.

I rolled over onto my back, my breath rising and falling as I recovered from pounding into Madeline's pussy. Sweat beaded my brow. Maddy liked it fast and rough and had given me quite the workout.

"I want a bigger advance," she said. "A Time of Change is going to surpass my previous sales; I just know it. My readers are ready for this new series. So I want an extra hundred thousand dollars." *She stroked my cock.* "You know I'm worth it."

My cock was in need of a rest anyway, but her words had poured a bucket of ice-cold water on my libido.

"The advance we've offered is all the company **can** offer, Maddy. It's the highest advance Book-ish has **ever** offered."

Her gray eyes fixed on me and she looked like an entirely different woman with her narrowed gaze and the look of repulsion on her face. Suddenly she didn't seem attractive anymore, her breasts no longer with their pebbled nipples were lying there as flaccid as I was.

"I'm sure we can come to some arrangement," *she said as she tried to work my cock into being a willing participant. But neither of us were. My cock and I weren't participating in this game of sexual blackmail.*

I removed her hand from my dick. "That's Bookish's final offer, Madeline."

With that she swung out of bed and walked into the bathroom. After showering, Maddy dressed and walked out of my apartment. She hadn't said a further word to me.

No, Maddy had saved them all for Eli as she informed him that she was going to BookLover who'd offered her more money and who hadn't sleazed on her.

That had resulted in a phone call from Eli telling me he'd be at my office first thing, delayed only by the birth of his third child.

I stood by my decision anyway. Her book wasn't worth more than we'd offered, and I'd find a new author who would put Madeline Sylvester and her women's fiction in the shade.

And that's where I was going now. We had an acquisition's meeting where my commissioning editors would come and tell me what books they'd discovered and why we should buy them.

I walked into the boardroom thinking that if there was a God then one of these editors would have the best women's fiction book I'd ever seen, one that we could pitch against Maddy Bitchvester's.

I looked around at my staff as I walked toward the refreshment table acknowledging the familiar faces. A new woman was assisting in fixing drinks and making sure staff had what they needed. A new editorial assistant it seemed. Eli had obviously decided that the way to get me to not sleep with my employees was to give me the dowdiest looking he could find. The new woman was dressed in a suit more befitting a fifty-year-old. It was at least two sizes too big for her. She had her chestnut hair in a bun. For fuck's sake, he couldn't have been more transparent if he'd tried. The poor woman had clearly been told to dress dowdy as fuck. I just knew that underneath those too-large clothes would be an absolutely rocking body. But I wouldn't sleep with any other employees now. My job was my only focus going forward until I turned this company back into the number one publishers in New York.

The assistant came up to me. "Would you like a drink, Mr. Ford?"

My eyes swept to her name badge. "That's okay, Jessica. I can get my own. Just like the rest of these people. You're not expected to get everyone's refreshments, just to order them for the meeting. And it's all first names here, so call me Barnett."

She nodded. No smile. Then she walked away. Eli had obviously also told her to stay a cold fish. I swear I could feel the arctic breeze left in her wake. I grabbed myself a coffee and took my seat. Colleagues followed suit and then I started the meeting. Probably not the way most bosses did if the expression on the new woman's face was anything to go by. Her eyes bulged so far out of her face I was surprised they didn't roll down the table for me to catch them.

"First things first. I fucked up. As you know, office gossip isn't my thing, I'd rather everything be out in the open. I took Maddy Sylvester on a date. One thing led to another and then it led to blackmail. End result is that she hasn't got the extra advance she wanted from us, because I didn't think she was worth it, and I mean that in a business manner before you speculate. She's gone to BookLover and that means we now have space in our schedule for a women's fiction title, so what do we have? Oh, and also, my apologies to all for the disappointment, but I'll no longer be mixing any business with pleasure."

There was a beat of silence and then one of the editors spoke. "I've been in discussions with Natalie Sinclair regarding her debut. It's based on her real-life trek through Peru where she almost died and…"

I shook my head. "No good against Maddy's. Pitch that later. Maddy's book is all Scottish landowner, rugged male, and then a historical story. While that's what she usually writes, this time she's gone with an older heroine, early fifties. Her readers are around that age now and so she's decided to write a book specifically for them."

I noted an amused smirk on the new assistant's face. It softened her features and made her look so much hotter. Jesus, I needed to book into a sex addict clinic if I was getting a boner for the office 'mouse.' Eli had made a terrible error because all I could think of was trying to find out what was hiding under that tragic suit and pulling her hair down from that bun. I really was a dog and Eli was intent on neutering me.

Concentrate on the fucking meeting, Barnett.

"Anything else?"

"I've been reading a historical like Maddy's. It's Trudy Carter, who has an established readership. Same modern-day story with historical back story running concurrently. Woman is in her thirties though," Paula Wild, one of my best commissioning editors stated.

I sucked my front teeth while in thought. "See if there's any chance she can make the woman older. If not, we'll still bear it in mind. Right now, that's the best we have. Great work, Paula."

Paula blossomed under my praise. She'd also blossomed within my sheets before now on a couple of occasions and had given me a look of pure evil when I'd talked about fucking Maddy. I had to admit that Eli was right. No more fraternizing with my colleagues. It created unnecessary complications. What if my staff deserted the company like Maddy had because of sex? Why women couldn't separate the two was beyond me. Just have a fuck, a real good fuck, and then move on. Or have a few more fucks. Without complicating it all by bringing up the word *date*, or *girlfriend*, or the worst one, *'exclusive.'* I shivered.

"Would you like me to turn the air-conditioning down, Barnett?" Jessica asked, jolting me once more from my thoughts.

"No, it's fine, thank you. I just seem to be finding I'm feeling an extra chill in the air today," I replied. And I did, but it was coming from the new assistant not the AC. She didn't like me. I could tell. What I didn't know was why. Was it something Eli had told her? Well, I would make her like me. That would be my new endeavor. Make the new woman like me and then she couldn't have me because I no longer fucked my employees. I was a new man.

I got out of my seat, refilled my coffee, then sat back down.

"Okay, what else do we have? Richie, do you want to tell me about that Peru one again?" My boss hat was firmly fixed on my head now. I had everything to prove to Eli and to this company. We would wipe the floor with BookLover and Maddy Sylvester would regret ever fucking with me, literally and figuratively.

CHAPTER TWO

Jess

A few days earlier...

I walked through the door of The Global, the luxury hotel where I was the deputy manager, and I cast my eyes at the reception desk. Good, Liberty wasn't there. Instead, Michaela stood behind the desk, looking the epitome of helpful professional as she dealt with a client.

My heels made a rhythmic tapping against the marble floor as I walked across the lobby and headed for my office. The sound was soothing and I made sure to focus on that rather than on the too-loud beating of my heart.

Boom. Boom. Boom. That's what it felt like in my chest. Echoing in my ears.

Concentrate, Jess. Clack. Clack. Clack. Clack.

Two days ago, I'd discovered that my boyfriend had been sleeping with Liberty. If that wasn't awkward enough, that I had to face his conquest at some point, right now I had to face the man himself as I pushed open the door of my office and found him sitting there. He was the other deputy manager and we had a regular meeting on a Wednesday at eight am.

I didn't think slapping my co-worker across the face was on the agenda, but I did it anyway.

Connor rubbed his cheek but nodded to himself. "I deserved that. I fucked up."

"It's usually the direction a cock goes up a pussy," I snarled, placing my coffee on my desk, and my purse in my drawer. I shrugged out of my coat, moving away from Connor as he stepped forward to try to assist me. I hung it in the small cupboard in the corner of my office.

Sitting behind my desk, I powered up my laptop and took my meeting notes out of the prepared file.

"Okay, so we need to discuss an alternative supplier of the hotel's complimentary toiletries as Aidan wishes us to reduce plastic waste."

"Stop this, Jessica." Connor's raised voice had me raise an eyebrow.

"Stop what? We're at work. This is what we're paid to do, run the hotel. Not to talk about where you've decided to put your penis."

"Well, you won't talk to me outside of work, so we're going to do it here instead."

I sighed and then took a drink of my coffee. It was delicious, hitting the spot perfectly.

He watched me. "Maybe if you'd reacted to me like you do coffee..."

I threw it at him. My paper cup sailed across the space between us and hit its intended target, the top separating from the cup as it bounced off Connor's forehead. I watched the hot, but unfortunately no longer scorching liquid tip out of the descending cup and splatter all over Connor's lap. He flung himself out of the seat, dancing as if trying to escape the liquid and heat.

"Are you out of your fucking mind?" he snapped.

"Are you? Cheating on me with Liberty. You're lucky I've not punched you in the balls, but give me time, it's still early."

"Fuck this," he spat out, looking down at his wet crotch before his furious gaze settled back on me. "You're clearly a psycho and it looks like I've had a narrow escape. Forget the meeting. Order whatever toiletries you like. I'm going to dry off and then find a clean suit."

With that, Connor walked out of my office.

I sat in my seat and smiled. The only thing I regretted was wasting the coffee.

When the hotel's major shareholder, AKA my 'big boss' Aidan Hall walked into my office an hour later, I figured Connor had ratted me out.

"Hey. How's Skye?" I asked out of politeness. Skye was his four-month-old daughter and the apple of her daddy's eye. While I agreed she was a beautiful baby, I wasn't all that maternal.

After showing me a slew of photos on his camera, Aidan finally put away his cell, grabbed himself a bottled water from the fridge in my office, unscrewed the lid, and took a sip while situating himself in the chair opposite my desk.

"So, I hear Connor has been putting it around?" It was a question, not a statement.

"With Liberty for sure. Who knows who else?" I shrugged.

"I'm sorry to hear that, Jess, truly. I thought I was as good at matchmaking as I was at business."

That made me laugh. Our general manager

Ashley had married her co-worker and deputy, Lucas; and Aidan himself had married his former bartender.

"Not in this case and I can tell you for definite that this is the last workplace relationship I'll ever be having," I assured him, folding my arms across my chest.

"Yeah, Ashley and Lucas said they wouldn't date a colleague. Now they're married and about to have a baby..."

"Yes, well I mean it. In fact, I'm having a break from men for a while. I'm going to throw myself into my career."

Aidan looked at the floor and kicked at something imaginary.

"Why can't you make eye contact with me? What's going on? Are you getting rid of me because I threw my drink at Connor's head?"

That had Aidan's attention. His head snapped back to mine and he sniggered. "You threw your drink at his head?"

"I may have done," I hedged.

Aidan lifted his shoulders up and down. "Sounds like he deserved it."

"Waste of damn fine coffee," I muttered under my breath.

Aidan straightened up in his chair, suddenly all

business. "I'm here because I have a business proposition for you, but it's a strange request."

I was intrigued.

"Go on."

"Eli called me. Eli King. The minority shareholder and CEO of his business, Barnett, has lost them a major client because he can't keep his dick in his pants. Now both Eli's wife and his daughter are due to give birth any day now, so his hands are full. He reached out to me to ask if I knew of anyone who could go there to Book-ish undercover. To make sure that Barnett was concentrating on work rather than any female within flirting distance. I immediately thought of you."

Could I do this? Go to a business I had no knowledge of and spy on someone? My heart beat faster with excitement. "I absolutely love books, but I've no training in publishing. Isn't that a problem?"

Aidan's hand flung around in front of me as he waved my concerns away.

"You'd be an editorial assistant. Way below what you are capable of, but I still remember what an amazing secretary you were. Of course, you'd keep your same salary as now and Eli would also supply a bonus payment to sweeten the deal. All you'd have to do is to keep an eye on Barnett, then let me or Eli know if you hear rumors of any more dalliances with book professionals. Because he's been warned. Any more cost to the business because of his libido and he's out. Eli will mount a hostile takeover on Barnett's share."

"And when would this begin?"

"Tomorrow."

My eyes widened. "Tomorrow? What about my work here, and don't I need to go for an interview?"

"Never mind about interviews and your current post. Eli needs you there ASAP. No one at Book-ish will have a clue who you are. They'll believe you are Jess Wallis, new editorial assistant. The only person in on this will be Eli's head HR person. So what do you think?"

"What about my job here?"

"Your current job will still be here when you return. Think of it as an opportunity to spread your wings a little. See how good a boss I am. You'll appreciate me more when you return."

I rolled my eyes and then took a moment to think about it.

An opportunity to get away from Connor, Liberty, and the gossip?

A chance to play at being an undercover spy?

"I'll do it," I said.

"Fantastic. Get anything done here that you need to do and pass everything else to Connor. I'm also pissed he banged Liberty. She was a great receptionist and she quit yesterday. So let's pile on the pressure, shall we?" He winked.

"Are you sure you're my boss and not my guardian angel?" I joked. Then I thought of something that turned my expression serious once more. "What will you tell Connor about where I've gone?"

"I'll say you're doing research for me on a separate project outside of The Global temporarily. Sound good?"

"Sounds perfect."

"Great. Eli will see you in his office, bright and early at 8am. Then he'll send you over to Petra in HR at Book-ish."

"You knew I'd say yes?"

"Course I did. You never shut up about true crime documentaries and soap operas. A chance to work undercover? You were never going to turn that down."

And with that, Aidan exited my office. He'd always been like a hurricane. I guessed that was the driving force in him that had made him as successful as he was. A billionaire no less. I spent the rest of the day passing as much of my workload onto Connor as I could. Email after email. He wouldn't have time to fuck another receptionist. He'd hurt me. We'd been dating for over four years and I'd been patiently waiting for him to propose. But there'd always been excuses about us living together and about anything more permanent.

I'd just not wanted to see the major red flags that had been in my face as clearly as a red rag to a bull. At least there was nothing to have to split. No joint record collections or a much-loved pet. One day he was in my life, the next he was out.

As I walked out of my office that evening, my best friend Ashley waddled up the hall. "I hear it's been an eventful day. I've told Lucas I'll be late home. Come on, let's go get a burger. My treat."

"A burger?"

"Please. I reaaallllyy want one. The baby is craving meat."

"Figures. I mean they got in your belly because Mommy did."

She laughed. "So, can we get a burger, and bitch about Connor?"

"Sounds good to me."

"I called Connor into a meeting today and said while work relationships were not forbidden, his behavior with Liberty had been unbecoming for a manager. She said he'd been a real sleazeball, but she still chose to sleep with him, so that's as much as I can do."

"And what was his response?" I asked, though I had a damn good guess it involved major sucking up, given Ash was a minority shareholder in the hotel and the general manager.

"He groveled and said he should have ended his relationship with you first, rather than have caused a scandal."

"I feel like an idiot, Ash." I fiddled with the paper napkin, shredding it.

Ash reached over and put her hand over mine, stopping me. "You didn't ask for him to cheat on you."

"I'm wondering how many more there were."

"Does it matter? Do you want him back?"

I shook my head. "I should have known. Four years and no ring."

"Some people go their whole lives without a ring and you two lived between each other's places. It wasn't like he pushed you away. So how could you have known?"

"I'm now querying his sports nights with his friends."

"Look, if you need answers, talk to him. Just know he won't necessarily tell you the truth. But if it helps you to put this behind you then do it. Then move on. And give yourself time, Jess. No matter what he did, you can't expect yourself to get over it quickly. You were together a long time."

"At least I'm getting the chance to escape seeing him at work."

"Yes, the job with Book-ish. Just make sure your personal experiences with Connor don't get mixed up with dealing with Barnett."

"Barnett screwed up a business deal, he didn't cheat. I'm there to do a job, and I'll do it well. I'm looking forward to getting first-hand experience of the publishing industry."

"You'll be amazing, just like you've always been at work. I hope you understand why I brought it up though. I didn't want you dead-eying Barnett on your first day. He's bound to flirt with you, you're gorgeous."

I smiled. I fully intended that Barnett would not find me gorgeous. Not in the slightest.

CHAPTER THREE

Barnett

Back in my office, I dealt with a few messages that had come in while I was in the meeting and then I sat still for a moment, apart from scrubbing a hand through my hair. If only I could reverse time and never have crawled under the covers with Maddy. Now I had this pressure on my shoulders of needing to bring my A-game more than ever. Damn it.

There was a knock on the door.

"Come in."

In walked the 'mouse.'

"Hey, Barnett. Paula asked me to print you off a

fresh copy of the manuscript that she spoke about in the meeting for your perusal." She placed it on the desk.

"Has the author indicated she can make the character older?" I queried.

"Paula didn't say."

I sighed.

"Sorry, Barnett, I'll go ask her."

I indicated to the seat in front of me. "Oh I wasn't sighing at you, Jessica, I was sighing at Paula. She's been here long enough now to know that I won't look at that manuscript unless I know it can be altered. Take a seat. I always welcome new staff personally and I'm usually in on any interviews, but I guess Eli was in a rush with the babies coming." I raised a brow, hoping this would indicate that I found the circumstances of her employment more than a little suspicious.

She hesitated and I pointed at the chair again. The fact I seemed to be making her uncomfortable was entertaining me. I wondered what Eli had told her about me. Fuck it, I'd ask.

"So, I'm Barnett Ford as you are no doubt aware by now. I'm the CEO of Book-ish, and a partner, though Eli is the major shareholder. Do you know Eli personally? It's just—don't take this the wrong way—but he put you in position as our new editorial assistant without consulting with me which is unusual. So I find myself a little wrongfooted this morning. Let's get that sorted by having a chat now."

She sat down in the seat opposite me, looking like she was waiting for her execution on Death Row. Was I that scary? What had Eli told her?

"So, how did you get the job?" I pinned what I hoped was an intimidating stare at her. Well, Eli shouldn't have done it. It's not my fault I was now playing cat with his mouse.

But the 'mouse' straightened up in her chair, crossed one leg over the other and stared right back. "I'm Jess Wallis. I sent a prospective letter to Book-ish addressed to the manager and Mr. King invited me for an interview. You'd have to ask him about why he didn't include you." She paused for a moment. "Although given what you announced at this morning's meeting it sounds like you've been otherwise engaged. Maybe that's why?" She shrugged her shoulders in a nonchalant manner. New staff were usually nervous when first faced with their boss, but not this one.

"Yes, well Mr. King has just become both a father and a grandfather so I shan't disturb him on this occasion."

"A father *and* a grandfather?" Her eyes widened.

I smiled. "Within the space of a couple hours.

Younger wife. Grown up daughter. Rather him than me."

"My best friend is about to have a baby. I'd rather have a burger."

It was such an honest and unexpected statement that I laughed and I eased up on her with my next questions. "So what's your background? Experience?"

"I've worked as a PA for years. Had a personal crisis that made me question everything. I thought about my dream job, and after drinking too much wine I sent my letter here. The rest is history."

"And has your crisis passed now?"

Her eyes dulled. "It will."

Immediately I knew that this 'personal crisis' involved a relationship. And that in turn reminded me that I needed to keep things here strictly professional.

"We do have staff counselling available. If you ever wish to take it up, just ask HR."

"I'm sure I'll be fine," she said. "I'm just glad I have this new job. I'm looking forward to developing my role."

A silence developed between us. What more could I ask? She'd said how she'd got the job and told me she had a background relevant to applying. If she was lying, I had no way of checking. For now, I would let her go, but I'd still be keeping an eye on her, to see if she was a spy in the midst.

I pushed the manuscript back at her. "I'd like you to read this manuscript and report back to me. I know you're nowhere near fifty, but imagine you are and let me know if this is the sort of book you'd want to read."

"Seriously?" Jess' smile widened, and I was taken aback by just how pretty she was. Even with her severe hairstyle and terribly oversized clothes, her face looked radiant.

"Seriously," I replied. "You might be asked to do this kind of thing. We like editorial assistants to dip into the slush pile occasionally. You'd be amazed at what you might find there. If you happen to find a book that will rival Maddy Sylvester's, be sure to let me know."

"Thank you, Barnett." She looked toward the door. "I guess I'd better get back to my desk before someone sends out a search party."

I nodded. "Welcome to the team, Jess. And we have no formal style here, as long as you're clean and presentable, so feel free to ditch the suit."

"Oh, I like my suits," she said. "I thought I looked smart."

Fuck. Was I projecting my idea of seeing her in a figure-hugging dress here? I really did need to look at my behavior in the cold light of day. Maybe I was the one who needed counselling?

"You do look smart. By all means keep wearing

them. I just wanted to let you know that we were pretty chill with the rules around here."

"Maybe that's your problem," she said.

I sat up straighter, feeling like my chin had hit the floor.

"What did you just say?"

"I said I was glad wearing my suit wouldn't be a problem." With that she rose from her seat and walked out of the door carrying the manuscript. She clicked the door closed behind her, giving me a nod of farewell. I swear she was wearing a smirk on her face, but the hall behind her was too dark to be sure.

I stared at the back of that door for a good five minutes while I decided that she'd most definitely said that my relaxed rules were maybe the problem.

And I thought that just maybe she was right.

I had a date with two women straight from work that evening. One had commanded me to her home and said I must meet the other one. So I grabbed the gifts I'd sent for from a local store and exited the building to get in my car in the underground lot, then made my way to the home of Bree London.

Bree had become a friend years ago when I'd just

taken the post of minority partner and she was a new-to-town event organizer. She'd arranged an event for Book-ish which had really put us on the map and had launched her business with aplomb. We'd been friends since. The fact I'd found out shortly after the event that her father was Eli King had been the only small hiccough in our friendship. Of course, I'd tried to hit on her within the first few minutes of meeting and had been quickly rebuffed. Thank God she'd never told her father and I'd respected her decision. That was one principle I had at least. If someone said they weren't interested, I listened. I wasn't a total jerk.

After negotiating security, I was let into the luxury home she shared with Toby, who was an Oscar winning actor. I took one look at my friend. "Jesus, this is why I never want kids."

"You fucking asshole. I do not look that bad."

I blinked my eyes at my friend. Her usually straightened hair was mussed up. Her clothes might still be designer, but I didn't think Christian Dior had added the spit up, and she was barefoot, not a Louboutin in sight.

"You look like a beautiful new mother," I said with honesty. "You're glowing."

She beamed. "Come and meet Saskia." She gestured through to the living room. "We might be able to prize her out of her father's arms but I'm not promising."

When I saw Toby, I had to do my best not to laugh because with the look of sheer joy and protection on his face as he looked from his daughter and then to me, I thought he might raise her skyward a la Lion King.

I walked toward them. "Hey, my man." I patted Toby on the back gently. "Congrats, Daddy."

He beamed with pride. "Thanks, Barney."

"Hello, little future wife," I teased back looking down at Saskia. Toby loved to call me Barney because he knew I loathed it. Women called me that when they were trying to indicate an intimacy between us that was non-existent.

"The fact I trust you to be near my wife is because I have no doubt in her undying love for me. The fact I shall trust you with my daughter is because I know that you don't want to face an early death. There shall be no imprinting here. This is not a remake of *Twilight*."

I sniggered. "Look at you. You've gone all alpha male. Shame your wife won't be able to make the most of that for six weeks."

Toby's eyes narrowed at me. "How come you know that? Are newly delivered women also on your fuck-it list?"

I snorted. "My elder sister has two children and no filter. I got a warts-and-all commentary of both her births that left me celibate for six weeks too. Now hand her over," I ordered.

"Aw, look at you two. Saskia already has men eating out of the palm of her hand."

"And that's the only part of her men will be eating from if Daddy has his way." I guffawed.

"Do you want to hold my daughter, or shall I pass her to her mother and punch you in the face, mate?"

"Ooh you've gone all British."

"Barnett, stop winding him up and take the baby," Bree ordered. "Then come sit on the couch because your arm will ache in no time."

Me being the asshole I was took the baby and stood there. Until a few minutes later my arm, ripped and toned as it was, started to ache just as she'd said.

Bree sighed at me as I made my way to the couch. She fluffed up a cushion and fixed it under my arm. "One day you might listen to a woman instead of always thinking you know best, you arrogant ass."

But I ignored Bree because I was looking at the little dot in my arms. This tiny bundle of ten fingers and ten toes, a smattering of fair hair, cute button nose and rosebud lips, had reminded me of my niece and nephew and of the fact I hadn't been to see Toni in so long. I was a shit brother and uncle, just like I was a shit in general at times.

Saskia heralded new beginnings in general and

maybe I needed one too. "She's beautiful," I said truthfully, looking from Bree to Toby and back at the baby.

"Well, I never thought I'd see the day. Barnett Ford brought to his knees by a woman," Toby teased. And I didn't mind it a bit, because little Saskia had done just that.

CHAPTER FOUR

Jess

Finally home, I walked into my apartment, kicked off my shoes, threw my coat and bag on the floor at the side of the couch and threw myself on top of it. Grabbing my thick blanket, I pulled it across myself, and stretching, I let out a deep exhale.

I'd thought this job would bore me, but with getting used to new systems and people, and then finding out I could read manuscripts from the slush pile, I was actually enjoying the change of scenery.

My career had changed a lot since I'd first taken a job as a PA years ago for a guy who ran a property empire and a sex club. When Henry had sold up, I'd been retained by Aidan, and had grown along with him. From a PA to a deputy manager, initially for the club and then for the hotel chain, I'd always let life's circumstances dictate my fate. Maybe that's why I was single and living alone at twenty-nine years old.

It was time I took more control over my life. Looking around the apartment, I decided that the first thing I was going to do was adopt a cat. Pets were allowed here and it would be nice to come home to someone. I could still have a significant other in my life and this one would actually be willing to live with me.

The more I thought about how I'd taken on Connor's excuses, the more annoyed I became. Thoroughly vexed, I ordered myself a Chinese takeout and pulled the manuscript out of my bag and started reading while I waited the arrival of dinner.

The twelfth Earl of Liversidge put down his shotgun and sighed. "Do you know what I need, Atherton?" he said to his assistant.

"Glasses?" Atherton said with a nod toward the sky where the earl had failed to hit a single clay pigeon.

"A woman," he announced. "Then I wouldn't need to be out here trying to take out my frustrations about the family finances on fake pigeons. Instead, I could be..."

"Please don't finish that sentence, sir." Atherton grimaced.

"I'm talking about Frances Timson, the accountant." The Earl shook his head. *"She's saved so many earls from having to sell up, but she's in major demand. Booked up for months. Somehow, I have to get her here to Liversidge. Any ideas?"*

"My first would be to put the safety back on the gun," Atherton retorted.

By the time my dinner arrived, I'd also poured myself a glass of wine and I was well into the opening chapters of the manuscript. It was a great book, with its touch of humor, and everything I expected the fans of the author and of the genre in general to love. But it didn't need changing to an older character. To me it had to stay exactly as it was, as the Earl needed to carry on the family line, and we needed him and Frances to have lots of babies.

I managed to fill myself to the brim with my dinner and was around halfway through the book when my cell rang.

It was my mother.

"Hey, Mom. You okay?" I asked her.

"Yes, darling. Me and your father are fine and still alive. I thought you might like to know."

"Sorry, Mom. I've had a lot on."

A sigh came down the line. "When haven't you?"

Guilt hit me then because I became aware that my mom did do all the work for us to keep in touch with each other, and I had been all consumed with my job and Connor.

"No, really. I changed my job temporarily and…" I swallowed. "Connor and I split up."

There was a pause.

"Temporary or permanent?"

"Permanent. I, er, I found out he cheated on me."

"Thank fucking God," came down the line, and then I was deafened as she shouted, "Grant, she's rid herself of the rat. Yes, gone for good."

"Mom, I thought you liked him? I expected you to be devastated," I queried.

"Couldn't stand him, but of course, we didn't want you to know that. You seemed to be in love. All we'd decided was that if you decided to live with or marry him, that your father was going to take him to one side so he knew he was being watched."

I felt like I'd entered some kind of alternate universe but that was usually how I felt talking to my mother. She tended to not hold back, which was why I was surprised that this was the first I'd heard of her not liking Connor.

When she was thoroughly caught up on all things Connor the rat, as he would forevermore be known, she asked me about my new job.

"That sounds amazing. I want to see this Barnett for myself. I'll come to your office tomorrow and we'll go for lunch. You get a lunch hour, right?"

"I do, but…"

"No 'buts.' I want to come and see for myself that my daughter is okay, and while she's vulnerable from a breakup she's not at the mercy of some strapping, hunky lothario who's going to take advantage of her."

"You mean you want to come and perve?"

Her voice lowered down the line. "Your father still has it, and we still have a great sex life, but having a new man in my imagination for the times when your father is not around…"

I held the phone away from my ears wanting to puke or be struck deaf. "Mom, what have I told you…?"

"Oh, yes, of course. Heaven forbid you think us women in our fifties still have sex or that if we do it's boring. I don't just raise the edge of my nightie you know and lie back and think of England. The things I could tell you…"

"But you'll not, because I'm ending this call. I'll text you my work address. See you tomorrow."

I couldn't hear anymore right now. I'd go back to the Earl and his accountant and psych myself up for another day as a corporate spy and for lunch with my mother.

I was in dire need of caffeine the next morning due to the fact I'd finally put the manuscript down at three am when I'd finished reading it, and I needed to be at my desk for eight thirty. I drank my first coffee as I got myself ready and poured a second into a travel mug for my journey to the office. Luckily, as I was trying to look as unattractive as possible, I didn't need to do much with my appearance. I just scraped my hair into the bun, then put on a light coating of foundation and I was good to go.

I was surprised to realize that I had a spring in my step as I closed my apartment door behind me and headed for the subway. It was all due to the manuscript tucked into my work satchel. Hopefully, I'd get a chance to talk to Barnett today and give him my opinion. My first ever manuscript review.

Reality soon hit the moment I walked into the office I shared with the other assistants, and found my phone was ringing, while my desk was piled with papers with attached sticky notes. Paula came waltzing in and over to me, looking all tall and willowy, her long, blonde curls bouncing as she walked. "Hey, Jess. Can you pop out for coffees? We're having an impromptu meeting to discuss a book."

I tried not to let my face show my annoyance. It

wasn't Paula's fault that there was a last-minute meeting that couldn't be catered, and this was my job. I'd had plenty such meetings in the past myself.

"Of course, no problem," I said, noting the order down on my phone, grabbing my company card out of my desk drawer, and then picking my purse back up.

With coffees collected, I pushed open the door to the meeting room. Other than everyone looking at me like I'd brought Gold, Frankincense and Myrrh rather than some hot beverages, I wasn't able to discern anything about what they were discussing.

"Do you need me for anything else?" I asked Paula, hoping she'd tell me to pull up a chair and take notes.

"No, we're fine here, and I saw that your desk looked like it had a lot of things for you to *assist* on," she said, with a sickly, saccharine smile.

Hmmm, it seemed Paula's mood had soured toward me for some reason, and I wondered what had brought that about. Then I caught Barnett's bemused expression as he looked from Paula to me. If this was some stupid game he was playing, using his female colleagues as pawns, then he ought to be careful. Because a man had made a fool of me this year already and it wasn't going to be happening a second time.

I was completely oblivious to the hour and had forgotten my mom was calling in until I saw her heading in my direction. Her head moved from right to left as she took in everything around her until she reached me.

"I am so pleased you warned me about this make-under because I'd have been worried to death that the rat was the root cause of this..." she waved her hand over my face and body, "...disaster." She cast her gaze around again. "So where's the hot boss?"

"He rarely ventures into the assistant's zone. He's the boss," I replied, just as the man himself called me a liar by walking right in. He strolled over to another assistant without looking my way. I breathed a sigh of relief.

"Is that him?" Mom said. I quickly changed the subject.

"Shall we get to lunch then, Mom, because I do only have an hour."

"Of course," she said. I should have known better though. I should have delayed moving until Barnett had left the room because as we got within twenty feet of him my mother yelled, "Aaargh, my head hurts," and promptly mock-fainted, ending up 'miraculously' splayed right across the only sofa in the room, rather than on the floor.

"Mom, get up. You're making a complete show of us both," I said out of the side of my mouth, but my mother continued her act, to the point where after a few seconds I wondered if she had fainted after all.

A few assistants came over.

"Do you want me to call 911?" one asked. That got my mom moving. She groaned and opened her eyes.

"Wh-what happened?"

"Have you eaten today, Mom?" I asked her, giving her an excuse for the faint.

She sat up and looked up at me pathetically. *And the Oscar goes to...*

"No, I haven't eaten since yesterday evening."

"Can I get you a glass of water?" another colleague asked.

"Yes please, if it's no trouble."

And then I heard Barnett's voice from behind me. "Is everything okay here?"

Fuck. With a glare at my mother that hopefully warned her to behave, though why I bothered making the effort I wasn't sure, I stood and turned to my boss.

"Sorry, Barnett. My mom came to take me to lunch, but she's not eaten since yesterday and she went faint. Once she's had a few sips of water then we'll be on our way."

"Nothing to eat, you say? Well, I have some leftover pastries from the meeting I just left in my office, so if you pop up there and fetch them, Jess, she can have a nibble on something before you go. We don't want you fainting again, do we, Jess' mom?"

"You can call me Tammy," she said, and then she sat up and fanned herself.

I left to get the food and crossed my fingers she didn't tell Barnett that pastries weren't what she fancied having a nibble on.

CHAPTER FIVE

Barnett

It sounded conceited but this wasn't the first time a woman had pulled a mock faint in front of me. I could tell by Tammy's coloring and features that she was related to Jess and hazarded a guess at it being her mom. However, I took my time before I went over and that's when I'd made the decision to send Jess on an errand run, giving me time to interrogate mommy dearest.

"More water?" I indicated the glass, although Tammy had only taken a few mouthfuls.

"No, I'm fine now, thank you. In future I'll not come all this way without having eaten. Poor Jess. Her first days here and her mother has made a fool of her. I hope you won't hold it against her." She tilted her head down and looked back up at me in a demure manner. "No, I'm sure you won't. You look like a perfectly decent man."

I refrained from saying Jess clearly hadn't told her about me then.

"You can't help hunger. What's important is that you're okay."

"I feel perfectly fine now. Hungry, but fine."

"Jess will be back soon and then you can get something and be on your way."

And this meant my interrogation time was dwindling by the second.

"So, do you live near Jess?"

"About thirty minutes away. We're very close but I haven't seen much of her while she was dating her rat ex. Now he's out of the picture I hope to see more of her."

I almost choked on thin air. "Rat?"

"Yes, the insipid, spineless, cheating asshole she wasted four years of her life with. She'll realize she was better off without him, but it takes time to heal a broken heart, doesn't it?"

"I wouldn't know."

"Oh, bless you. Barnett, isn't it? Have you never known love?"

How had my interrogation turned around so quickly to Tammy zeroing in on *my* private life? I appraised her closely. Because she was a minx that was why. Mischief was written all over her face.

"From family, yes. From meeting 'the one,' well I don't believe in that. Why put all your eggs in one basket, hey?"

My joke fell on flat ears and left me with the feeling as if my shirt was itching my back as Tammy leaned forward and patted my arm.

"My husband, Grant, was like you. He'd just not met the right person. Then I came along and rocked his world. Just when you least expect it to, it'll come and knock you on your ass." I saw Tammy's attention go elsewhere and sure enough Jess was back. All I'd managed to find out was that she'd been cheated on in a long-term relationship by a 'rat.' I'd never be recruited as a spy.

Jess put the basket containing the breakfast pastries and muffins on the small table in front of the sofa. She sat down next to her mom and I took the armchair adjacent.

"If you're busy, Barnett, you can leave us now. As soon as Mom feels okay, we'll be off for lunch."

I grabbed a muffin. "I'll just eat this and then I'll be on my way. I've not got time for lunch today, so this will have to do." This was a total lie. My PA had got me a peanut butter and jelly, which I realized would have still been on my desk and which Jess would have no doubt seen.

"Oh, you poor man. You must eat properly. Look what just happened to me because I was hungry and there's a lot more of you to fill."

"Mother!" Jess admonished.

"I meant it in a tall, clearly athletic, ripped kind of way, Jess."

I snuck a peek at Jess' face. Her eyes were closed but her expression still clearly said, 'Kill me now.'

"So what do you do when you're not seeing Jess then, Tammy?" I asked around a small bite of muffin.

"I teach English at a small community college part-time, and I have a very active social life including running a small book group for my friends."

I was about to ask her about the book group, but she'd carried on talking.

"Then of course my husband keeps me busy, if you get my drift. Hence only working part-time. I have to rest at some point and it's certainly not any night of the week."

"Because of all your social engagements you mean?" Jess added forcefully.

"Of course, sweetheart." Tammy smiled at Jess and then looked at me and shook her head.

"I'm right here, Mom. Have you finished? Because

I'm not going to have time for lunch if we don't go soon."

"Oh take a full hour still. What sort of a boss would I be if I took your mom's fainting spell time out of your lunch break?"

"What a fantastic boss. I thought Aidan was amazing, but..."

"Time to go." Jess basically yanked her mother out of the seat, but in doing so she inadvertently made me realize that Tammy had been spilling some beans. *Aidan*.

As I watched their departing backs, a lightbulb suddenly went off in my head. Aidan, as in Eli's friend Aidan Hall, the person Eli had bought the company off. My former boss? Did Jess work for him? There was one way I could find out.

I rushed back to my office at breakneck speed and found out the number for the hotel that I knew was now Aidan's only business.

"The Global. How may I help you?"

"Oh hello there. I'd like to speak to Jess Wallis please?"

"I'm sorry, Jess is currently not working at The Global. Could I put you in touch with one of the other deputy managers?"

"No, that's fine. Thank you." I ended the call, while my fingers flew across my keyboard. I put up

The Global hotel's website and I clicked on the staff section. And there she was. Looking nothing at all like the Jess who worked here. The Global's Jess was polished within an inch of her life.

"Thank you Momma Wallis," I said triumphantly, and then I reached over and grabbed my sandwich.

CHAPTER SIX

Jess

"You know I'm here undercover and you just blurted out the name of my boss," I hissed as we walked out of the room.

"Oh don't be silly. I only said his first name. Unless Barnett is Sherlock Holmes, I'm sure you'll be fine. Anyway, I was just coming around from fainting. I wasn't thinking straight."

"Mom, please do not blame a fake fainting fit. Aidan owned the publishers before Eli. He was Barnett's previous boss, although my understanding is he wasn't very hands on."

I prayed that my mom hadn't just fucked everything up. What had I been thinking letting her go there? And why hadn't I at least changed my surname, like a decent spy would have done?

"Actually, Barnett is a little Robert Downey Junior looking, isn't he? I'll have to dig out my box sets when I get back home. Now, where are we having lunch?"

Realizing I was wasting my time trying to get my mom to show an ounce of regret, I steered her out of the building and toward the close by bistro I'd chosen for lunch. We ordered and I decided to have a glass of wine regardless of the hour. Call it survival.

"I'm not surprised Barnett has a reputation as a manwhore. He certainly is a fine specimen. Can't blame him for dining out if it's on a plate."

I spluttered my wine. "Mom, that's my boss. Please stop."

"But he's not really, is he?"

"Barnett is forbidden from dating any work colleagues and likewise he's informed everyone that he is now forbidden to employees."

"He actually said those words?"

"More or less. He's certainly a boss with a difference." I laughed thinking of his speech on my first meeting with him and how shocked I'd been.

"I forgot how pretty you are when you laugh, Jess. You need someone to bring that smile back to your face."

"The rat only just left the building, Mom."

"I know. But I'd love for you to rebound straight onto the love of your life. It would serve Connor right. Anyway, the main reason I wanted to meet up with you was to discuss your birthday party. It's all still going ahead, yes?"

It was my thirtieth in a couple of weeks and my mom had insisted on me having a party and had thrown herself into arranging it.

"Yes. Why wouldn't it?" I said firmly, but I couldn't maintain eye contact when met with my mother's sympathetic gaze.

The truth was that I'd thought Connor might propose at my thirtieth. Had given myself the excuse that he'd been saving his declaration of wanting forever with me until my special birthday. What a joke.

"I'd have understood if you'd not felt in the mood. For as much as I didn't like Connor, you loved him. That's why I never said anything before."

I took another sip of my wine and then placed it down on the table. "I thought I did. I really thought I loved him. But the man I was 'in love' with." I air-quoted. "Didn't exist. I think I was in love with the idea of love." The more I pondered it, the more I felt my words were true. "I think I did love him at first, but then as time passed, I settled."

"Only you know your true feelings, Jess. I'm so

pleased you're still having your party though. I promise it's going to be amazing."

"No male strippers now Connor won't be there, Mom," I warned her.

She just laughed.

"Am I boring you, Jessica, or can you not handle the wine? You've not stopped yawning all lunch time," Mom said as our mains were cleared away and we ordered coffees.

"I was up until the early hours reading a manuscript for work."

Mom's lips pressed in a firm line. "Surely they don't expect you to work through the night."

I smiled. "No, Mom." I went on to explain about the manuscript and the slush pile. "...and I just couldn't stop reading it."

"You always have loved reading. You got that from me."

"I know. What's the latest book club book? Anything I should check out?"

Mom cackled. I didn't think I'd ever heard her make such a noise before and she'd made plenty.

"I don't think so, Jessica." She smirked to herself. "No, I shouldn't think so at all."

"Mom..." I pestered, intrigued. "Spill."

Raising a brow, Mom leaned over into her purse and took out her e-reader. Swiping across, she then handed it to me and I read the title, written across an impressive piece of man chest.

Mounted by the Mountain Man

"You cannot be serious." I handed it back to her like it had set my hand on fire.

"It's incredible. That's actually book four in the series. Monica brought in the first one and since then we decided that every book club would be the next in series until we either got bored or ran out of titles. I've been reading all sorts of jealous and possessive heroes in between. I wish your dad would slam me up against a wall and take me by force occasionally."

"Mom!"

"Oh I know, I know. You don't want to hear about it. Next, you'll be telling me I'm too old. You'll be here before you know it, Jess, and you'll realize then that age is just a number. Some women are never interested and others are just hitting their peak. Believe me, we don't just talk about the book at book club."

"Well, you might want to make room for Maddy Sylvester's next release in summer next year. She's focusing on women your age apparently."

My mom cut me a look. "Women my age? If there's one mention of a sagging tit, I don't want to know. When I read I want to be the character, not myself. Anyway, she's the one who defected and wronged Barnett so her book can fuck right off."

Our coffees came then and Mom changed the conversation to how she was redecorating the living room. I half listened while the other part of me giggled inwardly at how protective my mom had become of my manwhore boss.

When I made it back to the office, I figured it would be a good thing if I thanked Barnett, if he was free. That way I could also hopefully feedback on the manuscript. Having checked with his secretary, who'd told me I had fifteen minutes maximum before his next appointment, I went to his office, knocked on his door and entered at his instruction.

"Ah, Jess. I trust lunch went fine and your mom is now fully recovered."

I nodded. "I just wanted to say thank you and also to apologize. As you might have noticed my mom can be a little... over the top."

He grinned. "I thought she was wonderful. A breath of fresh air."

What the hell was going on? Barnett and my mother had seemingly formed a mutual appreciation society.

"So she runs a book club. Is that where you got your interest in books?"

"Yes," I replied and for once I was telling the truth. "Mom always had books around the place and like most bookaholics, as an extension of her, my collection was vast too."

"Well, if she'd like any copies of our titles for her club let me know. Like our upcoming knock-the-middle-aged-ladies-socks-off book."

"I'll ask," I told him, because there was no way I was informing him that the book club were only currently interested in rugged males and rough sex. Also, he'd opened up an opportunity for me to talk about the manuscript. Holding it up, I waved it a little. "I read the manuscript last night and made some notes. I couldn't put it down." I looked over to the chair in front of Barnett's desk, expecting him to tell me to take a seat, but he didn't.

"Already? Wow. As it happens that's what we were talking about this morning. Paula said it's not possible to change the story. It weaves around the characters ages, so it's being published, but not being our 'big' release. However, do let me know if you find anything in the slush pile. At this rate, a book a day, you might find us something fast, hey?"

"So you don't want any more of my feedback on the book?" I felt like a deflating balloon. I'd been so hyped.

Barnett shook his head. "Paula's the commissioning editor on that. I told her this morning that I'd asked you to take a look at it. So feel free to report back to her and she'll give you advice on what other things to look for."

"Oh, okay." At least I knew now why Paula had been cool with me. She obviously wanted me nowhere near her project.

"Is something wrong? You look a little put out," Barnett queried, tilting his head. I felt awkward standing in front of his desk, having been so excited to give my findings, and find myself effectively gagged. The fact was I'd moved on from being a PA. There was nothing wrong with the role and I'd enjoyed it when I'd worked as one, but spending all these past years in management, in roles where I could participate in business decisions and have a voice—one that was heard—meant that right now I felt frustrated.

"No, nothing at all. I'll find Paula and see if she can spare some time to hear my thoughts and give me some feedback. Once again, I just wanted to thank you for your help with my mom." I turned and began to walk out of the office.

I'd just reached the door when Barnett said, "Oh, and Jess."

I turned back around. "Yes?"

"I'm only joking when I said about reading a manuscript a day. You do it at your own pace. I don't really expect you to find our next big book. That's what the commissioning editors are trained and paid to do. It's good practice, but I just thought I should emphasize that your main role is to support the CE's with admin: tea, coffee, emails, etc."

At that moment I was annoyed that unglam Jess wore flats. Instead, as I fake smiled at my boss, I had to settle for only mentally launching a stiletto at his head.

"Thanks for the reminder. I'll get back to doing just that."

If my mood had already turned like sour milk, Paula being sat on the edge of my desk as I returned, made it curdle further.

"There you are. May I remind you that lunch is one hour, not ninety-minutes."

"Oh I'm not late from lunch; I'm just back from Barnett's office. What can I do for you?" I asked her as I took my seat, throwing the manuscript down on my desk.

"Oh yes, what did he want?" she asked, not the slightest bit bothered that it was none of her business.

"I just wanted to thank him for helping me with my mom earlier."

"Oh." Paula looked bored until she spied the manuscript. God I was stupid. Why had I thrown it down face up?

She picked it up and began looking through it. "Please don't tell me you went to talk to him about this?" She shook her head as she looked at it. "Jess, Jess. You're not trained in this. Did he laugh at your comments?" she sneered.

I answered her defiantly, my chin tilted upward. "No, he didn't. Actually, he advised me to see if I could talk to you about my first attempt at reviewing a manuscript."

"Ah, good. Well, quickly looking at this, I'd say don't give up the day job, but I'll tell you what, I'll look it over at some point because like Barnett says, I'm the one who should do so. I'm not sure when I'll get time though as I'm incredibly busy. In the meantime, if you could photocopy me twenty copies of the manuscript I've left on your desk at your earliest convenience and go fetch me a latte I'd be very grateful." She said 'very grateful' like 'you've no fucking choice, bitch.'

After giving her a sickeningly sweet smile, I said, "Sure thing. I'll bring everything to your office. And I'd be ecstatic if you do manage to take a look at the manuscript. I know it's not a priority, but your opinion would be valued by me with you being a respected commissioning editor."

She appraised me as if waiting for an extra-bitchy retort, but if I'd learned anything in my own management roles it was to not antagonize, and that killing with kindness was a far superior form of ammunition.

"Make it twenty-five copies, and actually, get me a latte and also a cappuccino. It's Barnett's favorite and I have a one to-one with him at three. If you can have everything ready for then." She flicked her hair off her right shoulder.

"Absolutely, Paula. I'll be at your door at two fifty-five so you can be at Barnett's on the dot."

A feeling of smugness rose inside me as she walked away with nothing further to say. I quickly looked at anything that had come in over lunch time and then I picked up the document and headed to the photocopier. Paula and Barnett really should get together. They were both absolute assholes. And if they did, well, he'd have broken his work rule again and would be in the shit with Eli.

You can't get him fired just because he's annoyed you, Jess, I berated myself. But then as I waited for the copier to spit out all the copies, my mind wandered back to my mom's conversations over lunch and an idea came to mind of just how I could make my boss extremely uncomfortable.

I delivered Paula's documents and her coffees right on time and with a spring to my step, and I went home sans manuscript, because I was going to spend the evening doing something for myself.

I was going to visit a sex club. When I'd worked at Abandon, I'd gone to Masquerade nights in order to watch and participate incognito, but now I could move around the club freely. Though I doubted I'd get involved tonight, I would go and remind myself that I was a woman with a healthy sexual appetite, and this time I'd take note of what the other women there were like and what they wanted.

And then I'd work on my plan.

CHAPTER SEVEN

Barnett

Fuck, I'd got Paula coming to see me in a minute. I was going to have to show her the new professional boss I was, given that previously I'd fucked her over the desk. I really had been an idiot, ruled entirely by my cock and now it was coming back to fuck me up my own asshole.

Anthea, my secretary, knocked and opened the door and Paula sashayed past her without a backward glance or a thank you.

Despite what I'd said at the commissioning meeting yesterday morning, Paula had clearly opened a couple of further buttons of her blouse since this morning's meeting and I swear her skirt was three inches shorter too.

She passed me a coffee, put her own on my desk and then sat on the chair in front of me, her leg crossed revealing an 'accidental' flash of creamy flesh above her hold up stocking.

I wonder what Jess has on underneath her suit? I thought, before catching myself. I really did require therapy.

"I just had a little chat with Jess and offered to look over the manuscript she reviewed, although I had a quick look and oh dear," she snarked. "But she said you'd told her I'd look it over and of course you know I'd do *anything* for you." She played with the pendant that dangled between her breasts.

"Only if you have time. She's an assistant after all, and a new one at that," I replied dismissively. "Now, I'm going to have to cut our meeting short as something's come up, so what's happening in terms of getting the cover illustration for this book?" I asked, pulling Paula's attention back to the point of the meeting.

The fact was that Paula was excellent at her job and as we chatted about the book in question I was engaged and enthused. But every point she made came accompanied with a hand through her hair, a suck on her pen, an eyebrow wiggle. It was endless and exhausting and entirely my fault.

From out of nowhere my brain decided to leave the building via my mouth.

"Paula, if I could just say something personal to you. Something outside of work for a moment?"

"Yes," she practically purred the words, and yet my brain via my mouth didn't acknowledge the car crash it was about to cause by continuing.

"You are a very beautiful woman."

"I'm glad you think so." She flicked her hair and thrust out her chest.

"But I'm so very sorry that I took advantage of that. In my role as your boss, it was wrong of me. I want to reassure you that it won't happen again."

Her eyes dulled and then narrowed. She rubbed her chin for a moment as if confused. Then, like a chameleon under attack, she decided to try something different.

"Barnett, we're two consenting adults and I never even acknowledged the fact that you're my boss. Okay, maybe we shouldn't have fucked on office time, but I'm still happy for us to get-together outside of work if you'd prefer."

Oh Jesus, I was going to have to spell it out.

"After the Maddy disaster, I'm not fucking anyone else for a while, Paula, so it's best if you just move on and find someone else. I'm physically and emotionally unavailable. It's time for me to show my worth as a CEO, rather than show my cock."

Her lips parted and I waited for her next words. Paula got to her feet. "I understand that you have to tread carefully for a while." She winked. "Just know I can be very discreet." I pictured a flapping fish on the ground gasping for a final attempt at water. With that she left the office. I smacked myself in the forehead because she wasn't taking the hint. I was wired and actually could do with a fuck, but instead, I decided to leave early, go home, and get into the gym. I'd pound the treadmill instead of some pussy.

Having parked in my space in the lot, I headed up to my apartment and shucked off my suit, discarding it to the floor. It felt restrictive and I was glad to change into my trackpants and a t-shirt. I took the elevator down to the second floor of my condo building and checked in at the gym reception. Not five minutes later I was on the treadmill.

My mind flashed with Paula's seduction techniques and Jess' disappointed face when I'd failed to acknowledge her feedback. God, why was that woman so under my skin? Was I still annoyed that Eli had put her there? Was it that I wanted what I couldn't have?

I quickly ended up moving onto the punching bags and still my mood was one of frustration and annoyance.

Dripping with sweat, I wiped my face and chest on my towel and decided to give up and return to my apartment to shower, rather than use the communal ones. I felt like a shaken bottle of soda. I needed a release. Heading straight to my bathroom, I turned on the shower faucet and stood underneath the water once it started steaming. Maybe I'd have been better off with a cold one?

Wrapping my hand around my dick I attempted to picture Paula and how I'd bended her over the desk, but my mind wouldn't get the memo and changed the mental image to Jess. Knowing that one way or another I needed to ejaculate, I gave in and imagined ripping those fucking goddamn awful clothes off Jess' body, pushing her thighs apart and thrusting my cock in her warm, wet pussy. I came hard; so hard I almost saw fucking stars.

But it did the trick. I felt the endorphins blast through my body, sending a rush of relief through me. I sat down on the floor of the shower stall and let the hot water tumble over my body for a few minutes, savoring the feeling of being sated, and then I washed myself down, got dressed, and decided that I'd order a takeaway and spend the rest of my evening with a bottle of Jack.

When I got to my office the next morning, I was tired, grumpy, and had a dull headache—the after-effects of binge drinking. I was tired because I'd woken up at four am and been unable to go back to sleep, and I was grumpy because even though I'd passed out on the sofa with a full stomach and copious amounts of alcohol in my system, I'd been tortured by dreams of Jess where she'd walked around my office wrapped in yellow tape that said 'crime scene' on it.

The only thing I could think to do was to drink coffee, send Anthea out for something to eat to take the edge off, take a couple of Advil, and bury myself in work. It made a change from pussy. As I still needed to find a book to rival Maddy's, I had a purpose at least.

I sent out a memo to the team.

I am still looking for a women's fiction title to replace Maddy Sylvester's ASAP. Please make available to me anything you feel could be suitable. At this stage it doesn't have to be agented. Hit me with any wildcards.

And with that, I sent for Anthea to get me my hangover cure.

Two days later...

It was the end of another week and despite my memo there had been nothing come to my desk of any use. I could have punched a hole in the wall, such was my frustration. My intercom buzzed.

"Barnett, I have Jess here wondering if she can see you for a moment. She says she has a potential manuscript."

"Send her in," I said. I sat up straight. I'd not seen Jess since she'd last been to my office and I'd sent her away.

She walked in and I wanted to laugh. She was wearing a mustard-colored turtleneck with baggy black trousers. Her hair was pulled back into a severe bun. The turtleneck looked like the inside of a baby's diaper.

"Good morning, Jess. Take a seat."

She did so, and I watched as she took a deep breath. "I'm currently on organize the mail duties as the newest editorial assistant, and a part-manuscript came through the mail, just addressed to Book-ish. It's very different, but you said to bring 'wildcards.' The thing is that it's only a few pages and there was a note inside saying that the rest will be sent the same way. It's called 'Confession,' and well, I'll let you look."

She passed me a few sheets, and as my gaze wandered around the first few sentences my jaw almost hit the floor.

"Wildcard? This is so wild I feel like it's biting my vision!"

She nodded. "I know. But I received it yesterday, and I decided to do some research on online forums and the women in there said if this was a book, albeit with a plain-ish black cover, they would buy it. Yes, there's a market for Maddy's stuff, but there are just as many women of an older age who don't want to be reminded of the fact. So I'm thinking maybe don't publish an out and out rival to A Time of Change, but instead publish something cutting edge and conversational that makes BookLover look outdated."

I considered what she was saying and while I did Jess got back to her feet. "But then again what do *I know*? I'm just an *editorial assistant*, so I'll leave that with you and get back to my emails and coffee pick-ups." Her smile registered with me like a raised middle-finger.

I ignored her jibe, mainly because I was invested in what she'd just handed me. "Thanks for this, Jess. I'll let you know what I think when I've read it and tell you if I need to see any more," I told her.

She nodded and left my office. I called Anthea.

"Hold my calls for the next thirty minutes or so, could you? I'm reading."

"Yes, sir. Just let me know when you're done."

I sat back and began reading.

Confession
By Anonymous

I'm not giving you my age. I'm not giving you my name. Neither is necessary. All you need to know is that I am a woman. Full of desire, I wax and wane, I ebb and flow. Sometimes I desire constant satisfaction; at other times I require nothing more than it to be acknowledged that I exist. Whether my body is firm or slack, slim or Rubenesque, scarred or smooth, I am still a creature with feelings and desires. Not one of us are the same and yet we are treated like a whole. A demographic. Here are my wants, my needs, for now at this moment. Maybe by tomorrow I will have changed my mind, and this desire will only reside in the mind of another woman? Who knows? But for now, here is my first confession...

I walk into the club. It has changed since I was last

here. From noir and silver stars, to contemporary and cool, now it's red and full blooded. It's like the rooms have a deep, lustful heartbeat. I've only ever been here before incognito, but now I've taken off my mask and removed my inhibitions. I like to watch. It turns me on, and I will no longer be restrained, well, unless I give my permission, of course.

Standing at one of the windows, I watch as one woman is caressed and fondled by two men. I will not describe them. It is irrelevant. All I wish to note, to see, is arousal and enjoyment. No matter why any of them come here that is the ultimate goal of all. To be desired and to be satisfied. All without judgment. For who is anyone else to pass such? If it's consensual, what does it matter if one person wants to be blindfolded, while another wants an audience? Whether I'm eighteen, or eighty-two, who are you, dear reader, to decide how sexual I should be?

As the reader you can do as you see fit. Imagine me as you wish, in the body you desire. It matters not as long as you have reader satisfaction. It makes no difference to me. I give you my confession and that's all I wish to do. Do with it as you please. My pleasure has already happened.

The woman lies back upon the bed. Her thighs are parted, and one man is between them, licking her pussy. She rises to meet him, pushing for her climax. She knows what she wants. There is no mask on her face, other than one of desire. The other man sits above her head caressing her breasts. Right now, this moment is for her. She arches her back, her breasts pushing into the man's hands. Her mouth is parted. I hear her soft moans and gasps and her request for 'more' through the sound system.

I am one of many gathered around the window. Some are merely observers like myself, some are being fucked while they watch. Others stay for just a moment and move on: to look in another window, or to find a room to participate in. Not one of us the same, remember?

Tonight, I will only observe because it has been a long time since I was here. I lost myself for a while, and now I need to find myself again. Though my panties are soaked through, I will wait until I get home before I replay in my mind what I have seen and move my fingers between my thighs and pretend it was me.

Over the next few pages, the writer explained in great detail how a man offered to bring her off in front of the window; about the ride home, with the cab's movement almost making her come on the slippery leather seat, and she left it teasingly where she was about to go to bed.

My cock was rock hard, and what I couldn't get out of my mind was that I knew Aidan had owned a sex club called Abandon. Was this anonymously sent through the mail? Or had it been written by someone Jess knew, or... was it written by Jess herself? Was she the one who had these wild fantasies?

The writing was amazing, the subject matter incredible. It could indeed rock Book-ish's readers' worlds. And I was all too aware that I needed Jess to rock mine.

But she was off-limits and so was I, so I'd just have to suffer in silence until Eli's little project ended and Jess was no longer an employee.

And then, well... I'd no longer be a forbidden boss.

CHAPTER EIGHT

Jess

Back at my desk I wished I had cameras fixed on Barnett's face right now as he read the confession. Would he think it was suitable? Would he want to read more? I hoped Anthea walked in and it was 'hard' for him to disguise his reaction.

Like he and Paula said, I had no experience of what sold books, but I felt sure readers would be intrigued by the confessions.

My desk phone rang and without looking I picked it up, expecting it to be my boss.

"Hello. Book-ish Editorial. Jess speaking."

"Jess. Thank fuck."

My shoulders tensed immediately at the sound of Connor's voice.

"How did you find me here? In fact, forget that. What do you want? Ringing me at work isn't appropriate."

"How else am I supposed to contact you? You've clearly blocked me on your phone."

"You don't need to contact me. That's the point. We're done."

He sighed. "That's the thing, Jess. I don't want us to be done. They say absence makes the heart grow fonder, right? And it has. I realize now how much I love you. I miss you, Jess. I want us to get back together."

Unbelievable.

"Well, I don't. I'm ending the call now."

"I'll prove it to you," was the last thing I heard before I cut him off.

Now I was annoyed. I'd had a good morning dropping off the confession and then Connor had called and spoiled it all. I didn't know what his next actions would be, but I figured he'd send flowers. He could send the entire contents of a florists. He could send all the tulips of Amsterdam. I'd still tell him to go to hell. Connor clearly thought I'd taken this job because I was a broken-hearted mess, unable to work in the same building as him. He'd never believe Aidan had specifically asked me to do this project for him. Connor only ever thought about himself being the center of the universe.

Wow. That was true. It was like the blinkers had dropped from my eyes and now I saw Connor for what he was. A good-time guy who wanted to work and play. To be a bachelor boy, but also to have regular sex. I didn't know why he suddenly wanted me back, but I doubted it had anything to do with him realizing he needed me.

I picked up my cell and called Aidan.

"Jess! I was wondering how you were. How goes it in publishing?"

"I'm quite enjoying it actually," I answered truthfully. "I'm a little bored with not being able to use my management skills but seeing how a publishing house works is cool."

"Phew. I thought you were calling to say you wanted out. Has Barnett tried anything yet?"

"No. He's on his best behavior. The reason I'm ringing isn't about business per se, it's about Connor."

"Oh yeah?"

"He's just called to say he wants me back. Now forgive me, but this is quite a turnaround and I wondered what your opinion was. Is he looking depressed and like he misses me?"

I wasn't expecting a snort.

"Connor is getting shit from all angles. The staff hate him because we've lost you and Liberty, though they know your move is temporary. He can't cope with his workload, and the charm he's relied on before isn't working. I'm guessing in the past he's done a lot of consulting with you, because he can't seem to make good independent choices regarding business. For fuck's sake, he hasn't even ordered the new toiletries line yet. It's just fucking soap. If I hadn't already agreed to let you do this for Eli, I'd be the one begging for you to come back. Instead, I have Lucas riding his ass."

"I thought as much. Don't worry, I'm sure I'll be back soon. Barnett really does seem to have decided to turn over a new leaf. Another week or so and I'll hopefully be able to tell Eli that his business is back in safe hands, rather than ones touching up his colleagues."

"Good. We miss you, Jess."

I ended the call, feeling happy about being missed and ecstatic that Connor was struggling. As I thought about the past, he had always asked me a lot of work-related stuff. I'd not even realized with the way he phrased things that he was using me.

Oh Jess. You must do better. You're worth a million Connors, I thought to myself.

Checking my emails, I found one from Paula.

Are you able to minute the commis-

sioning meeting on Monday again? I've looked over your notes and they are comprehensive. We usually rotate between assistants, but I'd prefer it if you were there again on Monday as I have some important information to feedback.

Wow. Praise from Paula. Okay, it seemed like she'd had to prize it out of her tightly clenched asshole, but she wanted me there again. That was something. A recognition of a job well done.

Over the weekend I threw myself into giving the apartment a face-lift. Nothing much, but I re-arranged some furniture and created a reading nook for myself. We had access to new books at Book-ish and a selection I'd brought home were placed on a new bookshelf I'd assembled and put in the corner of my living room besides a loveseat. A new throw to pull over myself while I read meant it was somewhere to relax, and that was what I did Sunday evening. As thoughts of my upcoming birthday swirled around my mind, I found that instead of being fixated on proposals, I actually felt okay. I had a good career that I enjoyed. A great apartment that I would decorate how the hell I liked now, instead of making it neutral so Connor didn't complain about it being 'too girly' as he had when he'd first stayed over. I didn't need a man. Next time I had a relationship, and I was in no rush, it would be because I wanted a man. Craved him heart, body, and soul. I was still determined at some point in the near future to get myself a cat. *I was feline fine* I thought and then I laughed.

And with that, I got out my laptop and I typed up another confession.

Monday morning soon came around again and I got the meeting room set up ready for the commissioning meeting. This time when they came in, I directed them to the coffee machine instead of making them a drink.

Paula appeared and I walked over to her. "Good morning, Paula. Is there anything you need from me?"

She smiled. "No, I'm good. Just maybe sit beside me so you can hear what I say clearly?"

"Sure." I reckoned she must have got a book to replace Maddy's as she seemed very self-satisfied. Fuck. I hoped Barnett didn't reject it and say I'd already found something. We were only just beginning to get along.

The man himself walked in and as my body reacted to seeing him, it was like I'd been de-fibbed. As if my eyes were dehydrated and he was a tall glass of water, as if I were the ying to his yang, as if he was a hypnotist and I was in his thrall... I slunk back in my seat as a cold stone sober fact hit me.

I was in lust with Barnett Ford.

With the way his hair shone, the way his eyes twinkled, with how his mouth curved when he smirked. With the way his slacks accentuated the firmness of his butt. My nipples hardened and my pussy basically cried for his milk as he walked past.

"Jess."

Paula's words pulled me out of my reverie.

"Sorry, what?"

"Richie just asked if there are any cookies."

I swung my head and torso around to see Richie standing looking everywhere but at the packets of cookies which were on the shelf below him.

Sighing, I got out of my seat and pointed them out to him. Did he not realize I'd just discovered something both momentous and disastrous? I'd got a crush on my asshole boss. You know, the forbidden one, who had sworn off work relationships. Who would be fired if he had one. The one who used women and... Was. An. Asshole.

Clearly, I'd had some kind of a mental breakdown. It was the only explanation. I decided this could be my last week here. If Barnett behaved himself for another week, I'd tell Eli that I was sure everything would be fine. I'd take my accrued leave from working at The Global and have a good month's vacation before returning to my original job. Then I'd make sure I didn't 'carry' Connor any longer. As I sat there, I vowed there would be no more of me keeping myself small for others. I might have to do it right now in my post as spy, letting Paula boss me around, but after this I was done letting people control me. I'd also make sure the staff at The Global were always treated respectfully too. I'd update our staff training program now I'd spent a little time back on the floor. I'd bet Connor hadn't treated all staff with respect, but I needed to ensure my motives were for the greater good and didn't look like a personal vendetta.

For now, as the meeting began, I'd take the minutes, and I'd avoid looking at my boss, given my newly realized crush.

"Thanks for the agenda, Paula." Barnett said and I could have thanked him because it annoyed me and turned down my lustometer. I mean I'd used the last one as a template and Paula had scribbled a couple of things on it and then I'd corrected it, distributed it, and brought extra copies to the meeting, but yes, let's thank Paula.

"Anytime."

I just knew she'd be making 'Come fuck me' eyes at

Barnett. I kept my face firmly on the iPad where I was taking notes.

"So, some potential good news," Barnett said. "Last week I received a small part of a manuscript. It's very risqué, and as yet, I don't know who the author is as it was sent anonymously." My eyes raised as far as his knees where he had papers resting on his lap. "If you could hand these around, Jess."

Fuck. I was going to have to go near him. Keeping my eyes firmly on his knees and then on his raised hands with the papers in, I took them while ensuring I touched no part of him. Unfortunately, my initial position meant that he could easily think I was staring at his crotch. I passed the copies around and sat back down.

There was silence for a few minutes and then Richie spluttered on a cookie. "Goodness, do we really want to be known for selling porn?"

I couldn't help it. My eyes darted to see Barnett's reaction. He was looking at Richie like a fly he wanted to swat.

Paula began to speak. "Oh, Rich. You need to get up to date with the modern woman, darling. This is incredible. It demonstrates both how women want all their desires to be met and for them to be treated as individuals. But at the same time, the fact it's anonymous shows that women still can't actually stand up and demand what they'd like. It's such a juxtaposition. And you say you don't know the author at all?" she said having turned back to Barnett.

"No," Barnett replied. I could feel his eyes boring into me. I was sure of it. "It came in the mail, with a Post-it saying there would be more. We can only wait."

"Well, I'm on board with this being a potential against Maddy's. It's modern. It speaks to all women. Dependent on what the rest of it describes obviously."

"Thank you, Paula."

More people added their agreement to the possibility of this being 'the book.' I actually felt sorry for poor Richie. His colleagues had seen Barnett's reaction and agreed with their boss.

The meeting got caught up with the other agenda items and then Barnett asked if there was any other business.

"Just a few things about Swansong, the book of Trudy's, that I thought of over the weekend," Paula said.

"Go ahead."

"Firstly, I feel that the main character, although she wants a family, should demonstrate some inner strength during the story. It's missing a conflict she has to battle. So although she ends up with her happy ever after and of course the man saves her from the final problem, the reader is acutely aware that she would have been able to save herself anyway."

My fingers clutched my electronic pen in a death grip. Because what Paula had just read out was directly quoted from my notes on the manuscript, and as I sat there Paula went through almost all of my notes and claimed them as her own.

"Absolutely fantastic, Paula. Great work. I'm on board with all that and it will be a much stronger book because of it. Carry on like this and I'll have to see about a promotion."

Breathe, Jess. Breathe. It doesn't matter because this isn't your real job.

Fucking bitch, I might just knock her off that chair on my way past.

"If there's nothing else, I'll call the meeting to a close," Barnett said.

I was glad because I couldn't get out of there fast enough.

"Did you manage to take note of everything said, Jess?" Paula asked with fake politeness.

I raised my eyes up to hers. "Yes, everything was made perfectly clear," I answered.

CHAPTER NINE

Barnett

I hoped that Jess wasn't too cross that I'd not mentioned that the confessions had come via her, but I'd detected some resentment toward her from Paula and didn't want it making any worse. Given the currently unstable situation I had with my former fuck buddy, I was trying to satisfy her at work while I refused to outside of it. It wasn't ideal, but while ever there was a spy in the midst and my career on the line, that was how it had to be.

I therefore wasn't surprised when it was Anthea who brought in the next confession. Jess had clearly knocked and run.

Placed in a plain manilla envelope, I drew out the next pages. Clipped to the top was a note from the author.

I will announce my identity with the final pages and then if you are interested in publishing my work you can get in touch. Until then I wish for you to read this like the readers would do. With no idea of my true identity.
Anonymous Author.

While I desperately wanted to know the author's true identity: whether it was indeed being mailed to the business or if Jess was somehow behind it, the author was right. I would be reading it like any other reader. I requested a fresh coffee from Anthea and once I'd dealt with a few urgent tasks, I once again settled to read.

While a good lover can make your body sing, getting to know your own body and then sharing that knowledge brings greater satisfaction.
  I'm back at my apartment after being at the club,

and while the guy who offered could have brought me to climax, I had no way of knowing if he was any good at it. Tonight, I preferred my imagination and my own experienced fingers.

Stripping out of my clothes, I slip between my bedsheets totally naked. As I close my eyes, I take in all the other sensations around me. The sheets are cool against my skin, making my body goose bump. Anticipation has my heart beating a little faster. The sheet touches my erect nipples and sinks around the dip of my belly. I run my hands over my body, feeling the soft skin beneath my fingertips. I imagine I brought the man back home with me and it's his hands that currently caress my flesh. He had dark hair, dark eyes, and was jaw-droppingly attractive, but it's not what's important as my eyes are closed. Now I remember those large hands, thick digits, and tidy nails as 'his' fingertips continue to tease my body by touching me everywhere but where I need to be touched, where I crave to be touched. I would beg right now.

I imagine his amusement and a growl in my ear of, "You're so fucking wet for me," as his fingers dip into the heat between my legs where I am indeed soaked, my juices slick and dripping.

'He' rubs my clit with his fingers, knowing exactly what I need. A slow, gentle, rhythmic rub to get me in the running for my climax. I respond to his touch, tilting

my hips to push my clit further into his fingers. He expands his touch, moving to pushing a digit inside me, while his thumb continues to flick my nub.

I gasp under his ministrations, my breaths becoming faster and shorter as my desire builds.

"I'm going to fuck you now," he informs me, and I piston my fingers together, part my legs wide and fuck myself, imagining his clenched buttocks as he thrusts inside me, giving me everything I desire. I climax around my fingers as my entire body shakes. Wrung out, I collapse back onto my sheets while I enjoy the feeling of being spent.

If I ever do bring him back from the club, I will get him to touch me exactly like this, exactly how I like first, and then I'll see if he has anything else to show me. Because it's entirely possible that someone else can know how to play a hit tune on my instruments.

Jesus fucking Christ. As I sat there with yet another painful erection, I decided that this was all a con. A trick. Jess was an evil plant, sent to test my conviction. She was trying to get me all worked up to see if that made me go and sink my cock into an employee. It had to be. Well, I wasn't going to fall for it. I would not succumb. Jess could continue sending her daily fantasies. I mean, come on, it said he had dark hair and dark eyes. The ultimate revenge would be this book being a huge success and it putting me firmly back in Eli's good books, so Jess could *bring her A-game*. And tomorrow if there was another confession, well, we'd handle it a little differently.

I thought about bananas. Disgusting things that gave me the heaves and switched off my being turned on, and then I got on with my day. I sent Jess an email.

Thanks for dropping off the manuscript. If another comes tomorrow could you call into my office with it ASAP.

I got an immediate reply.

Yes, I will bring it to Anthea as soon as I am able.

I wrote again.

No, if you could actually bring it to my desk this time. There is some work I want to do around what we have so far. I need some editorial assistance.

I smirked while I waited for her response.

Okay.

I was so looking forward to tomorrow.

The next day I had an early morning meeting, but I told Anthea to interrupt me if Jess arrived as the new manuscript took precedence. Yet, the meeting finished and there was no sign of either. I typed into my laptop.

Has a manuscript arrived?

No. Looks like there isn't anything today. Sorry I can't assist you further on this occasion.

Sassy. I liked it. But she wasn't winning.

That's fine. Please come to my office for 12:00 and we'll work with what I already have.

I considered asking her to bring me a coffee but decided against it. She'd probably piss in it. I sent Anthea for one instead and insisted she got herself a drink and a bun for her trouble.

I was all fired up by the time Jess knocked on my door. She'd deliberately avoided my gaze for some reason in Monday's meeting, but now she had no choice but to look at me.

"Take a seat, Jess. You can put your tablet down on the desk. You only need your voice."

"Okay."

Today's outfit was a wine-bottle-green flouncy blouse and an A-line chocolate brown cord skirt. While the outfit could have been titled 'classy' on another body, on Jess it looked like a tent on top and a teepee on the bottom. Her hair was, as ever, back in a severe bun.

"So how can I *assist* today?" she asked.

I sat forward in my chair, my fingers steepled together as my hands rested on my desk. "It's about this manuscript."

For a split-second apprehension flickered across Jess' face in the form of a slight grimace.

I continued. "I don't really feel I can keep talking to the commissioning editors about this until I have the whole thing and have chance to meet the author, given that just like today, the rest may never actually arrive. So, the first thing is, obviously to ensure that if we receive more you bring it to me ASAP and also, if there's ever any indication of a chance to meet the author please bring that to my attention too as this is high priority."

Jess nodded. "Not a problem."

It was time to have my fun now. "Okay, the thing is, if this is going to be our lead book in women's fiction, I need to get my audio team on it. We'll need a strong female voice to narrate. However, I initially need to know what, if any, kind of changes would have to be made to the manuscript for audio, so," I paused and passed the papers over to Jess. "If you could read this out to me."

Jess didn't reach for the pages. She blinked twice as

if checking she wasn't hallucinating and then said, "Pardon?"

"I need you to read this out to me."

"I don't think so," she huffed.

"Why not?"

"Because it's inappropriate. It's... explicit."

I nodded like I fully understood her hesitation, when really I was inwardly highly amused at the fact she was agitated. Served her right. "Honestly, I understand why you would think that, but Jess, in women's fiction, even in Maddy Sylvester's and other authors' work, there are sex scenes. It's part of publishing. You have to see them as just words. I don't want you to act out the scenes, this is a purely professional job. Something that happens regularly." It was only a half-truth. Staff did read out manuscripts to me, but I'd never had one this explicit before.

"Fine," she said, grabbing the papers.

"I'll close my eyes. I need to forget it's you reading, and just get my ear in to the flow of the words."

This was absolute bullcrap. Audio went straight to the audio team. I didn't worry about any of that. I had an established team who handled it very well. But Jess hadn't trained for the job properly and so didn't know that. I closed my eyes and listened.

Jess began. "I'm not giving you my age. I'm not giving you my name..."

I sat until she'd read the entire first two sections.

She'd read it as plainly as she could. Giving no cadence to her voice. I'd thought about bananas more times than I cared to remember and as she finished, I opened my eyes.

"Is there anything else?" she asked, and I got the impression that murder wasn't far from her mind.

"No, that was perfect. I don't think we need to change much at all in terms of the words on the page. I'll let you go get your lunch."

Jess rose and grabbed her tablet.

"I really hope we do get some more pages as I have every confidence that this could be a bestseller," I mused as Jess reached the door.

"I'll bring them if there are any. Do you want me to leave them with Anthea now?"

"Hmmm. No, I'd like your opinion if that's okay, given I don't want to involve anyone higher yet."

"But my opinion isn't of interest given I have no experience."

"But you'll be getting experience, won't you?" I raised a brow.

She sighed. "Look, why don't you ask Paula? I mean she's up for a promotion because of her amazing feedback."

She sounded jealous. My eyes met hers, but I realized she wasn't envious, she was pissed.

"That was your feedback, wasn't it?"

"I don't expect you to believe me." She sighed. "But yes."

I tapped my fingers on the back of my other hand while I considered her words and thought back to the meeting. "I do believe you, Jess. I've worked with Paula for years and she's good at her job, but she's not good at hiding her true feelings, and now I realized why she kept looking at you and making what I realize were barbed comments in your direction."

"So why tell her she might get a promotion?"

"Because I thought it was her feedback until now. I will deal with Paula. I just need to think of how." Without her making my life increasingly difficult. "I am sorry that she did that though. I wasn't kidding. The feedback was excellent. You're wasted as an assistant if that's what you're capable of."

Jess shrugged. "I am what I am. Paula doesn't bother me. It shows her insecurities. She can be damn sure I won't be reading any further manuscripts that she can steal my ideas from though."

She left the office and left me feeling more confused than ever. I had a fake editorial assistant who was showing a true aptitude for editing, and my feelings for her veered from teasing her as revenge for her fakery, actively wanting to encourage her to consider a career in publishing, and then fantasies of wanting to strum her clit exactly as she'd just described in her monotone voice.

As I once again thought of the yellow fruit I detested, it came to my attention that Jess was driving me bananas.

CHAPTER TEN

Jess

The absolute fucking ASSHOLE.

The only saving grace was that he shut his eyes, otherwise I would have *died*.

I didn't think for one minute that he had assistants come and read out erotica in his office. Acting it out, yes. Reading for audio. Hell no.

What I was going to feedback to Eli I didn't know. Barnett was supportive one minute, cold toward me the next, and now he seemed to have taken liberties with me, before going back to being supportive. He had more personalities than James McAvoy in *Split*. I could not work him out at all.

Then all of a sudden it came to me.

Was this what he did with women at the company?

Yes! I'd bet this was his MO.

First be affable and approachable, then cool off so the woman tried harder to get his support and admiration back. Then see how far he could get away with pushing the boundaries, like getting me to read erotic literature to him. He probably expected that after I'd have been begging for his touch. Maybe he'd make a pass at me next and then I could report back to Eli or Aidan and get out of here.

The trouble was, I hadn't been expecting him to like the book and think it could be a bestseller. Yes, my mom taught English and had brought me up on books as much as she'd nurtured me with love and food, but me, a bestselling author?

Talking of my mom, she'd insisted I went to her book club tonight to talk to the others about life working at a publishers.

I hoped her book club wasn't expecting too much from me. I was only an assistant after all. I'd not met Stephen King.

As I returned to the office, I was hit by a sea of red. Red roses and red balloons were placed all around my desk. It looked like St. Valentine had thrown up. I knew who was responsible for this. I'd anticipated it.

Sure enough there was an envelope on my desk.

Sliding the card out, I noted the teddy holding a heart on the front. Inside it said:

Jess
To show you how sorry I am.
I love you.
Connor.

Now I was doubly pissed. I was pissed at Barnett; I was pissed at Connor. As I spotted Paula walk into the office stalking toward me, I realized I was triple pissed. Picking up my letter opener, I stabbed a balloon just as she reached my desk. I smiled inwardly with satisfaction as she startled.

Placing the letter opener down, I folded my arms over my chest. "What can I do for you, Paula?"

"Oh, don't worry about that at the moment. We need to do something about all this." She gestured around my desk. "Only this is far too distracting. Desks should be kept clean and tidy. I'm going to need you to tidy it all away."

"That's what I'm doing," I said, and I picked up another balloon and stabbed it, after which I grabbed a bunch of roses and with a silent apology to their beauty, I threw them in the trashcan.

"Wow, who pissed in your cornflakes this morning?" she asked and the fact she was clearly basking in my misery made me even angrier.

"Barnett. Barnett pissed me off this morning," I announced. "And these flowers I've just come down to, are not an apology... *from Connor,*" I whispered the last two words under my breath so that I wasn't lying but so she didn't hear them.

"Let me help you." Paula demanded I hand over the letter opener and she stabbed all the remaining balloons. The rest of the assistants were clearly staring at us both, but as I looked back at them they would look away.

"There," Paula said when my desk was empty, and then she stomped off.

I bet I knew where she was going, and I didn't care in the slightest. Barnett had made his business his bed and he could fucking lie in it.

"Sweetheart, I'm so glad you could make it," my mom said, air-kissing me on both cheeks before introducing me to all her book club friends. We were in the living room, my dad having been made to go to the sports club for a few hours.

I sat and listened as they discussed the latest mountain man book.

"I felt the words were, erm, very compelling," Mom's friend Missy said.

"Yes, I agree. They nailed the descriptive text. I felt like I was there," another woman said.

The discussion stayed this way for around three more minutes until my mom clapped her hands together loudly.

"What is going on tonight? We're not reading literary genius, although I agree the writer is excellent. We've been reading about a ten-inch cock and not one of you has mentioned it."

Faces were turned down toward the floor.

"It's because of me, Mom. I think people feel embarrassed because I'm here." I cleared my throat. "Let me tell you a bit about my job," I said, and I began by describing the day to day and then I described the erotic manuscript that had arrived, although I didn't say I'd written it. "So you see, there's nothing that you could say in front of me now that would shock me. I'd rather you were just yourselves. In fact," I announced. "Why don't some of you write your confessions and maybe they could be included in the book? I know the author and I'm sure she'd be willing to include some. If it's published, it's being published under Anonymous. There'll be no knowing who wrote the words inside. You could even post them to me at work and not add your names."

"Oooh, I will. I've lots of fantasies after reading this latest mountain man book. Hey, shall we do it now? Have you got any paper, Tammy?" Missy asked her.

"Of course. Oh how amazing. My daughter is hosting an actual writing workshop for us. She is so very talented." Mom went off to get some paper and pens. I think she was overplaying my role, but I knew better than to challenge her.

"I won't be putting my name on, but if it makes several million pounds, I want my share," Bonnie said.

"All contributors would be paid. I don't know how much. It would have to be negotiated. I think millions might be slightly optimistic," I replied.

With everyone in agreement that they would be compensated if their confession was used, the room went quiet as pens scratched across paper. Mom was writing furiously. I leaned over. "I can't read your confession, Mom. That would be entirely inappropriate."

"Then get one of the others to do it because there is no way I'm not being part of this book," she hissed. That was me told. "Anyway, it's not about your father."

I sat and wrote another confession of my own

and then a while later people passed me their sheets of paper. Some asked if a 'ghost writer' could tidy theirs up. Others folded theirs up as if shy, but every single one of Mom's book club handed me a confession.

I wondered how many involved ten-inch dicks. After everyone had left, I sat with Mom for a while.

"How is the lovely Barnett?" she asked.

Something must have flitted across my face because her forehead creased. "Is everything okay, Jessica?"

I told her about Connor having called me at work and him now sending me flowers.

"The fact he must have stalked you to discover where you're working is disconcerting. Not only that, but as if you'd take him back." Her eyes perused mine. "You wouldn't, would you?"

"No of course not. Over my dead body."

"Good. Now tell me about Barnett."

"What do you mean?"

"My original question was about Barnett. Your face went weird, and then you avoided the subject by talking about Connor. I'm your mother. I know when you're being evasive."

I sighed. Then I figured I would destroy her perfect image of him.

"...and I felt so embarrassed at having said those

kinds of words in front of him, Mom. Do you agree with me, that it's some kind of MO?"

"Maybe. He's definitely hot for you though. I saw it the moment I met him."

"Don't be ridiculous."

"Darling, I was laid on the couch after my 'faint,' looking at him with one eye screwed shut and the other opened just a slit. He never took his eyes off you the whole time; especially when you bent over to check my pulse."

"He did not."

"I know what I saw, Jessica. Guess what else I noticed too?"

"What?" I said as a sigh.

"You like him too. That's why you avoided my question and that's why you're annoyed that this might be what he does as standard to every woman at Bookish."

I was about to protest again when my mother put a hand on my arm.

"Jess, it's me, your mom. If you can't be honest with me, you can't be honest with anyone. It's not like I'm going to tell you you're stupid for having feelings. I'm just glad they're not for the rat."

"But Barnett's a rat too. He's a manwhore, Mom. And an asshole. And I'm there to make sure he doesn't take advantage of his staff. Which means it's ridiculous that I'm attracted to him."

"Darling, he's a very attractive man. And do you actually know that he's a manwhore? Or has he just had an unsuccessful dating history and been a little naïve and lazy to choose his workplace as his dating pool? I think you need to find out all the facts before you present them to Eli, don't you?"

"I can't exactly just interrogate the man about who he's slept with and why, can I?" I whined.

My mom grinned.

"What? That's your mischief face."

"You can't openly interrogate him, no, but you can stop dressing like Miss Marple and see how he copes with seeing the real Jessica Wallis. Throw him for a loop and see how he reacts. If he gets handsy you know he's a rat too."

Somewhere in the midst of my mom's madness was some actual sense.

"Mom. You might just be onto something there." An idea bloomed in my mind.

CHAPTER ELEVEN

Barnett

I entered the office with trepidation and the hope that Paula had a) now got the message and b) had calmed down. I think I had post-traumatic-shouted at-disorder, and every time Anthea came in the room, I startled.

"I won't let her through this door, Barnett. Not without your say-so. You can relax."

I beamed at my assistant. She was a superstar. "Thanks, Anthea."

"I can see you're trying, Barnett. It's a good idea, you no longer mixing work and pleasure, if you don't mind me saying."

It was like having a work mom, which made up a

little for the fact my real mom had passed a few years ago.

"I don't mind at all. If you can't talk to me straight, no one can."

"Of course if you were to meet someone here you could see yourself settling for, like Mr. King did, that's different. But you'd need to keep it on the down-low and not pick a potential psycho."

My forehead creased as I tried to work out what she was saying, but she was already escaping, shouting she had, "A lot to get on with."

Thank goodness she was metaphorically out on reception with a fire extinguisher, ready to fight the fire of Paula Wild.

Yesterday afternoon...

My door burst open and banged into the wall, making me jump. In front of me stood an angry looking Paula. Anthea was close on her heels.

"I'm so sorry, Barnett, she went straight past my desk."

"It's fine, Anthea, I'll take it from here," I reassured her, though it was all fake bravado and I wondered if I should have updated my will seeing Paula's face.

Anthea left and closed the door firmly behind her, though through the office door window she held up her fingers to spell out 911. I smiled and then looked at Paula.

"Erm..."

"You said no fucking of employees. You said you were being a boss now. Yet I find out you've sent Jess red roses. Balloons. What the fuck kind of idiot do you think I am? How dare you."

"What on earth are you talking about? I've not sent anyone roses or balloons."

"That's not what she said," Paula snarled.

"Then she's either mistaken or she's lying, because I swear on my own life, I have not sent Jess anything. Why the fuck would I?"

Paula stood stock still. All the rage emptied from her body and then her face turned from puce to vivid pink. In all the time we'd worked together I'd never seen Paula embarrassed.

"Oh my god. She played me. She fucking played me, because I..." She stopped.

"If you were going to say because you claimed her feedback as your own, then I already know."

Paula flopped down onto the chair and placed her head in her hands. "Oh God, I have made such a fool of myself, and now my job..."

"Paula," I said firmly. "This is exactly why I'm

done with blurring the lines of professionalism with sex. You've just gone batshit because you thought I sent another woman flowers, when in any case we are not a couple. We're ex fuck buddies. I'm sorry to spell it out but that's all we were."

Tears welled at her eyelids as she looked back at me. "I hoped for more."

I nodded. "I know. But I didn't. I'm sorry."

She nodded. "My job..."

*"Your job is safe, Paula. I wasn't lying when I said you're one of the best commissioning editors we have, if not **the** best."*

"But I was giving Jess' feedback..."

"This time, yes. Usually, no. Look, let's just forget everything unprofessional we've done before on both sides, shall we? We've both made mistakes and if you can overlook the fact I don't want anything beyond a professional relationship, then I can look beyond what you did earlier."

Paula nodded. "Would it be okay if I went home early? I just need a moment to think about my actions today, because I've lost myself somewhere along the way."

"Take as much time as you need." I paused. "Although it would be great if you were back tomorrow because you're a fabulous commissioning editor."

She grinned. "I am, aren't I? When I'm not acting insane over my boss."

"Go home, go have a bitch about me with some girlfriends. Chat shit and drink wine. Your desk will still be there when you're ready. But... whatever you have going on with Jess, it ends now. I'll have a word with her tomorrow about her lying to you about the flowers too. I'm going to switch her over to a different editor. I think that's best."

"Yeah. I'm sorry for how I acted today."

"And I'm sorry for leading you on if I did."

She shook her head and her lips drew into a thin line. "I knew what you were offering. I just thought I could be the one to change you."

I scoffed. "There's no such person."

She smiled wanly and rose from her seat. Then with a slight wave, she walked out of the door.

I breathed a massive sigh of relief that just maybe, that was the end of women trouble at my place of work.

Now I had back-to-back meetings for the rest of the afternoon, so I'd have to wait for tomorrow to confront Jess about her role in inciting Paula's behavior.

I'd asked Anthea to set up a meeting for Jess to come see me at eleven. Anthea buzzed through on my intercom.

"Jess is here. Are you *ready* to see her?" she said breezily. There was something underlying in her tone, but I was fucked if I could work out what it was.

"Yes, send her through." I smartened myself up, adjusting my tie and sitting up straight. It was time to call Jess out. Her very presence was causing chaos in my world and I was done with all the game playing. Eli had told me to behave and I had. I didn't need a spy in the midst. I realized that somehow I seemed to have woken up cranky.

Probably due to the lack of bedroom action of late.

More likely because Jess gets to you, and you don't want to admit it.

Inner voices were very annoying.

A knock, and then she came in. And my mind obliterated.

Like Doctor Strange doing his weird shit where he has pieces of the universe everywhere, my mind no longer functioned, as one bit was trying to maintain reality while another was under the impression I was hallucinating. Another, connected to my cock was going, 'Down boy.'

Jess was not 'Jess the Dowdy Assistant,' today. Jess

was... well... I currently had no words due to my brain explosion.

Her hair was long and straightened. Her eyes catlike with flicked black liner. An emerald-green wrap dress fitted like a glove, and those endless legs ended in kitten heels.

She took a seat in the chair opposite my desk and spoke clearly and concisely, as if she hadn't just caused me to completely malfunction.

"I have another confession. Shall I read it to help with the audio?" she asked.

While I figured hearing it might kill me, I nodded, because it was all my body was currently capable of doing.

But I knew before she even opened her mouth, the monotone Jess of yesterday wouldn't be here. She wasn't going to play fair.

This was open warfare. The 'If I'm going to get Barnett to show his true colors, they'll be coming out now' mission. If I'd had a white handkerchief in my suit pocket, I'd have waved it. Instead, I just sat there while Jess' 'battle cry' came forth.

"My confession will surprise you," she read out. "Well, I hope so anyway, because it surprised me as I wrote it. Dear reader, I had no idea this was my fantasy, but I found the words spilling out across the page, and so here they are. I'm bared to you in more ways than one."

She took a breath and then with every undulation in her tone, I fractured further apart. I was somewhere in the ether wondering if I'd ever recover from Jess in all her glory. Because I could no longer deny it. I'd fallen for the woman in front of me. I might not know much about her yet, but I wanted to know. While I also desired her physically—yearned to plunge into her warm depths—the fact remained that she captivated me mentally too. I wanted to know what was behind her drive, wanted to, *oh my fucking God*, get to know her family and everything about her. I was having a mental breakdown. It was the only possible explanation.

The confession unfolded.

"I work with a guy and he's, well, he's hot. But he's my boss and for many, many reasons, he's forbidden, and well, that just makes him hotter. The more I shouldn't want him, the more I desire him. At first, I just looked forward to being at work around him. Catching a glimpse of him and wondering if when he looked back at me, he was seeing his colleague, or seeing the woman I am. But then I noticed I wanted to dress up for him. Wanted him to see me as desirable. Wanted him to want me. Even though this will never become anything in real life. It is a fantasy and it's where it will stay. For all the many reasons I will tell you later, but for now. Here's my fantasy.

"It's late at night and I've stayed behind to finish off some work. As I walk down the hall, I see a light on in his room and can't help but walk in. I'm only intent on making polite conversation, in order that I can spend moments in his presence that I can play back that evening. But my pre-considered question of, 'What are you doing working so late?' dies on my tongue as I walk in and find him lost to his desire. He's sitting on his chair behind his desk with his eyes closed as he fists his cock.

"He's not heard me come in and as such I can watch undiscovered. His eyes are closed, his lips parted, and moans and groans slip from between his pillow soft looking lips as he works his cock. 'Yes, yes, just like that. Just like that.'

"I imagine that it's me he's thinking of as he jerks off. It's taking all I have in me to not make my presence known. To not either take his cock in my own hand, or in my mouth. Yes, to let him fuck my mouth. His hands grasping the back of my head, guiding me as I take him all the way to the back of my throat.

"It's not enough. He wants to sink into my depths. He pushes up my skirt and lays me across his desk, face down. My panties are pushed to one side as he plunges into me. Fuck, it's everything I imagine and more.

"Desire unfurls inside me. Tendrils free themselves from where they were tied up, restricted. Now they are free, and as my fingers caress myself in reality to my climax, in my fantasy he does not see the sixty-three-year-old woman I am, he sees the twenty-three-year-old woman I was. The woman I was before I entered a mentally abusive and sexless marriage that I've never had the confidence to get out of. Until now. Because as my desires unfurl upon the page, they unfurl in real life. I married the wrong man for many reasons, but it's never too late to go in search of the right one."

My eyes widened in shock. Lost as I was in the image of Jess confessing she had the hots for me, I now fixed my gaze on her face. Sixty-three? Sixty-fucking-three? Never had I lost a hard-on so quickly as the Jess before me suddenly became an old woman with my cock in her mouth.

Jess was smiling. A large smug grin all over her face. Because she knew exactly what she was doing.

"If you are now thinking 'Ugh,' and imagining some old lady with white hair, you're doing her a disservice. She's glamorous as fuck, looks like Jennifer Aniston, and would show any boss a good time as a cougar. And that's why this book needs to be published. To challenge stereotypes about women and their sexuality."

She stood up, "I'll leave you to your day, now," she

said. I rose too and walked around to stand in front of her.

"Our meeting isn't finished. Reading the confession isn't why I called you to my office. I wanted to talk about your position." A groan escaped me at the word, exposing my true feelings. *Not now, Barnett!*

"Did you picture me, Barnett? Did you imagine it was me with your cock in my mouth?" Jess arched a brow. "Did you imagine fucking me, like you have your other employees?"

I leaned down toward her, my mouth dangerously close to hers.

"You'll never know," I whispered. "Because I no longer sleep with my employees."

She snapped her head up straight and stepped away from me.

"So what else did you want to discuss with me?" she said, folding her arms across her chest, which served to accentuate those fucking gorgeous tits.

"Oh, just how long Aidan or Eli had asked you to stay here," I said, tilting my head, and watching as she became the one knocked off her perch.

CHAPTER TWELVE

Jess

One minute I thought he was going to kiss me. To break his rule about him being forbidden. To show that when it came to a hot female he was weak. But then he'd pulled back and I felt a confusing mixture of feelings. From being pleased he'd managed to stay professional so I could leave and tell Eli he had nothing to worry about, to what alarmingly felt like a crushing disappointment that he didn't want me.

However, his own confession, that he knew I was a plant, had now brought me back firmly into the present moment.

I sighed. "How long have you known?"

"Since I met your mom and she said Aidan."

"My goddamn mom."

"It wasn't her who gave it away, it was your reaction when she said the name."

I moved and sat back in the chair, and Barnett returned to his own.

"So why didn't you call me in here and tell me you knew and to get the hell out?"

"All truth from now on, Jess?" he asked.

"No point in anything else is there?" I replied.

"I liked having you here," he admitted. "First of all it bemused me, seeing you in the oversized clothing with your hair scraped back in the bun."

"Look…"

He held up a hand. "Casting no aspersions to the dress sense; my colleagues can wear what they like. But yours was just so over-the-top horrendous."

I felt my lip curl up at the corner for a moment. "I did my best."

"Anyway, I know you'll now feel that because I knew who you were that it's behind the fact I've behaved, but I want you to know it's not. Full confession time, Jess, and this has knocked me for six, but for the first time in my life I have found a woman attractive and not because of how they look. Well, not completely anyway. I've not suddenly been struck blind."

I felt my heart rate quicken. Surely he didn't mean me?

"You are just so captivating, Jess. I don't know why your idiot ex treated you like shit, but he obviously didn't know what he'd got until it was gone. You're intelligent, beautiful even when wearing a sack, caring, and far too good to be an assistant. You could train as a commissioning editor. You have the right qualities. You put people in their place without being a complete bitch. You're excellent at narration. I could go on, but in summary you are someone who I admire, as a person, not just as a hot female, and I'm just going to tell you that you are exactly that, and no amount of dowdy outfits can disguise it."

I had no idea what to say to him.

"So thank you for showing me that I am actually capable of getting to know someone and potentially having a grown-up relationship with them, not just hot sex. You were sent here to teach me a lesson and believe me I've learned several. How were you approached to come here anyway?"

"It was just perfect. I worked with my ex, found out he'd cheated on me and needed to get away for a while. Aidan had spoken with Eli and they thought I'd be the perfect person to keep an eye on you."

"And now what will you tell him?"

"The truth. That while I've not been here long, all

I've seen is someone who's professed the error of their ways and no longer is going to mix business with pleasure."

"Thank you."

It was odd him thanking me. Odder still that I would face Aidan or Eli and tell them Barnett was back to his best professional self when he'd just admitted all these feelings for me. He hadn't however said he wanted to do anything about them, and he couldn't, could he? Because Eli would take that as he hadn't changed at all. Aidan would think I'd lost all my common sense and rebounded onto the manwhore. I could see it now, him apologizing repeatedly at sending a vulnerable woman into the lair of a manwhore.

And what was I even thinking anyway. I didn't want to date Barnett, did I? All this was just confusion and that rebound. I needed to get out of here.

"You're welcome. I guess that's all there is to say then really. I've no longer any reason to stay here so I'll go pack my things."

"You won't consider staying? I mean, regardless of what was behind the 'confessions' that really has turned into a viable option for our lead book. Is there no more?"

"If you'll take it as an anthology, there's a lot more. I wrote the first ones and my mom's book group have supplied so many more."

"Could you put a full manuscript together as soon as possible?"

"Yes, of course, but are you being serious?"

"Deadly. I'm not the only man who needs teaching about how women really feel. I'm honestly so glad I met you, Jess. Eli wanted to test my faithfulness to the role, but you've actually taught me so much more. So, will you stay?"

I shook my head. "No. I belong at The Global. I love my job there, and you aren't the only one who's learned about themselves. I know now to not hold myself back for a man. I'm going to step fully into my management role and shine. My ex better watch out, because I'm no longer the naïve idiot he treated me as."

"Okay, well, good luck, Jess. If you ever change your mind..."

"I won't."

There was nothing else to say, so I stood up and walked out of Barnett's office without looking back.

"Bye, Anthea. Thanks for everything," I said as I walked past his lovely secretary.

"Why does that make me think you're leaving? You can't leave. That man needs you. I've never seen him so... human."

I burst out laughing and she joined in.

"I'm sure he'll explain. It's a long story, but I was only ever meant to be here temporarily. I'm going back to my proper job now. I work at The Global." I wasn't sure why I was telling her all this. She just had that kind of reassuring face that invited you to open up.

"Oh, what a shame. Well, happy birthday for Saturday. I hope your party goes well."

My brow creased. "How do you know...?"

Anthea grabbed and waved a gold card at me. "An invitation came for Barnett."

"Oh my lord, my mom," I said, outraged.

Of course she would fucking invite him. And I would continue with my indignation and not acknowledge the fact that my stomach had just fluttered with a million butterflies at the fact I might see Barnett again, and outside of work too.

I was packing away my few belongings into a bag when Paula walked into the office and over in my direction. For God's sake she was like a dog with a bone. No doubt she'd come to give me a piece of her mind about my letting her believe Barnett had sent the flowers.

"Paula," I acknowledged.

Her mouth dropped open as she looked at me and then stared at what I was doing.

"Have you been fired?" she said, but it was with surprise, not pleasure.

"Nope. My position here was never long-term. I just had a project to do, and it's completed." That was all she was getting from me.

"Well, I'm glad to catch you before you leave. I came to apologize."

That had my mouth dropping open.

"I'm sorry, I think I must have misheard you. I'm sure you just said you came over here to apologize."

She nodded. "I shouldn't have passed your work off as my own. There's no excuse. I completely forgot how to be professional, and I'd just noticed how Barnett seemed captivated by you, and…"

I tried not to react to her comment, but she gave a half-smile.

"Wow. It's mutual."

"There's nothing between Barnett and myself. Never has been. I'm leaving and I have no further plans to see him again." I left out my mom's invite as I doubted Barnett would show his face at my party.

"He's only ruled out dating people he works with, and you'll not be working with him anymore. It's all I'm saying."

I'd had enough. "You've been a bitch to me the whole time I've been here, so what is this really about? And by letting you think Barnett sent me those flowers rather than my stupid ex, I wasn't any better. You're free to go and do whatever you want to do, Paula. It doesn't concern me." I carried on gathering my belongings.

"I wanted him, but he doesn't want me. I've got my head out of my ass and back into the business. Like Barnett, I will no longer be mixing business with pleasure. I love my job and I'm going to focus on grabbing the books that will have BookLover crying into their coffees."

"For what it's worth and I'm really a manager for a global company, not that it should alter your opinion of my advice, but it's where I've learned this... do your job to better the company and yourself and forget any so-called rivals. It takes your attention away from what's important. Nailing it. Remember why you do your job, do it to the best of your ability and you'll shine. It's Barnett's job to worry about the competition, and if he's doing his best, the company will rise anyway."

"You're right, and I promise, I won't be treating any other staff like they're the shit off my shoe. I'm appalled at how I acted."

"Good. Because I'm going to recommend someone else for my replacement and they've already been treated like crap by a manager in their previous employment, so I want to know they'll be okay here."

"They will."

"All the best, Paula. I honestly mean that."

"Thanks. Good luck to you too wherever you go next."

"Thanks." With that, I grabbed my bag and handing in my cards and ID at security, I left Book-ish.

When I got home, I changed straight into some comfy loungewear and collapsed onto the sofa. It was done. I'd finished my short time at Book-ish. Now I wouldn't see Barnett every day, I'd see Connor.

Deciding I was done thinking about men and work for the day, I put on a cheesy movie and ordered takeout, and blocked everything but the movie plot from my mind.

The following morning, I went to meet Aidan to discuss my vacation time and my subsequent return.

"Eli is very grateful to you for your work, and also very happy to accept Liberty as your replacement."

"She deserves a fresh start as much as anyone else. Connor hasn't lost his job so I don't see why she should suffer any further."

"True. Although Connor has now been given several warnings."

"Oh?"

"He's been arranging personal things on work time and sneaking off."

"Were any of these personal things roses and balloons?" I queried.

"So they were for you. I didn't know given Connor's indiscretion."

"He stalked me to work."

"He also was seen at a rival hotel where he booked in for the evening and then gave me a list of suggestions the following day. I make it my business to know what my close rivals are doing and his suggestions were so close to their ideas that I immediately rumbled him. One more mistake and he's out, Jess."

"Good. It's what he deserves for not working to the best of his ability."

"He should have done what Barnett has. Owned up to his mistakes and then set about to show he meant business."

"Absolutely."

Aidan leaned in and stared at me. "Oh my god."

"What?" I felt at my face for where I clearly had ink or food.

"You've fallen for Barnett. Please tell me that you didn't sleep with him."

"I didn't do anything with Barnett. I was there to work. To check he didn't sleep with anyone from work. It would therefore hardly have been very professional of me to sleep with him myself."

"But did you secretly want to?"

"Aidan, I swear you're worse than any girlfriend I have. Stop with your matchmaking. It didn't work out so well for me last time."

"Do you think he likes you?"

"It's irrelevant. Now my job there is done and I'm going to enjoy a month's vacation. See you on the flip side, boss."

"I'll see you on Saturday. Lori and I have a babysitter."

"Fabulous. See you then," I said, and I left work behind for a while. I had time to get massages, my hair done, my eyebrows and lashes tinted, manis and pedis, and everything waxed. I was taking myself off to a spa.

CHAPTER THIRTEEN

Barnett

It had been so cathartic. Laying my truth out on the table. I'd dealt with Paula, spoken with Jess, and now here I was, reminded that I was Barnett Ford, CEO and partner of Book-ish. My company would be the best fucking publishers in New York. I was back in the game.

Anthea came in the next morning with my mail. "Sorry, Barnett, I totally forgot to give you this invite yesterday. I checked your weekend schedule and didn't see any conflicts, so I RSVP'd yes for you."

She handed me the gold invite. I took it and read

what it was and then I folded my arms across my chest after placing the invite down on my desk.

"Since when have you ever RSVP'd a social event for me without asking, and especially one on a weekend?"

Anthea smiled, doing her best to look innocent. "It's Jess. I just knew you'd at least show your face there. Now, shall we talk gifts? You can't go empty-handed after all."

"What are you up to, Anthea? Jess is just an ex-colleague. I've no need to go to her birthday party or get her a gift."

"With all due respect, Barnett, I don't agree. In fact, I think your words are a complete crock of shit."

If I'd been drinking or eating, I'd have choked to death. As it was, I was rendered speechless, which gave Anthea time to tell me in no uncertain terms that I clearly liked Jess and so should at least turn up with a gift and wish her a happy birthday.

"But if you asked her on a date that would be even better."

"Anthea," I part-snapped, given I felt entirely called out, vulnerable, confused, and excited in one fell swoop.

"I'm sorry, Barnett." Anthea fidgeted with her sleeve. "I stepped out of line. It won't happen again."

"Anthea." I sighed. "What can I buy Jess for her birthday?"

Anthea grinned.

CHAPTER FOURTEEN

Jess

The spa had been glorious. I'd fully relaxed while I'd been primped and pampered from top-to-toe. It had been a good couple of days and then when I got back, I'd bought myself a birthday present, in that I'd adopted a small, six-year-old rescue cat called Kismet.

She was perfect, had settled in like she'd never lived anywhere else and had made the sofa her own whenever my lap wasn't available.

I'd had an amazing birthday so far. Gifts, cards, and flowers had been arriving at my apartment all day, and Ashley had sent the most beautiful necklace: a platinum chain from Tiffany's with a small square diamond pendant on it.

I enjoyed a relaxing day with Kismet until it was time for me to get ready. The truth was I felt a little foolish having a celebration based around the fact I'd reached this milestone age. But my mom had insisted, and I knew better than to try to swim against the tide where she was concerned.

I slowly got ready, putting on the silver strappy dress I'd bought, and then the cab came to take me to my party. When this was done, I could get back in my pajamas and enjoy my month off. I was going to hang with Kismet, and work on putting 'Confession' together.

"Darling, you look absolutely sensational," My mom greeted me with air-kisses. She then proceeded to stay at my side while every guest greeted me and got them to all agree that I was looking amazing.

Finally, I managed to make an escape and grabbed a glass of champagne from a passing waiter.

"Aww, she's just proud of you," Ashley said, coming to my side. She grabbed my glass.

"What are you doing?" I panicked as my heavily pregnant friend moved the glass nearer to her face.

She took a huge sniff. "I miss champagne. I need this baby out, so I can partake. It's not fair."

I took it back away from her. "Loved up mummies-to-be don't need alcohol. Save it for those of us left on the shelf at thirty."

"Well, I'm just hoping hot ex-boss comes here to sweep you off your feet," she said. I gave her a glare for being too loud.

"I told you all that in confidence. Sssh."

She mimed zipping her mouth.

I spent the next ninety minutes floating from guest to guest, but I couldn't help but watch the door looking for Barnett. As time went on and I realized he wasn't coming, I instead started watching the clock, hoping it would soon get around to a time where everyone would leave and I could go back to my cat and pjs.

The dance floor had begun to warm up and my mom came and grabbed me and pulled me onto it. "Come on, Jess, get into the flow of things. Dance like no one is watching."

That wouldn't be a problem. No one was. I wondered how many cats I'd have by my fortieth.

As more of my family and friends joined me on the dance floor, I finally started to relax a little and let go. My mouth dry and my heeled feet hurting, I gestured to those around me that I was getting a drink and I began to make my way off the dance floor. Tripping over a purse, I reached out and grabbed an arm and heard a, "There you are."

Closing my eyes, I couldn't believe he was here. I took a deep breath, opened them back up and I looked up into the face of Connor.

"Wh-what are you doing here?"

"I was invited, remember? No one said I couldn't come. Anyway, I've been looking for you, to give you your present. Just a moment."

He went off toward the DJ as I tried to think about how I could eject him without making a scene. Trust Connor to think it was a good idea to turn up to my special party, and it never enter his brain that he'd not be welcome. Either that or more than likely, he knew full well and put his own needs first anyway, like he'd always done.

Fuck it, I'd throw him out. But as I turned to take a step toward him, his voice came over the DJ's microphone.

"If I could have your attention please, ladies and gentlemen."

Everyone stopped what they were doing. I mean the music stopping had already alerted them to the fact that something was happening.

"If the birthday girl could make her way to the stage."

People began cheering me on. A lot knew Connor,

or knew of him, and didn't yet know that we were over. Not knowing what else to do right now, I decided to go and accept my gift. Then once this ordeal was over I could make him leave.

I stood in front of the DJ booth and tried to look for my mom in the crowd, but there were so many people I couldn't spot her.

Connor was talking to the crowd and then back at me. He walked in front of me, blocking my view which was highly annoying. I zoned him out as I thought a familiar face came into focus at the back of the room, and I tried to look over his shoulder. My view cleared, and I caught another view of the man himself.

"Yes," I said, ecstatic that Barnett had come and wondering what that meant.

"You will?"

I looked down, realizing that Connor was on his knees in front of me. Before I got a chance to protest, he leapt on me hugging and kissing me, and family and friends swarmed around us, congratulations on their lips. Only I could have been proposed to without realizing, and worse than that appeared to have said yes.

By the time I'd pushed Connor away, and got to my mom, there was no sign of Barnett. Maybe I'd imagined him anyway?

'What am I going to do, Mom?" I shrieked as she came into view.

"We've got this," she said, and she nodded over to where my dad held out a hand to shake Connor's.

"What?"

"Keep watching, honey." She dashed off ahead.

As Connor held out his hand, my dad pulled it behind his back and held it in an armlock. And while Connor grimaced in pain, my mom punched him in the nose.

"Kismet, I am so glad you are here so I can tell someone about the drama that happened at my party," I told my cat as she snuggled onto my now pj clad lap. Connor had left with a bleeding nose and clear instructions to come nowhere near me again. I'd let him know that my yes hadn't been for him and hadn't the fact I'd not even been looking at him given him a clue. He'd launched into a plea of wanting me back and that he was offering me everything I'd ever wanted now, but he was wrong.

I didn't want him. Not in the slightest.

My phone rang and I picked up my cell to speak to my mom. "Just checking in that the rat hasn't turned up there, because if he has your dad is coming with a shotgun."

"No, Mom. I think he got the message."

"That's good. Well, you get a good night's sleep

and don't let that man have spoiled what otherwise was a great celebration."

"Mom, did you see Barnett there?"

Mom paused. "No, sweetheart. Why, did you?"

"I thought I did, but I must have been mistaken."

"I'm sure if he had, he would have said hello to one or both of us. It would be strange to attend a party and not say hi to the host or main guest of honor."

"Yeah, you're right, Mom. I must have been imagining things. Anyway, I'm beat so I'm going to get some sleep. I'll call you in the morning, okay?"

"Okay, darling, sleep tight."

We ended the call.

"Time for bed, Kismet. Seems I was dreaming while awake, so I think the sooner I get to sleep the better."

CHAPTER FIFTEEN

Barnett

What the fuck had I been thinking? Anthea clearly had been watching too much Bridgerton and imagining all sorts of daydreamy romance scenarios.

I'd spent most of the day waiting to attend in some kind of stage fright, and eventually decided I'd turn up near the end of the party, so that it would be busy and I could hopefully blend in with the crowd until ready to make my move.

Instead, I watched another man propose to the woman I wanted. She'd seemed unfocused and I could have sworn she'd seen me, but then I heard her say, 'Yes,' and as that fucking jerk gathered her into his arms and everyone cheered, I hightailed it out of there. I must have been in that room all of three minutes. I'd not even left the card and gift.

So that was it. I'd lost my heart and now I had to suffer thinking that someone else had my girl. Someone who didn't even deserve her. All I could do was throw myself into work, ban Anthea from talking about Jess, and hand over the reins of the 'Confession' anthology to Paula. I'd only been keeping it as a tenuous thread to keep me in touch with Jess. Now I didn't want to see her again.

For the next five weeks I focused on work and going to the gym. So much so, that when Eli came to see me, he exclaimed at the sight of me.

"Jesus, Barnett. You're so ripped."

He stood staring at me and then he looked down at the very slightly rounded stomach he had.

"I've not been able to get to the gym and now my middle-aged spread is trying to make an escape."

I laughed. "How are Alex and the kids?"

He beamed. "They're really good." He lowered his voice. "But it's nice to be back at work. Sorry I haven't been able to drop in until today. Get me up to date with events."

I did, and by the time I'd done, my partner was looking a lot less stressed than he had the last time we'd met.

"So hopefully you'll not have to put another spy in the midst." I arched a brow.

"Oh that was Aidan's idea, not mine. I'm business minded but I don't mind admitting I have no idea when it comes to women. I'd just been moaning to him about you and he'd suggested sending Jess along. He wanted her out of the way of that slime ball other manager of his until he worked out what to do with him."

"Yeah, well now they're going to live happily ever after. I guess absence made the heart grow fonder, right?"

"Huh?"

"I was at Jess' party when he proposed."

Eli looked confused. "Hang on a minute." He took out his cell and dialed a number.

"Aid. Quick question and a strange one. Connor was fired, right, and he's not with Jess?"

He listened.

"Ahhhh. It's just Barnett here thought they were engaged."

There was another minute or two of conversation and then Eli handed me his phone. "Aidan wants to talk to you."

I took it, wondering what the fuck was happening.

"Erm, hello."

"Barnett, my man. Why did you think Jess was engaged?"

"I saw it. I saw him propose."

"You were at the party? I didn't see you there?"

"I was only there for a minute."

"Fuck, you left when you thought she was engaged. You dick."

"I don't understand."

"About two minutes after the proposal, Jess walked away from Connor, and Tammy punched him in the face. There's no engagement. And ever since, my deputy manager has been throwing herself into her work and pretending everything in her life is coming up roses. But when she doesn't know I'm watching I can see she's not herself. I thought it was just the fact she'd had a turbulent couple of months, but are you behind this? Did something go on between the two of you after all?"

"No, nothing at all. I mean, I told her I liked her, but I also said I wouldn't mix business with pleasure."

"So why were you at the party? You might as well fess up now."

"Okay. I wanted to see her again."

"Be at my hotel at eight tonight. I'll leave a key on reception for a suite. The suite's on me, the rest of it is on you. Don't let me down. Jess means a lot to me."

My heart beat faster.

"Thanks. I won't."

I passed the cell phone back to Eli.

"Yes, okay. You've won the bet after all. A month's worth of babysitting. Fine. As if I don't have enough babies in my life right now."

Eli finished his call and looked at me. "This better not get in the way of work, but I wish you all the luck in the world. Go get your girl," he said.

I waited for him to leave.

"Don't you want to go buy flowers and things and get prepared? Take the rest of the day off," Eli instructed. "For once, you're making the right decisions in your personal life as well as your professional one."

I didn't need telling twice. As I went past Anthea, I grabbed her and gave her a huge hug. "Wish me luck. I'm going to get my girl," I shouted after her.

I heard her whoop as I hurried down the hall.

CHAPTER SIXTEEN

Jess

Things at the hotel had largely run smooth of late. Don't get me wrong, you got disgruntled guests on a daily basis, but in the main things were good. Life was good. I'd got into a routine of seeing friends, going to the gym, visiting my parents once a week and then going to book club, and cuddling Kismet. There were worse ways of living.

I'd finished the 'Confession' book while on leave and submitted it to Paula. Now would come editing and everything else needed to get the book out there. The book club were so excited. From being bashful about submitting their confessions, they were now hoping they'd be an Oprah or Reese book club choice, and strangely, that wasn't beyond the realm of possibilities according to Paula.

In another weird turn of events, Paula and I now got along. I'm not sure it could yet be termed a friendship, but we'd put the past behind us and were focused on the book release. She'd told me she was dating a guy she'd gone to school with and met at a reunion. She seemed happy. Her one attempt to ask me about Barnett had been met with a firm, 'There never was a me and Barnett,' after which she didn't bring up the subject again.

Ashley was now on maternity leave and so Aidan had asked me to step up my duties as a general manager, given that Lucas would also disappear on paternity leave as soon as the baby made an appearance. I'd wound Aidan up then about his matchmaking reducing our staffing ratios.

The man himself was here now and his face wore the look of harassment of a boss wanting to get home. He strode toward me.

"Jess. There's a guy in the Rose Suite and he's complaining about almost everything in the room. He's upsetting the staff. I want to get home, so would it be okay for you to go see him and try to work out what exactly the problem is?"

"Sure. Go home. I'll handle this guy. You know

how it goes. They book a suite they can't afford and then complain to try to reduce the price."

"Thanks, Jess." He looked at his watch. "Oh, but aren't you finished now too? I can't ask you to stay and me go home."

"I don't have a little one waiting for me to kiss her goodnight. Go. This won't take me long and then I'm out of here."

"Okay. I owe you one," he said and then he dashed away, no doubt before anyone else could grab him with a problem.

I took a deep breath, ready to brace myself for whatever awaited me in the Rose Suite, and I pressed the elevator button.

Knocking on the door, I reminded myself that this was nothing I'd not faced a hundred times before.

Then I heard the words, "Come in," and my heart stopped.

It couldn't be...

Pushing open the door of the suite, I didn't think it was possible for my heart to beat any louder. It threatened to punch through my chest. Barnett stood in the room dressed in a smart gray suit. The room was filled with silver balloons, and a giant banner saying 'Happy

Birthday.' A table was set for two and a champagne bucket with Cristal on ice was the centerpiece.

Barnett walked past me and closed the door.

"Now I know you don't like my opinions on what you wear, but in the bedroom are a few of your dresses if you'd like to pick one to change into for our meal."

"How...?"

"Aidan, your mom, Anthea, Eli. I didn't do this all by myself. It's been a team effort."

"I'll go change," I said. Because I needed a moment to gather myself, and to work out what this meant.

"It's dinner, Jess. There's no pressure here. Just dinner and talking."

No pressure. Was he kidding me? You could cut the sexual tension in here with a knife.

I nodded and went to get changed.

Sure enough, in the bedroom of the suite I found five of my dresses hung in the closet. I picked a plain black wrap dress and quickly changed, after first visiting the bathroom and freshening up.

Then I returned to the room, met with Barnett's nervous but welcoming smile.

He gestured to the table and we both took a seat. Barnett popped the cork on the champagne and we laughed as it sprayed everywhere. After pouring us a glass each, he held his up to mine to chink together. "Happy birthday, Jessica."

We chinked glasses and then I took a nervous sip. "What's going on, Barnett?"

"What's going on is that until earlier today I thought you were engaged to another man."

I gasped. "You *were* there! I thought I saw you."

"I thought I saw you accept a proposal."

I laughed. "Oh, Barnett, when I saw you, I said 'Yes,' happy that you'd made it. I had no idea I'd accidentally accepted a proposal while entirely focused elsewhere."

"You saw me and you were happy I was there?"

I laughed. "Yes. Then I was caught up in stupid Connor's theatrics and when I looked again you were gone. No one else said they'd seen you, so I presumed it was like when you imagined you'd seen water in a desert. That I'd just wished you were there."

He shook his head. "Meanwhile I thought you'd taken the rat-bastard back."

"God, not a chance."

"I've wasted over a month. It's only the fact Eli and Aidan corrected me today, that I found out at all."

"Well, we're here now," I said.

"That's so true. Jessica Wallis, would you like to be my date?"

"I'd love to," I said honestly.

"Excellent. If you'd like to look at the menu..." He

passed it to me, and I pretended to peruse it even though I knew the menu off by heart.

And that began my first date with the asshole manwhore who it turned out had completely captured my heart.

The more time passed during the meal, and the more relaxed we became with each other, I found we had lots in common. Barnett had had a childhood pet cat and couldn't wait to meet Kismet. He told me about his sister and his nieces and nephews. About being raised by a single mom who had sadly passed on. We both loved the gym, good food, and of course books.

"You reading those confessions almost killed me, Jess."

I giggled. "That was the point. I never intended for them to become the book they have. It was all just to torment you."

"It worked."

"I take it you're now a changed man then? Redeemed, and done with your workplace manwhore ways?"

"I am, but my past is what it is. I regret dabbling in the workplace pool for the difficulties it caused, but I don't apologize for enjoying sex."

"You shouldn't. Your relationships are your business."

"They weren't relationships."

"You know what I mean. Anyway, I dated my co-worker too. I also don't intend to date a colleague again."

"Well, that's good news, that neither of us wishes to date a colleague again," Barnett teased.

"Oh yeah?" I teased back.

"Because we don't work together."

"Technically speaking I'm a client of your publishers, so doesn't that make you a forbidden boss?"

"Then I resign."

I giggled. "Actually, on a technicality, the 'Confession' book is written by Anonymous…"

"I'm not your boss. Therefore, I'm not forbidden."

He reached into his pocket and brought out a long rectangular black velvet box. "Happy birthday."

Reaching for it, I felt the soft fabric and then I opened the box to reveal a charm bracelet with one simple charm on it. A key.

"That's the key to my heart if you'd like to take it," Barnett said. My eyes flashed over the box to Barnett. Seeing this hunk of a guy looking so damn vulnerable.

I passed the box back to him and watched his eyes dull a moment. "Could you put it on for me?" I said and I held out my wrist.

His eyes sparkled.

After the meal, Barnett put on some music and we swayed together in the middle of the room.

"Let me know when you want me to call you a cab," Barnett said.

"You're sending me home?" I arched a brow.

"I didn't want to presume anything."

"Barnett." I looked him directly in the eyes. "Take me to bed, and I'll confess *exactly* what I want you to do to me."

I was whipped off my feet so fast my head swam.

Barnett carried me into the bedroom and set me down on the edge of the bed and then he brought the chair closer to the edge of the bed and sat down.

"Okay, Jess," he ordered. "Confess."

CHAPTER SEVENTEEN

Barnett

The evening couldn't have gone any better if we'd have been actors in a play. The date had gone well, the conversation had flowed, the food had been excellent. I'd decided to end the night with a romantic dance and then ask her on another date.

But Jess had other ideas.

Now I sat in the chair in the bedroom opposite this beautiful woman, who was a perfect blend of confidence and vulnerability, and I did not want her thinking she was out with a man who would fuck her and leave. The old me had left the building where Jess was concerned.

My behavior had been called into question right at the same time that Jess was placed in my office, and this woman: sassy, badassy, and yet with the surface scars she bore from being treated like crap from a supposed lover, had taught me that not only was being a 'love them and leave them' lover assholery at its finest, but so was leaving someone dangling on a string. Connor and I had been opposite ends of assholedom.

"I want you to know that this isn't a one-off for me, Jess," I told her.

She smiled. "While I'm hopeful we have something good sparking between us, let's not put pressure on it, Barnett. I like you, you like me, and right now I want you to rock my world."

"Okay." Fuck, was I now coming on too strong? I still had a lot to learn it seemed.

"Strip," she commanded.

I obeyed. Taking off my clothes slowly and as seductively as I could. Jess watched every move I made, hungrily; her eyes feasting on my flesh as it became bared to her.

"Now strip me," she ordered.

As I took off her clothes, I also took my time, revealing naked flesh and caressing it with my hands, taking in the smoothness of her skin, the freckles and moles, small scars from years ago that I'd find out in the future were from falling off a bike as a child.

Her breasts bared to me were utter perfection.

"You should have been jailed for covering this body up with those dreadful clothes."

She laughed.

"On second thoughts, Richie and the rest of the guys would have been put off their work, and maybe trying to claim what's mine."

That earned me an eyebrow arch. "Yours?"

I pouted.

"Hmmm, well if I'm yours, I guess I'd better get you to claim every inch of me," she said. "So, Barnett, I must confess, that I want your hands over every inch of my skin, teasing my nipples, my pussy. I want your tongue re-tracing the steps of your fingers, and then I want your cock deep in my center."

I picked her up and pulled her further onto the bed.

"Tell me again slowly," I commanded.

And she did. My hands traced over her skin, teasing her nipples, before delving lower and finding how wet she was at her core. I teased her nub until she demanded more, craving my fingers and rocking against them until she exploded. I couldn't get enough of watching her come, as I repeated everything with my tongue. While I couldn't deny my cock was ready to ride himself home, I was completely focused on Jess' pleasure. She came over my mouth and I tasted her delicious honey, and decided that if I suffocated this way, I could think of no better way to go.

But then Jess confessed how she wanted me to fuck her, and who was I to deny her what she desired?

With my hand gently resting against the back of her neck, I pushed her thighs apart with my knee and positioned myself over her. And then I thrust in deep.

"Fuck, Barnett, yes. Exactly like that. Harder. More."

And then when we were exhausted and sleep took over, I confessed that I never wanted to be anywhere else.

CHAPTER EIGHTEEN

Jess

Eighteen months later...

It was the launch party for 'Confession' and although the book had been published under 'Anonymous,' everyone from my mom's book club was there. My mom was working the room and coyly telling anyone that she may or may not have a confession in there. Pre-orders were so high, the book was set to hit The New York Times bestsellers list, USA Today, and The Wall Street Journal, which was far too much for my own brain to take in.

Book-ish had contracted me to put together a sequel. Soon, I'd be in a position where I no longer needed to work at The Global and could spend my time with Kismet while I read people's desires and wrote more of my own.

And my boyfriend... well he liked it if I took the best parts of those confessions and we acted them out.

Things had just progressed so easily between the two of us, to the point where after eight months, we'd got an apartment together. It had become crazy to live apart as we spent most of our time together.

Barnett came with me to visit my parents and of course my mom loved him. Actually, so did my dad. I'd met Barnett's sister and her husband and kids. We went to the gym together. We'd become one of those really annoying couples that didn't want to be apart. But we both had busy jobs and so we still had our own space. Plus, I'd never been a 'ditch my besties' kind of girl and so I met up with Ashley regularly when she needed a break from mommy duties. She now had a beautiful baby girl called Delia.

Paula did a speech about the book and gave away hardback copies to everyone there. The paperback wouldn't be released for another six months. Then Barnett went up to the front to say a few words.

"Thanks everyone for being here with us today as we launch our latest book. Reviews have been mainly absolutely sensational, although there have been the odd comments about just how hot the contents within the pages are. But we've answered every such comment the same way; that these are the frank and open confessions of a group of ladies who want to be heard."

He thanked Paula and the rest of the team who had been involved in the book: from editors, to cover designers, to formatters. The list went on. It took a team to make a book at Book-ish and they'd all been amazing.

"Finally, I'd like to thank Jess." He pointed to me. "Jess was the one who received the confessions in the mail and brought them to my attention. It wasn't the only thing brought to my attention; I also became aware after she'd left that I couldn't get her out of my mind. I have a special copy of the book here for you, Jess, if you could come forward. A limited edition."

He hadn't told me he'd done this. How wonderful that I would have a special edition of the book I was now so proud of. Smiling at the others gathered around, I walked to Barnett's side to receive my gift.

Barnett signaled and I saw he was getting Eli's attention.

"Although I did promise never to mix business and pleasure again, you'll have to forgive me, Eli, on this occasion."

He dropped to his knees in front of me. Only this

time my attention was nowhere else. Just on the wonderful man in front of me.

"Don't worry, I didn't dismember a book," he said jokily, knowing how precious I was about turned over pages and coffee-stained covers.

My 'limited edition' was a rectangular box that looked like a book, but when he opened the cover, inside was a velvet lined box with a diamond engagement ring nestled in the center.

"Will you marry me, Jess?" he asked.

"Yes. Absolutely yes." I answered.

Barnett slid the ring onto my finger as everyone cheered and then he dipped and kissed me in a movie-star kiss that made my knees turn to jelly. He picked me up and spun me around.

"Thank you for making me the happiest man, alive," he said.

"Well, if you had have damaged a book my answer might have been different," I joked, and then I kissed him again.

The End

PS

Maddy Sylvester's book sold well at first and then received poor reviews from women who indeed said that just because they were older didn't mean they wished to be portrayed with saggy boobs, an extra roll of fat around their middles, suffering from constant hot flushes and having to break off before sexy scenes to be smeared with lube. It's rumored that her next book will revert back to her previous target audience.

Note from the author: this is the final book in the Love in NYC Series'
If you've not yet read all the series and books, start the first book now with SOLD, Romance in NYC: Double Delight which you can get FREE here: https://books2read.com/u/bwoPWO
If you've enjoyed this book, please leave a quick **review** for it to let others know they should read it.
Thank you. Angel xo

ROMANCE IN NYC SERIES' INFO

ROMANCE IN NYC: Double Delight

Sold
Submit
Share

ROMANCE IN NYC: The Billionaires

The Billionaire and the Virgin
The Billionaire and the Bartender
The Billionaire and the Assistant

ROMANCE IN NYC: Forbidden Bosses

Abandon
Exception
Confession

FREE STORY WITH NEWSLETTER SIGN UP

Did you know I have a newsletter? I love it because I can write to you with news of work-in-progress, sales, giveaways, and general updates about my life!
You also get a FREE short story, the prequel to Rats of Richstone, BAD BAD BEGINNINGS.
So sign up today. I look forward to connecting with you.
Angel xo

https://geni.us/angeldevlinnewsletter

ABOUT ANGEL

Angel Devlin writes stories about bad boys and billionaires. The hotter, the better.
She lives in Sheffield with her partner, son, and a gorgeous whippet called Bella.

When not working, she can be found either in the garden, drinking coffee, watching too much TikTok, or daydreaming about her ideal country cottage.

She's a firm believer in living in, and enjoying every moment and hopes her words bring you that enjoyment. Let her know, by leaving a review, joining her newsletter, or dropping her a line via Facebook or email.

Facebook page: https://www.facebook.com/angeldevlinbooks

E-mail: contact@angeldevlinwriter.com

Printed in Great Britain
by Amazon